METEOR MAGS
RED METAL AT DAWN

AND OTHER TALES OF INTERPLANETARY PIRACY

PRODUCED BY
MATTHEW HOWARD

IN CONJUNCTION WITH
MARGARETA'S ALLIANCE FOR
GRAVITATIONAL STUDIES

Meteor Mags: Red Metal at Dawn
And Other Tales of Interplanetary Piracy

The Adventures of Meteor Mags and Patches
Volume 3

Papberback ISBN-10: 0692594582
Paperback ISBN-13: 978-0692594582

MeteorMags.com

CONTENTS

7

The Western Route

Tracing the right of property back to its source, one infallibly arrives at usurpation. Theft is only punished because it violates the right of property. But this right is itself nothing in origin but theft.

—Marquis de Sade; *L'Historie de Juliette,* 1797.

PART ONE: SHOTGUNS IN SPACE

September 2029: Vesta 4.

"What in the *hell* are you doing to *my cat*?!" Meteor Mags stood in the doorway to the room, one hand on her hip and the other waving in the air.

Patches looked up and froze in Tarzi's lap. "Meow!"

"Oh, Auntie, settle down. She's fine. Look at her!" He scratched Patches' cheek.

Celina just laughed. "Now you can say you've seen it all." As Tarzi combed the bushy fur, Celina worked a sizeable ball of it onto a spinning wheel. From Patches' tail, through Celina's fingers, and around and around the wheel grew a thread of calico.

Mags shook her head and walked over to inspect the proceedings. "Now," she said, "I have seen it all. Where did you get that spinning wheel? It looks ancient."

"You don't recognize it? It's from your gramma's place!"

"No way." Mags let the edge of the wheel brush her fingertip, and she smiled.

"Yeah, it was tucked away in the corner of the barn with all the pool tables. I only saw it when they were putting the last one on the truck. I just put it with the stuff to go to the club." Celina stopped pumping the wheel with her foot. "Look, don't be cranky. I made you something." She reached into a bag at her feet. "Okay, close your eyes!"

Mags closed her eyes.

"Hold out your hand."

Mags held out her hand.

Celina filled it with something soft, then closed her fingers around it. "Now open up!"

Mags opened her eyes and laughed. "Nice sock. Where is the other one?"

"Patience was a virgin. This takes *forever* the old-fashioned way."

"Yeah, but watch this." Tarzi swiped the sock from her hand.

"Hey!"

He produced a lighter and held the sock over the flame. "Doesn't burn." The small fire did not make a mark. "You can't cut it either. I tried."

"He tried a *lot* of stuff," said Celina.

"I'll bet he did! So, now I have a single indestructible sock. Great! One of my feet will be thrilled."

"We wanted to surprise you, but that's all gone to bollocks now." Tarzi handed back the sock. "It doesn't hurt her. She may be invulnerable, but she still sheds."

Patches jumped down to Mags' feet and rubbed on her calves, wrapping her tail lightly around a boot.

"We'll start a new comic strip called *The Invincible Yarn Man.* Listen, have you seen Plutonian? He said he would spin tonight, but I was hoping to talk to him first."

Patches whined, then got scooped into the air and cradled.

"Aw, that's right, dear. Party time tonight! We'll get you some earplugs." Mags scratched her behind the ears. "If you happen to see him, ping me. I'll be in the shop for a little bit."

As Mags walked down the hall, Tarzi turned to Celina and said, "I *told* you she would freak out!"

"She took it pretty well. I think this whole thing with Patches has her gobsmacked. One day she has a normal cat, and then..."

"Then the next, she has indestructible cat hair socks. Just wait until Mags finds out this wasn't our first."

"That," she said, fixing her gaze on him, "is why we will wait until her birthday to surprise her with the whole thing."

"Hellooo, Mister DJ! Are you busy?"

"Never too busy for my biggest fan." Plutonian set down his tablet. The waveforms on the screen showed he was quite busy assembling another one of his audio collages. But he never objected to a visit from Meteor Mags.

She peeked around the corner of his open doorway. "Hey," she pouted. "Who are you calling *big*, you scurvy pirate?"

"Arrr." He made a mock frown. "Don't tell me I have to walk the plank again."

She swept her white bangs back from her forehead. "Not this time. But look! I brought you something." Her arm appeared in the doorway, holding a black padded bag. "Wanna open it?"

"Oh, what have we here?"

She sauntered into his room.

He had grown quite comfortable at Club Assteroid in the two years since Mags rescued him from the MFA. He had his own quarters, freedom to play anything he wanted on the club's internal radio station, and enough parties to keep him amused. Tesla sprawled on their bed below a series of framed concert posters. The posters were all replicas, not the originals hung in their previous station, but they made the DJ and his cat feel at home.

Vinyl albums covered a table. "I see you've been rebuilding your collection of '6os freakbeat singles. Oh, the Easybeats. And The Poets! Love those guys." She laid the bag on top of them. "Now, I don't mean to knock your trusty old Remington double-barrel, but I thought maybe—just maybe—it might be time for a little upgrade."

Plutonian came to the opposite side of the table. "Just let me get these out of the way."

"Of course. Sorry, dear."

He swept the albums up and stacked them, placing them in an empty crate.

Mags rolled her eyes, shaking her head with amusement. "So organized." She held the padded bag in the air until he was done. Then, slowly unzipping it, she asked, "Have you ever seen one of these before?"

He drew a breath and placed a hand over his heart. "Mags! Where did you get this?"

"Do you like it?"

"*Like* it?" He ran his fingers over the length of the gun, from barrel, to stock, and back again.

"The pistol grip really isn't my style," she said, "but I thought you might like that kind of thing. You can take it off if you don't."

"Benelli," he said softly.

"Indeed. Best thing to come out of Italy since pepperoni pizza!"

"The M3. Mags, they don't even make these anymore."

"No, they don't. It's practically an antique at this point, you know."

"May I?"

"Of course! It's yours now. I mean, if you want it."

He lifted the shotgun from the bag. "I've *dreamed* of having one of these!" He pulled the bolt back, making sure the chamber was empty. He sighted it along the wall in the other direction. "Seven rounds in the magazine, one in the pipe. Pump action for light-duty rounds, and all you have to do to switch to semi-auto is—this."

"Now here is a man who knows his shotguns." She purred, and her tail flicked back and forth. "So I thought you might like these, too." She placed a pouch on the table and unzipped it. "Accessories! This will hold six more rounds on the stock. Here's a strap. This is a telescopic sight you can attach to it. And this is a laser you can mount for those annoying low-light shoot-outs. Did I miss anything?"

Plutonian admired the weapon in his hands. "I don't even know what to say. You're not going to tell me where you got it?"

She placed her fingertips on the table. Leaning over it she said, "I tell you what. I promise to tell you *all* about it, on one condition. You go outside with me right now and shoot the living fuck out of it!"

He laughed. "It's a deal. What kind of loads have you got for it? Buckshot?"

"Oh, I have buckshot if you want it. But listen. These creepy fuckin' lizards, have you seen them?"

"Can't say that I have. I've only heard talk. What's the score?"

"Armor. Body armor, and lots of it. And underneath that armor? Some seriously thick hides." She turned her hip, lifted it, and sat on the tabletop. "Now, Tarzi, he doesn't mind guns. In fact, he's kind of crazy about them! And Celina's no stranger to a firefight either. But these girls at the club, they're not exactly shooters. I think the closest any of them got is playing hand-me-down copies of Call of Duty."

"That's about as realistic as Tetris."

"That's what I'm sayin'! So if we get into a scrap with these reptiles, I need to know we can lay down some serious firepower. I need somebody backing me up with a weapon that can take them down. And I'm not talking about some pussy laser pistol, or nine millimeter bullshit, or even my thirty aught six. I mean take them *down*, motherfucker. That's why I got these." She slammed a box of shells onto the table.

"Hell, Mags! Three-inch slugs? You could take down a hippo with these things."

"You could take down a hippo if she was hiding behind a refrigerator. These bastards will rip a fucking hole in any armor the lizards can dream up, and then some."

"This is like, what? 3000 pounds of force?"

"Exactly. Within twenty-five meters anyway. It's like getting hit with a ton of bricks."

"A ton and a half."

Her lips curled into an evil smile. "Precisely. I don't care *what* they're made of. They're going down."

"At close range, at least. But even at a hundred meters, you can get a four-inch cluster with a Benelli. With a little practice."

"Does that mean you'll come practice with me?"

"Let's go! Tesla! We'll be back in a bit."

His cat lifted his head and blinked. Then he rolled on his back, stretched as far as he could, and closed his eyes.

Outside, on the surface of Vesta 4, Mags drove Plutonian to her makeshift shooting range. She handed him a pair of modified headphones which combined noise-cancelling protection with a built-in communication system. They switched off the mics to mute the noise from the shotguns, but a stream of music from the new PBN played in their ears. He had put on her favorite album for starters: *Armed Love* by The (International) Noise Conspiracy.

At the range, Mags had a table set up for boxes of ammo. Down the range sat a wide array of targets, expired household appliances, and other fun things to shoot. She also had a matching Benelli M3, freshly cleaned and polished, except she had removed the pistol grip. Seven slugs fit in the bottom, and she popped an eighth in the chamber.

Holding it to her shoulder, she aimed at a washing machine thirty meters out and clicked the safety off. She squeezed the trigger once, and a gaping hole ripped in the machine's metal casing. She waved at Plutonian to take a turn.

He followed suit, firing at a water heater. "Damn!" He rubbed his shoulder, then lowered the shotgun to just above waist level. He advanced on the useless appliance, firing from the hip.

The metal tore into shreds, sparking in the dim, cold light of space. Shell casings flew out to the right, one after another. On semi-automatic mode, it took less than three seconds to empty the magazine.

He raised his hand and made a circling motion in the air, then pointed forward.

Mags played along, advancing on the helpless appliances. Plutonian gestured at the washing machine. Mags, shotgun still at her shoulder, pounded three more rounds into it.

Plutonian pulled more shells from the holder on his stock, loading them into the bottom of his weapon. When she paused to reload, he blasted away at four targets surrounding the appliances. He only nicked the first two, but he put two rounds a piece into the centers of the final two. Then he was empty.

From his left side, Mags placed a shot into each of the targets' heads.

He raised his hand again, palm flat. They tapped their earpieces to turn the mics back on.

"Fuck yeah! Nice shooting, mate." She gave him a thumbs-up.

"I think it's safe to say the appliance rebellion has been crushed."

"That'll teach them to oppress us with their mechanistic bullshit. Death to laundry! No hot water without representation!"

"Mags, this thing fires like a dream. These slugs have a serious kick to them, though! I need to adjust my stance. Shooting from the hip is no way to go into a firefight."

She shrugged. "It worked out at close range."

"Yeah. But we don't want the lizards getting that close, do we?"

"No, we sure as hell don't. But I'd take you as point man any day. Nice lead."

"I'm a little rusty. Give me a smaller round and let me get warmed up, and then we'll take these fascists at two hundred meters."

"This is you *not* warmed up?"

"Mags, I've been firing shotguns since I was eleven. But that's not a story you want to hear today."

"Isn't it?"

"Not when you haven't told me where you got these babies yet."

"Fair enough," she said. "A deal's a deal." They walked together back to their starting point at the table full of ammo. "So, these things came out in '89, same as Nirvana's first album. But I didn't see them 'til a couple years later when I was on the West Coast in the States, and that's where I ran into Slim. Do you know my buddy Slim?"

"The guy who runs Below the Belt?"

"Yep, that's him. So, Slim wasn't always the fun-loving criminal he is today. In fact, when I met him, he was in some pretty deep shit."

September 1991: San Diego County, California.

She checked her mirrors again. Her van looked much like any other van on Highway 5, but the back of hers was loaded with crates of stolen guns. A single shotgun hid under a beach towel up front with her, just in case. A bottle of sunscreen and a pair of sandals she had no intention of using completed its disguise.

Mags cranked the tunes and sang along. She had only picked

up the new cassette tape *Ten* from Pearl Jam two weeks ago, but she must have listened to it a hundred times already. She especially liked the song *Deep*. Mags pounded the steering wheel and screamed the words.

The radar detector on the dashboard flashed its lights, but the speedometer hovered right at fifty-five miles per hour. When she hit Carlsbad, Mags pulled into a parking lot with a similar van. She parked in the empty space between the van and a large truck. Unseen, she stepped out and quickly switched her plates with the other van. She planned to do it again in San Clemente.

The tape deck kept playing the album over and over.

She made it through Los Angeles singing the verses to *Why Go* at the top of her lungs. Mags turned onto the 101 Highway and continued along the coast. She loved the scent of the ocean and the glorious views.

By the time she reached San Francisco, the setting sun looked like angels lit on fire. Mags was starving. She found the restaurant where she planned to meet her contact. But as she drove by, she glimpsed a man in the front window. A mask covered his face.

She circled the block and turned into an alley on the opposite side. She killed the van's engine and coasted to a silent stop. She took the stolen shotgun from under its towel and stepped into the alley. As she approached the small service door to the side of the restaurant, she heard a gunshot from inside.

Mags silently pulled open the side door. A small wall about a meter and a half tall extended from the doorway into the interior, providing her some cover. In a crouch, Mags made her way to the edge of the wall and looked in.

The shooter had his back to her. He stood at the cash register, waving his pistol and shouting. Two men in ski masks, pistols drawn, backed him up. One of them looked out the windows of the storefront into the street. The other brandished his weapon at the few customers who cowered in their booths. Mags decided he would be the first to die.

She stood, bringing the shotgun to her shoulder in one smooth motion. Two deafening blasts shook the restaurant. Before the man hit the ground, Mags swept the barrel to the lookout. Three more blasts rocked the restaurant in less than a second. People screamed, but their cries sounded faint and distant. Mags' ears rang.

The lookout had taken two slugs to the chest and one to the gut. Mags ducked behind the wall. The lookout smashed into tables and collapsed. The shooter at the register, in a panic, emptied his clip in Mags' direction. He reached for another, but she was too fast for him. She stood and put two slugs in his torso. He fell backwards into the counter. She put one more into him just to be sure.

"Police," Mags shouted at the terrified customers. "Stay where you are! Don't panic! SFPD!"

She stepped over the shooter's lifeless body to look behind the counter. A chubby sixteen-year-old boy sprawled on the floor with his back against the shelves on the wall. His left shoulder and chest were covered with blood. The stain on his shirt was spreading. "You're going to be okay," Mags told him, clicking the safety into place. "You speak English, kid?"

He nodded, eyes wide.

She stepped around the counter and squatted next to him. "Let me see how bad it is." She tore open his shirt from the bullet hole. "Today's your lucky day. Looks like your bone stopped the slug. Are you hit anywhere else?"

"No, no, officer," he stammered. "They—they came in—they tell me to—"

Mags bent down closer to his ear. "Listen, kid," she whispered. "I ain't no fuckin' cop. I got business here, okay? But let's keep that our little secret for now."

She could see in his eyes he understood.

In the clutter on the shelves behind the counter, she found a pair of pliers. "Fucking little pimp gun. Trying to hold you up with a .25? I'd have punched them in the face." She took a clean dish towel from the shelf and rolled it up. "Okay, bite down on this. Got it?"

The boy clamped his teeth on the towel. She grabbed a second one from the shelf and folded it twice.

"This will sting a little bit." Mags took the pliers and guided them into the hole just under his clavicle, where the slug sat lodged against an upper rib.

"Rrrrr," he growled, and squeezed his eyes shut.

Mags grabbed the slug and pulled it out of his body. She pressed the second towel onto the wound. "Okay, you need to press this here. Keep pressure on it! You're not going to die, but we can't have you bleeding out."

The young man reached across his chest to press the towel against him. His jaws clenched. He growled in pain, but he pressed anyway. He spit out the towel.

"Good man." Mags stood up and addressed the customers. "Okay, people. I need you all to clear out of here. This is a crime scene now. We need to seal it off. My backup will be here any minute."

They looked confused.

"Didn't you hear me? Clear out, people!"

A man stood up, directing his wife and children out of the booth with him. "Shouldn't we stay and make some kind of statement?"

"That won't be necessary, sir. We've been watching these punks for weeks, waiting for them to make a move. We've got everything we need now. But thank you for your concern. Come on people, let's go, go, go! Dinner's on the house tonight."

The restaurant was clear in less than ninety seconds. Mags locked the front doors and did the same to the side door. "You're Ching's kid? Your dad owns this place, right?"

"Yes, he does."

"Get him on the phone, and be quick about it! Tell him to meet me at his warehouse. We can't meet here now. Tell him he's got three bodies. And tell him to bring some hair dye, red or black, it doesn't matter."

"What if police come?"

"Hopefully those witnesses will be long gone, so they can't give a description of me. If the cops show up, you tell them I was a black man. Got it? A black man. About six two. This tall." She held her palm flat above her head to show him. "And you saw him making this sign with his hands." Mags showed him a gang sign. "Got that? Just like this."

"Uh, like this?"

"Perfect! That'll keep them busy for a while. This whole thing will look like a gang shoot-out. So glad I wore this turtleneck today. No identifying marks." Her eyes fell on the shelves again. "Christ, I could eat the arse end out of a low-flying duck." She grabbed a couple cans of soup. "Alright, kid. I got a hot van and possible hostiles incoming. Time for me to bounce."

The boy was already on the phone.

Two hours later, Mags watched the lights pull up outside the warehouse. She had let herself in with a code and parked the van inside. Six men stepped out of a pair of black cars. The last one, shorter and chubbier than the rest, held a hand to his chest. Mags slid the door open and waved.

An older gentleman in a dark suit led the procession. No one had guns drawn, but Mags knew everyone was carrying. "Meteor Mags," said the older man, smiling. "How are you, my friend?"

"Just glad we're still friends, Ching. Hope I didn't cause you too much trouble earlier."

"Trouble? You saved my son's life today." The entourage entered the warehouse. Mags slid the door shut behind them and latched it.

"Oh, it wasn't that big of a deal. Piddly little round. How's it feeling, kid?"

The portly boy smiled happily. He gave her the thumbs up.

"Did you have to talk to the cops?"

"Oh, yes," he said. "Black man in ski mask, very tall. He come and kill gang members. Take all my money." His grin grew even larger as he proudly flashed the gang sign Mags had taught him.

Mags laughed. "Do me a favor, Slim. Don't go flashing that sign anywhere. You'll get yourself killed in some places, okay?"

"Yes, ma'am."

"Brave little man you got there, Ching." Mags nodded respectfully to his father.

"And a smart one, too." Ching put his hand on the boy's uninjured shoulder. "He does quite well in school, especially at math. But I don't mean you saved his life from the bullet, Mags. Those men were there to execute him. Publicly. Because he is my son."

"They sure fucked that up, didn't they? What's their beef?"

"They're from one of the younger gangs. Chinese, but from Vietnam. They are unhappy with my efforts to keep heroin out of our community. So they aim to take, by force, a piece of my gambling business and weaken my territory."

"Ain't that a crock. Nothing good about heroin, Ching."

"Just look what opiates have done to my country in the past."

Mags nodded in agreement. "And now we got viruses spreading everywhere through dirty needles. The whole scene is fucked."

"Agreed. But this is why we have moved into imports and exports." Ching raised his hand and beckoned one of his men. "Before I forget, here is the hair dye you asked for." The bodyguard stepped up to Mags with a box of dye and a box of latex gloves.

"Ching, you are a doll! Oh, and jet black, too. Good choice. Mind if I use your sink?"

"Go right ahead. Are these our guns?" He gestured towards the crates she had unloaded from the back of the van.

"They sure are. I hope you don't plan on selling them anywhere near here, though. The MPs on the base in San Diego are probably looking for them already."

"No, they have another destination. As I said, imports and exports. But thank you." Ching gestured again. One of his bodyguards presented Mags with a briefcase.

"Another day, another dollar. Always a pleasure, Ching."

"Indeed. But I have something else which may interest you. Come." He walked to a corner of the warehouse to pull back a tarp from a stack of boxes on pallets.

"Oh, be still my beating heart." Mags grinned. "You mind if I take a pack?"

"Be my guest."

She opened a box and pulled out a carton of cigarettes. She took out a pack, smacked it sharply against the palm of her hand three times, then peeled it open. "You got a light?"

Ching snapped his fingers. A bodyguard lit her cigarette.

"Such a gentleman." She exhaled a puff into the musty air of the warehouse. Tendrils of smoke rose above her head. "Damn, that's good. You got plans for all these?"

"I'm confident we have a buyer in Canada, if we can get them up there. But my expertise is shipping from the docks, and in much larger quantities. I thought you might have ideas for a land route for a cargo this size, since you got here with no problems."

"Ching, I like your style. Assuming you haven't paid off the inspection stations all the way up the coast, you don't want to ship them by semi. You want a smaller vehicle, one to two-person crew, max. Could be a work truck, or a van, but you don't want it to look like construction trades. The locals tell me those get pulled over all the time by cops with a hard-on for unregistered immigrants. Make it something that can handle the back roads without looking suspicious, and a driver who knows how to stay cool and avoid trouble with the highway patrol. What you *don't* want, however, is that fucking van right there." She pointed her cigarette at it. "That thing is so hot right now, you'd be better off scrapping it for parts."

Ching smiled. He knew she had a rough way of talking. But underneath her bluster, Mags had a capable mind. If only she were Chinese, he thought, she would make an excellent General in his operation.

"So I think getting them *to* the border is a cinch," Mags continued. "A leisurely two-day run, maybe three if you stop to see the sights. One day if you got some decent coffee and do it non-stop. But what about the border crossing? What's the destination?"

"My son has an idea or two about that."

"Does he, now?" She could not imagine what ideas a sixteen-year-old boy could have that Ching had not already thought of, but she also knew he was no fool. "Did he cry when you stitched him up?"

"Not a tear," Ching said proudly.

"Okay, then." She waved the boy over. "Heya, Slim. Come help your auntie Mags dye her hair."

She stubbed out her cigarette on her boot heel, then flicked the butt into the nearest rubbish bin. "Oh, and Ching? I don't mean to impose on our friendship, but those Benellis are masterful shotguns. Do you mind if I keep a couple?"

PART TWO: THE CANADA CONNECTION

"Wow," said Plutonian. "You and Slim really *do* go way back."

"We sure do. We been through some shit, yo!"

"And you really held on to these Benellis all that time?"

"They got a history! Dude, I have stuff in my armory you would not even believe. You want the grand tour?"

"I'd love it."

They boarded the transport. Plutonian rested his empty shotgun beside him, safety on, to the other side from Mags. She steered the transport away from the club to her private hangar.

"So, what happened with the cigarettes? Did Slim really have a brilliant idea?"

"It was brilliant in its simplicity. See, Ching wasn't kidding when he said the boy was good in school. Turns out he had been on a field trip up to Washington to compete in some math tournament. And while he was there, he scouted around, took a little trip to Canada, and got the lay of the land. You gotta realize this was years before the Internet became a thing on Earth, and way before any idiot with a tablet could pull up satellite maps. Back then, it took a little more effort to figure things out. But Slim was nothing if not observant, and he was always thinking."

"Sounds like a good kid."

"He was. Ha! He still is. Just a big, happy kid. You know, Tarzi reminds me a little of him at that age. Well, not with the goofy smile all the time! And Slim would never mouth off to me like my nephew does." Mags laughed. "Not that I mind at all. But I tell you, that boy's mind is sharp as a razor. He's got big things in store for him, as soon as he gets this whole being-a-teenage-boy trip sorted."

"You really like that kid, don't you?"

"I love that little anarchist. And he keeps me young. Plutonian, when you've been around as long as I have, things get pretty fucking boring sometimes. It's sad. You see old friends and pets die. You outlive your family. Things you worked on and cared about just fall apart. But Tarzi makes me feel young again. Some of the shit we get into, man, it's insane. But we're having the time of our lives. I never laugh as hard as I do when we're hanging out."

Plutonian smiled. Mags had never really opened up to him like this before. He enjoyed hearing her stories and her unique perspective on life. "So, tell me what happened on the run to Canada."

"Oh, god. I could talk your ear off. But I will tell you a little bit, because it's got some more Benelli history in it. You're gonna love this."

She spread out the map on the table. A constant drizzle fell from the grey sky. Mags and Slim enjoyed the scenery from inside a sheltered picnic area in Washington. Evergreens surrounded the park, and in the distance lay the Pacific Ocean. "Okay. Here's where we are now." She tapped her finger on the map. Then she ran it along a thick line. "And here's Highway 5, which we've been enjoying so far."

Slim chomped happily on his sandwich. He gulped down a mouthful and pointed to several spots on the map. "And these are all manned border stops. We don't want those."

"That's right. So, if what you are saying is true, my idea is to turn off the 5 here and head inland. That will take us to a bunch of smaller roads, like here, and here, and here. We might even find a few service roads that aren't on the map." She crunched on potato chips. "Now, tell me again how we figure out where to cross."

"All we need to do is scout the crossings between 4 p.m. and 8 a.m. We park out of sight and walk to a decent vantage point. We use our binoculars to see if the station is manned. If it isn't, but it's open, then it must be one of the electronic ones. I'm sorry I don't have a specific one already, but that's the best info I could get." He took another bite.

"Don't sweat it, little man. You're doing great."

Slim smiled as he chewed.

"I still can't believe you got the locals to turn you on to this little trick. You must just have a likeable face."

"It helps if you know French. Not as much as on the East Coast, but still. Are there any chips left?" Like his father, the boy spoke English fluently, along with French, Mandarin, and Cantonese. The night he dyed her hair black, Mags discovered his broken English was just a show he put on for police or anyone else he needed to think he was stupid and harmless.

She passed him the bag of chips. "Help yourself. So, how long do you think we have to get clear of the area once we trip the electronic sensors? How long until the patrols are on our arse?"

Slim shrugged. "That's the tricky part. It could be less than a minute, if they're already in the area. But let's say their station is six miles away. If they can go at the drop of a hat and do, oh, sixty miles per hour on these roads, that would give us six minutes. Or it could be longer. Basically, we have no idea."

"That's why I'll be doing the driving, dear. Either way, we need to get the hell out of there fast, but not so fast we draw attention to ourselves." She sighed. "Your old man won't be happy if I get you in trouble up here. The whole point of this trip is to keep you *out* of trouble."

"You really think so?"

"I know so. Listen. If some guys showed up at my restaurant to kill *my* son, I know what I'd do. I'd suit up for war. I would start killing motherfuckers until there wasn't anyone left to kill, know what I mean?"

Slim frowned. He hadn't thought of that.

"Your dad wants you out of harm's way for a little bit. I mean, he didn't tell me that in so many words. But why do you think he has us messing around with a small cargo like this? He isn't doing it to get rich."

"He could be, though. Even if you're right, we can establish an important relationship here. I think he wants to find out if it's worth his time to set up major shipments from the Bay into a Canadian port. And he's trusting me to lay the foundation."

"I know he trusts you. And I can tell he loves you."

The smile returned to Slim's face. "He trusts you, too, Mags."

She laughed. "He probably trusts me to rack up a body count if anyone so much as touches a hair on your head. At the very least."

"Auntie Mags shall avenge me," he said with mock seriousness.

"Hahaha. That's right, darling. Okay, let's hit the road. You want to drive for a bit?"

"As long as we can listen to something besides that Pearl Jam album again. Don't you have any other tapes?"

"I have Mother Love Bone."

He rolled his eyes. "Mags, Mother Love Bone basically *is* Pearl Jam."

"Oh, they are? I had no idea," she lied.

"Yeah, right." Smiling, he took the keys from her. "First, we get some new tapes."

"Fine! I need to send Gramma a postcard anyway. Let's go."

She pulled the van into the driveway of a farmhouse, a two-story bungalow with a barn in the back. It sat on a large lawn on a wooded plot with no neighbors in sight. The sun had set. Two men sat on a bench on the porch below a single light. At the sight of the van, one of them got up and went inside.

"This must be the place," said Mags. "Stay here for a second."

"No sweat. By the way, nice driving."

"Thanks, little man. We should be able to wrap up this deal and use the same station to make our exit before dawn. I'll just be a second."

A third man came out onto the porch. He had pulled his grey hair into a pony tail. Tattoos covered his bare arms. He raised two fingers to his temple and flicked them towards Mags in a casual salute. "Welcome to Canada. Have any problems at the border?"

"Not a one."

Slim watched their casual banter from his seat in the van. Mags stood on the lawn with her pistol holstered. She wanted to take her time and get a feel for these men before going ahead with the deal. But then, as if she heard something, she spun around. Her hand went to her pistol.

Mags stumbled forward once, twice, and fell to the ground.

"Oh, fuck!" Slim clicked the door locks into place.

The man with the ponytail gestured, and the men on the porch ran to the van, guns drawn.

Slim climbed into the driver's seat, but the window on that side exploded inward. He shielded his face.

A muzzle appeared in the open window, and it shot him.

"Wake up, kid. We don't have all night." The man with the grey ponytail slapped Slim across the face. "Wake up! Jesus, how long does this stuff take to wear off?"

"Couple hours, usually," one of his associates replied.

"It's *been* two hours. Come on!"

"You said you wanted them taken down fast." The man shrugged his shoulders. "They went down fast."

Slim shook his head. He tried to speak, but the gag in his mouth stifled the sound. The world slowly came back in to focus. He could see the van parked in the barn with them now. It had come through a large sliding door which shared a wall with a normal-sized door for entry and exit. He heard Mags' muffled voice beside him, incoherent.

Like Slim, her hands were handcuffed behind her to a metal chair. The chair was bolted into the floor of the barn. Her feet were bound with rope. She seethed. She growled. But she could not escape.

"Alright, he's coming around," said the ponytailed man. "Bring the phone over here. Listen, kid. I'm gonna take this gag off. But if you yell or scream or pull any shit, I'll put a bullet right between your eyes. Got it?"

Slim nodded.

"Good. We just need you to say hi to your old man. Let him know you're alive. Let him know you'd like to stay that way. Okay?" The man removed the gag. "Here. Give me the phone." He held the receiver of a cordless phone up to Slim's ear.

"Dad? Is that you?" Slim listened. "The whole thing is a set-up! They shot—"

The ponytailed man pulled the phone away. "Quiet, kid!" He spoke into the phone. "I'll call you back."

He stuffed the gag back into Slim's mouth and tied it tightly. "Okay. The two of you keep an eye on them. No one leaves this barn."

"What if I gotta take a leak?"

"Piss in the corner! No one leaves this barn. Understand?"

"Got it, boss. What do you want to do with the girl?"

Mags forced her eyes to focus. They shone with pure hate. She uttered a string of muffled curses.

"Start dosing her with heroin. If she seems like she's coming out of it, shoot her up again. In a few days, she'll be so strung out she won't know what planet she's on. Then I suppose we can sell her off." He walked towards the door to leave.

"She's, uh—she's a little big for that, don't you think?"

The ponytailed man snorted. "She'll slim down after a week or two on H. Believe me. I'll send someone out to relieve you in a couple hours."

"Okay, boss."

The two remaining men sat down casually at a table where they set their pistols. Each pistol had a silencer mounted on it.

One man prepared a syringe of heroin. "You tie her arm with this tubing, and I'll shoot her up."

"Sure thing," his partner answered, picking up a length of tubing.

The man with the syringe got up.

Slim could only imagine the words Mags growled through her gag. But the man with the syringe only made it two steps. His partner snatched a pistol from the table and fired three silent rounds into his back. The syringe dropped to the ground, and the man quickly followed. A pool of blood spread on the wooden slats of the barn floor.

Mags and Slim stared in disbelief. The shooter stood and took his keys from his pocket. "Listen up, you two. This whole deal's gone south. But we can change that, if we work together, okay? My name's Paul du Maurier. I'm going to take your cuffs off now, but if you mess with me, I swear to fucking god I will put you down. Now pay attention."

Paul stepped behind Slim and unlocked the boy's cuffs. Slim rubbed his wrists. He set about untying the gag.

"This whole gang has been bought off," said Paul, "by your dad's enemies. Ching wants to smuggle cigarettes, but they'd rather go big and bring heroin up here. Nothing personal, you know. Just money." He unlocked Mags' cuffs.

Mags snapped her arms forward and furiously tore off the gag. "Motherfucker! Get these goddamn ropes off me!"

"Shhh! Keep it down, lady! You want to get us killed?"

"Oh, there's gonna be some killing, alright." She struggled to untie the knots which bound her feet. She reached for her boot knife, only to find it gone. "How many of them are there?"

"Ten of us." Paul's eyes fell on the dead man. "Make that nine. Eight if you don't count me."

"And why *shouldn't* I count you, Paulie?"

"It's just Paul."

"Whatever you say, Pall Mall. Now give me a reason or go to hell."

"You know, I heard you were a real tough girl."

"You heard right." Mags tore the ropes free. She knelt on the floor to help Slim with his. "You okay, little man?"

"I'm good. I think. Kinda fuzzy."

"Okay. Talk, Paul!"

"Listen, tough girl. I don't want heroin in my neighborhood any more than Ching does. There's not a single thing I like about that garbage. But if we wipe out the opposition here, you and me can do cigarette business all goddamn day."

Mags smiled. She flung the ropes aside and stood up. "Shit," she said, placing her hand on the back of the chair for support. "What did they shoot us with?"

"Animal tranquilizers. I hope you're up for a fight."

23

"Paulie, I am *always* up for a fight. And I have a little surprise in the van for these fuckers. Come here. You too, Slim. Oh, bloody hell. What happened to my window?"

"They busted it out," said Slim. "I saw you fall. I tried to get to the driver's seat. Then they smashed it in. I'm sorry, Mags."

"Don't be." She opened the back doors of the van, grabbed the corner of the plastic covering one of the door's interiors, and ripped it away.

In the interior cavity of the door stood two shotguns strapped in place with Velcro. In the bottom of the cavity, a half dozen boxes of buckshot shells sat on two pairs of bandoliers, also loaded with shells. Mags draped two of the bandoliers across her like an X. "Crew, this would be a real good time to come up with a plan."

"Paul could use that phone, call the house, and lure them out here," Slim suggested.

"Nope," said Paul. "The cordless is on the same line as the house. And if I know Anderson, he's got two guys watching the barn."

"Those two turds on the porch?" She shoved shells into the Benelli as fast as she could.

"Maybe. But the porch doesn't face the barn. I'd guess he's got two guys at the back of the house and then those two guys on the porch. And the rest inside."

"Anderson's the creep with the ponytail?"

"That's him."

"This barn got a hay loft?"

"Sure does," said Paul, pointing to a wooden ladder. "Right up there."

"Here's what we do then. Paul, you got a silencer, so you cover the door. Slim, you come with me and—" Mags suddenly grabbed the boy and shoved him towards the front of the van. "Take cover!"

Neither Slim nor Paul had heard a sound, but they lacked her sensitive ears. She brought the Benelli to her shoulder and aimed at the door. Paul turned just in time to see it open into the room. A shotgun blast destroyed the silence. The door splintered and filled with holes. It slammed back on the person opening it.

Mags advanced on the door. She fired twice more in rapid succession. A body slumped to the ground, its foot sticking through the doorway. "So much for surprise. Slim, get to the loft! Paul, shotgun!" Mags dropped to a crouch and opened the door.

Just as Paul had said, she saw two figures at the back. They had raised their weapons at the sound of the blasts. Her pupils expanded like a cat's in the darkness. Wood splintered above her head. Mags shot five more times in less than two seconds. The men fell to the ground.

She backed up and slammed the door shut. "Come on, Paul. High ground! Now!" She ran past him and up the ladder. "Come on!"

Paul shoved a final shell into the second Benelli and grabbed a bandolier from the van. He followed her up. When he got to the top, Mags had already taken a position at the open door to the hay loft facing the back of the house. Slim stayed back from the opening, in relative safety near the wall.

Mags got on her stomach on the floor of the loft. The two sentries at the front of the house ran around the side. She sighted them, leading the target. She fired. One fell. The second one looked up, confused. Mags looked into his eyes and fired twice. Buckshot shredded his shirt. He stumbled and fell on his back.

"Second story," Paul shouted at her. His ears rang. He dropped to the floor.

Mags rolled to the side. A barrage of thirteen pistol rounds tore into the wood where she had been a second before. She pulled more shells from her bandolier and pressed them into the magazine.

In the silence that followed, Paul lunged at the loft's open door. He aimed at the second story window of the house and fired all eight of his shells into it. The window exploded. His shots ripped holes into the house's wood siding.

"Reload!" Mags shouted at him.

She rolled back into the opening and pounded eight more rounds into the second story window. She scanned the grounds as fast as lightning but saw no one out there. She rolled back to cover.

"Three down for sure, five maybes. Paulie, you got a light?"

"The fuck? A smoke break?"

"Fuck you! Give it to Slim." Mags pressed eight more shells from her bandolier into her shotgun. "Slim, drag a bale of hay over here and light that bitch up!"

He caught the lighter. The boy pushed a bale of hay to the open door and held the flame to it.

"Are you nuts?" Paul asked.

"Yes! Kick it out and light another!"

Slim kicked the burning bale out the doorway. It fell to the ground. A second bale tumbled down on it. More return fire came from the second story window. Mags tried to count the shots and realized she had at least two shooters in the window. Puffs of hay and wood splinters exploded to her side. The barn wall below them began to burn.

"A couple more, Slim!"

"On it!" He set two more bales on fire and shoved them out the opening.

"You two go get the van," Mags ordered them. "Open the big door and drive it out."

"What about you?" Slim asked.

"Just make sure you drive it right by the front porch, okay? As close as you can. Then get away from the house! Got it?"

"Got it."

"Mags, what the—"

"Just fucking do it, Paul! Go!"

She rolled back into the opening and fired four shots at the second story window. She fired four more into the pair of windows on the first story of the back of the house. Glass exploded. Someone cried out in pain. Her lips curled in vicious satisfaction as she reloaded.

"Anderson, you gutless fuck! Give it up!"

"Go to hell," came the reply. Mags' ears twitched at the sound. She guessed he was in the second story. Two up top, she thought, and one wounded on the bottom. That left two unknowns. Smoke and flame curled up towards her from the burning bales. Then she heard the big door slide open below her, and the sound of the van starting up.

Paul then understood the reasoning behind her arsonist impulse. As he slid the door open, the burning bales provided him cover and chaos. He dropped behind them as shots rang out from the house. He crawled behind the bales, got out of the line of fire, then ran to the van.

Slim hit the gas. The van crashed through the burning bales in a fiery explosion.

Paul had cranked his window down and stuck his shotgun out. But a loud thud on top of the van startled him, and he fired wildly at the house.

Slim steered the van across the lawn and as close as he could to the porch.

The loud thud was Mags. She had jumped from the loft onto the van's roof. As the van sped by the front porch, she jumped again. Her feet landed on the second-story overhang above the porch.

Mags scrambled to the window hoping to gain the advantage. But the panes of glass exploded out onto the roof top. Bullets tore into the inside wall and whipped past her through the window frame. She cursed.

"She's over the porch," Anderson called to his men.

The porch door slammed open directly below her. Mags ran along the wall to a second window two meters away. Shotgun blasts ripped into the ceiling of the porch below her. She smashed out the window with the butt of her shotgun and climbed inside.

This window lacked a line of sight into the room where Anderson and his other shooter were. She could not see them, but they could not see her either. It put her on a landing right next to the top of a narrow stairwell set off with a wooden railing. Mags stuck her shotgun over the side of the rails and fired blindly. A man cried out.

Mags pointed her shotgun out the broken window. One of Anderson's men had left the porch and gone onto the lawn to get a line of sight on her. She dropped below the window as two more shotgun blasts ripped into the wall. Mags brought the Benelli back up and fired. The man in the yard fell backwards, his torso torn apart by buckshot. She leapt over the railing and onto the stairs.

The wounded man at the bottom of the stairs tried to draw a bead on her, but she obliterated him with a blast from the Benelli. She scanned the room, then headed to the kitchen.

Above her, two pairs of feet stomped into the hall. She called up to them. "Come on down and play, you little bitches!"

In the kitchen, she grabbed a roll of tinfoil from the pantry shelf. Opening the refrigerator, she purred. "It's my lucky day." She snatched up a two-liter soda bottle.

The footsteps stopped at the top of the stairs. Clearly Anderson and his companion had reservations about walking down the potential death trap of the narrow stairwell. She set her shotgun on the counter.

Mags dumped the soda into the sink. From below the sink she took a bottle of drain cleaner and poured its contents into the soda bottle. Her nose wrinkled at the smell. She crushed some tinfoil into a little ball.

Faint footsteps on the stairs. She swept up her shotgun and dashed to the edge of the kitchen.

Anderson's mate peeked around the corner of the stairwell. Mags blasted the wall then fired again and again. His body hit the floor.

She grabbed the fixings for her homemade bomb and ran to the corner she had destroyed. She stuffed the foil ball into the bottle and quickly sealed the cap. Giving it a few firm shakes, she flung it up the stairs.

It exploded above the stairwell. It rattled the remaining windows and sprayed toxic chemicals all across the landing at the top.

Anderson dropped his pistol, and a shot escaped it. But there was no escape for him. He screamed, and his skin burned, and his eyes.

Mags shoved more shells into the Benelli and charged up the stairs. The air reeked of drain cleaner. She fired at his legs.

Perforated by buckshot, he collapsed. More screaming.

"Shoot me up with heroin, will ya? Sell me off? Fuck you, Anderson!" Mags fired her remaining shells into his legs. Then she took her empty shotgun and beat him to death with it.

Moments later, she ran out the front door. The barn burned like a giant torch behind the house. The hay bales had set the lawn ablaze, too. She heard the van's horn and ran down the road.

Mags flung open the back door and jumped in. "Paul! Which way is the nearest fire station?"

"Just west of here," he said, jerking his thumb in that direction.

"Slim! Drive like hell the other way!"

"On it!" He put the pedal to the floor. "Paul's got a place just north of here where we can ditch this van."

She made her way to the front. There, the smuggler put her hand on his good shoulder and patted it several times. "Little man, you are one stand-up criminal."

Slim flashed her a huge smile in the rearview mirror. "You're not mad?"

"Mad? Oh, no." She laughed. "Now, Great-gramma Mad Dog, she probably would have been mad as hell. But me? I'm sweet as a little angel."

Paul snorted. "Give me a break, eh."

Mags patted him on the shoulder, too. "You know what, Paul? You're alright in my book. Thanks for saving our arses back there. You still want to do business?"

"As long as you promise not to set any more rendezvous points on fucking *fire*, I might be open to it!"

"Darling," she said, tearing open one of the boxes in the back of the van, "I'm going to set the whole damn *world* on fire." She ripped open a carton, then a pack, and pulled out two cigarettes. "Care to join me?"

"And that was pretty much the end of it," she said. "We got out before anyone showed up. Paulie hooked us up with some fresh wheels in exchange for the smokes, and we went out the way we came."

Plutonian sat with her aboard the *Queen Anne*. "And that was your western route?"

"Things were kind of hot in that neck of the woods for a while, what with a gang slaughter and arson and all. But Slim was right about his dad wanting to lay a foundation. Paul ended up being the perfect connection. He went all-in on establishing a new crew to handle our 'liberated' cargo through the ports, not just over land."

"Ching wasn't mad at you for getting his boy in trouble?"

"Hahaha! Let's say he wasn't thrilled about that part, but we ended up solving a major situation for him. We cleared out some traitorous scumbags! And he was taking care of business back in Chinatown, too. Old man Ching may have been a gentleman, but when it came to wiping out that rival gang, he made bloody sure he had a solid grip on the town by the time it was all over. He even had me keep Slim out of town a little while longer until he was finished—cleaning up."

"What did you two do, hang out on the beach?"

"Oh, that's another story entirely. I'll tell you all about it someday." Mags smiled and stood up. "So, do you want to see some more stuff in the armory?"

"Does it all have as much history as the Benellis?"

"Mister DJ, it's *all* got history."

"Lead the way."

ASTEROID UNDERGROUND INTERVIEW: SLIM

Slim, Welcome to the *Asteroid Underground*.

Thanks, buddy. Glad to be here. You don't mind, do you?

Oh, no. Go right ahead. That smells great! What is it?

Kung Pao chicken. Well, a vegetarian version. We make it with seitan. It's less traumatic for the chickens that way. Here. Try some. You don't have a peanut allergy, do you? Okay, try this.

Wow, that's tasty. Do you make all your own food at Below the Belt?

Oh, yeah. Our customers don't just come for the loud music and sexy dancers, hahaha. We're the only place outside the Martian Warehousing Zone where a miner can get a home-cooked meal.

Tell us how you got started cooking.

Oh, I don't even recall when I started. I worked in Dad's restaurant ever since I can remember.

Your dad was in the restaurant business, too?

No, no, hahaha. Dad was in the gambling business. Or more accurately, Dad *was* the gambling business in Chinatown. The restaurant was just a cover. A meeting place, a decent way to launder money, that kind of thing. Once he moved into imports and exports, it wasn't so important, but we kept it open a few more years anyway. I don't know if it was so he could always get a home-cooked meal, or if he just thought it would keep me out of trouble! Maybe both.

Does Meteor Mags still dance at Below the Belt?

No, though we'd love to have her back. She mostly dances at her own place now. When she has the time.

Is it because of the shootout?

Hahaha, no. Well, maybe just a little bit. Don't print that, though. Mags is *persona non grata* with the MFA, the Port Authority, and just about everybody else these days. So, it's probably not a good idea for her to be in a little club like mine. She has to be more careful about hanging out now. We all miss her, though. She's quite the dancer.

And you've known her a long time, too, haven't you?

Oh, forever. Since Pearl Jam's first album came out, anyway. I remember because she played the living hell out of the damn thing! Oh, I couldn't listen to that album for a couple years after that.

So, 1991?

That's right. Ah, I was just a kid back then. Good times. We still chat, of course. She's got a new project in the works and, I don't mind telling you, the math is pretty tough on it. I help where I can. Sometimes it just helps to have two minds working on the same problem.

A new project? What is she working on?

I can't really give you the details. But I think it could be the most important thing since the GravGens, if we can get it to work. Revolutionizing life in the Belt, that's about all I can say. And you know how Auntie Mags loves a good revolution.

She sure does. Thank you for joining us, Slim. Anything else you'd like to say before we go?

Yes! Come out to Below the Belt! We always have a good time, the dancers are always beautiful, and the meals are always cooked fresh to order! See you there.

8

Red Metal at Dawn

The attention of our readers is now to be directed to the history of two female pirates—a history which is chiefly remarkable from the extraordinary circumstance of the softer sex assuming a character peculiarly distinguished for every vice that can disgrace humanity, and at the same time for the exertion of the most daring, though brutal, courage.

—Charles Ellms; *The Pirates' Own Book*, 1837.

PART ONE: THE LABYRINTH

October 2029.

The asteroid known as Vesta 4 hurtled through yet another black orbit around the sun. In its relatively brief life of one billion years, it had more or less resigned itself to being caught in this orbit around the yellow star. Some centuries, Vesta 4 almost enjoyed itself.

But things had become more exciting lately. At the highest point on the rim of the massive crater at Vesta 4's south pole, there now stood a building filled with wondrous lights and sounds. The sign on the building read "Club Assteroid," but Vesta 4 did not appreciate the humor in that.

It did, however, enjoy the hustle and bustle. People came and went—all kinds of people. Vesta 4 had become so enthralled with their activities it hardly noticed when the woman with the tail renamed it from 4 Vesta. "It just sounds better that way," she exclaimed in one of her moods. "To hell with what the charts say!"

If you dropped a rock from Club Assteroid's lofty perch on the rim, it would fall thirty-one kilometers to the bottom of the crater. Only a few orbits ago, the rock would hardly have fallen at all. Vesta 4 had never been the gravitational equal of the only larger asteroid in the Belt, Ceres. And neither could approach Earth's moon in terms of gravity.

But now, buried at the base of the enormous mountain in the crater's basin, GravGens pumped out an Earth-like gravity. Thanks to the artificial gravity, Vesta 4 now held its very own atmosphere. This pleased it.

On nights when the parties on the rim grew exceptionally bright and loud, Vesta 4 felt a small tickle as a second set of GravGens kicked on. Club Assteroid housed the second set, which could lessen the gravity inside the club with the turn of a dial. Vesta 4, made of mostly rock, lacked the biology to appreciate the sensual effects this had on dancing bodies.

Tonight, however, no party raged in that strange building on the rim of the crater that held the tallest mountain in the solar system. Tonight, only a soft glow emanated from some of the windows. Faintly at first, but then stronger, came the sound of a single piano.

Meteor Mags sang softly. Her hands moved over the piano keys, falling on them like rain drops. Her voice floated above the chords like a borealis, shimmering in the darkness. Tonight, she felt like singing *Trains* by Porcupine Tree.

Celina stood outside the entrance to the small concert hall in this wing of the club. Closer to the living quarters of Mags, Celina, and all the women of the club, the concert hall provided a space for their private gatherings away from the rowdiness. In the few years since they built this club, Celina had listened many times to her friend playing solo after everyone else had gone to sleep.

On these nights, Mags kept the concert hall completely dark except for a single candle. She would sit at the piano on the stage in the small band shell in the room, playing sometimes for a few verses, sometimes for hours.

Mags hit the high notes like they were written for her. The piano grew louder, like thunder on the edge of billowing clouds. Celina felt an ache in her heart she could not explain, a longing. Then a hand slid into hers and held it.

Hyo-Sonn stood beside her quietly. The young woman raised her eyebrows in a silent question. Celina nodded.

Mags' voice filled the room and spilled into the hallway. Hyo-Sonn felt it, too: the longing, the ache, like reaching through the night for something she knew she could never touch.

Hyo-Sonn whispered, "Is Mags okay?"

Celina smiled again, the wetness in her eyes showing sparkles from the candlelight. "She's okay, sweetie" she whispered. "Ever since I've known her, Mags just has nights like this sometimes." Celina remembered. "She wakes up in the middle of the night and doesn't want to talk at all. But she will go the piano and..."

Hyo-Sonn hadn't known Celina very long, only a few weeks, but she knew she had never met anyone like her before. "And what?"

"I think she has dreams sometimes that make her sad, and this is just how she works it out. Then the next day, she's fine. Like nothing happened."

"What does she dream about?"

Mags announced, "I can hear you two out there, you know!"

Hyo-Sonn looked mortified. Celina just chuckled. She called out, "No getting anything past those little ears of yours, wagtail!"

Mags jumped down from the stage. She wiped her eyes with the soft suede of her gloves then strolled up to Hyo-Sonn. She placed her hand on the side of the young woman's head, mussing her hair slightly. "You two are about as sneaky as a herd of elephants." She kissed Celina on the cheek.

"Sorry, Mags. I was just worried about you."

"Don't worry about me, dear." The smuggler placed her hand on the young woman's cheek. "I'll be just fine."

Hyo-Sonn laughed. "Hmmm, why does that sound familiar?"

"What?" Mags feigned shock. "I *was* fine that time! Hahaha!"

"What are you two going on about?"

"Inside joke." Mags' belly shook as she laughed. She put her arm around Celina and squeezed. "Do you remember that night we showed up with Hyo-Sonn and the new girls?"

"Dear lord, how could I forget? It's impossible to get a night's sleep around here sometimes!"

"Let me tell you," said Mags. "When we were on that ship…"

Then she told the story, with Hyo-Sonn interjecting here and there. Mags did have a tendency to exaggerate, after all.

Below them, Vesta 4 listened quietly as it spun through the Belt. It too, remembered that night. Stone never forgets.

September 2029: Uncharted Asteroid.

Meteor Mags took her wire cutters and snipped through a few centimeters of the mesh barricade. She worked the tip of her saw into the opening. After drawing it back towards her a few times to start a groove, she sawed back and forth as fast as she could.

"That's going to take all day," said Tarzi. "Why don't you just torch it with your pistol?"

"Save your charge in case we really need it. Here." She pulled a smaller, foldable saw out of her kit, a tool bag on her belt. "Start on the other side."

Tarzi unfolded the saw and got to work. "Why would anyone make a mesh gate, anyway?"

She wiped a little sweat from her forehead with the back of her arm. "Do you know what a Faraday cage is? It's like a box you sit inside. The outside of the box distributes electrical charge evenly across the surface."

"Why would you sit in it?"

"You're safe from the current there. See, it isn't voltage that kills you. It's the amps. The current." She leisurely chomped a piece of bubble gum while she sawed. "So anyway, the box distributes the charge evenly across the surface. Since there's no difference in charge, you have zero voltage. And without any voltage, there's no flow of—Tarzi, are you even *listening*?"

"Um, not really. Can we just use the torch on this stuff?"

Mags laughed. "Whistle while you work! We'll be through in no time." She sang the chorus to *Breaking into Heaven*.

"Since when were you a Stone Roses fan? That band is so weak."

"Shut up! They had some great jams. Just because you weren't around in '89 to really appreciate what it was—"

"Oh yes, 1989. What a great year for humanity. Thatcher. Reagan. The—"

"Hey, it didn't *all* suck. We kind of had a baby Internet back then. And Nirvana's first album." She sighed nostalgically then went back to singing.

Patches watched her friends through half-closed eyes. She sniffed the air. Patches smelled fish, or things like fish. Fishlike creatures for which she had no name. She could only imagine.

She wondered if Mags could smell it, too. Patches wondered a lot of things lately. Something felt different after she woke up in that strange machine. She turned her head to lick a tuft on her shoulder.

"Patches loves it here! Listen to her little motor go." Mags peered over the rims of her glasses and smiled. "It's weird," she said, sawing away. "She doesn't even need her helmet anymore when we go outside."

"She doesn't catch on fire, either."

"What?!" Mags stopped sawing to glare at him. "Did you try to light my cat on fire?"

"It was her idea," Tarzi laughed. "Seriously. Check her chat history."

"Whatever. Don't you two come up with any more experiments!"

"So," he offered. "We're sawing through a Faraday cage?"

"Well, no. This is like the mesh version of that. You take a bunch of screens and layer them. The only holes in the resulting mesh are smaller than the wavelengths of the electromagnetic spectrum. In other words—"

"In other words, the holes are too small to get the juice through, and so you're safe on the other side?"

"Precisely! You're pretty smart sometimes." She kept sawing. "I'm guessing this mesh extends all the way around the laboratory. It wouldn't make any sense to electro-shield the front door and not the whole thing."

Tarzi sawed away at the mesh with a bored look on his face. He frowned. "So whatever is inside the mesh is safe from an electrical storm? Just how many electrical storms do you think they get on a little asteroid like this?"

"I was wondering the same thing myself. And my guess is: not many. So maybe—" She ripped away the remaining mesh on her vertical cut, down to the ground. Then she started sawing horizontally, just below eye level, cutting to where Tarzi had started a meter to her left.

"So maybe there's something else on this asteroid besides a storm."

"Maybe."

"But what?"

Mags smiled and kept sawing. "Let's hope we don't find out."

Two Days Earlier, on Earth.

"Hey little man. R U ready 2 Rock? The revolution calls."

Tarzi heard the gentle chime. He picked up his tablet. It felt weird when it talked out loud to him, interrupting his train of thought. He kept it on text-only most of the time.

"Right now?" He typed on the screen. "Kind of busy."

The MM icon showed orbiting stars as she typed, "Wrap it up dear LOL you do NOT want to miss this."

He wasn't actually doing anything at all, but she didn't need to know that. "Don't blame me for what happens then. Usual place?"

"Will be waiting xoxoxox ~M."

Tarzi stood up, tossed the tablet in his open back pack, and pulled the zipper shut. "Attention, house. Let me out and lock it down."

The voice command in his parents' house obligingly opened the side door into the yard. Tarzi swept up his backpack from the couch. He had dressed hours ago, hoping for this call. He stood in the side yard just long enough to watch the house lock itself down. Windows and doors clicked their locks into place.

He pressed his earbuds in and pulled up a playlist. It would take him thirty minutes to walk the trails to the dam. A low, growling buzz filled his ears, then the hammering beats of something being smashed into tiny pieces. A droning guitar bashed his eardrums. He smiled peacefully and disappeared into the forest behind the house.

When he reached the edge of the clearing where the *Queen Anne* had landed, he looked through the trees with amusement. Mags had set out her portable "stage," a piece of plywood in the grass where she danced.

She wore her favorite headphones. Unlike Tarzi, she didn't care for ear buds. She liked old-school gear, with big puffy enclosures around the speakers and an adjustable band across the top of her head.

Mags might have liked the old-school look, but she loved having several hundred terabytes of music running on phantom wireless power in her ears. Tarzi had listened to her arguments about the portable Gramophone and Victrola cabinets from the early twentieth century. "The only way to listen to tunes totally off the grid," she called them. But he knew she loved her massive music library more.

He watched Mags spin around, pumping her arms in the air as if cheering. She broke into a strut, walking a circle as wide as the board on the ground. She pumped her arms in the air again. Tarzi wondered if she was dancing or inciting a riot.

Mags' tail curled around her. She covered the headphones on her ears with her palms, whipping her head from one side to the other, singing along to *Smash It Up* by The (International) Noise Conspiracy.

Patches leapt out of the grass. She pounced on her favorite toy birdie and ripped at its feathers. "Meow!"

"Tarzi!"

He looked up from Patches to see Mags waving at him. How does she always know I'm here, he wondered. He pulled his ear buds out, letting them dangle around his neck, and walked into the clearing.

He called out, raising a fist in casual salute. "What did you bring me?"

She squeezed him in a hug. "So much stuff! Come on, come on. We gotta get in the air and get moving. Adventure awaits!"

As Tarzi followed her onto the ship, Mags told him all about the laboratory she planned to raid. "So the guy tells me it's just up there, and nobody's even watching it, because no one who *should* be watching it even knows it exists!"

He checked his laser pistol like he always did, adjusting here and there, polishing nonexistent smudges just to watch it shine. "But he doesn't know what they were creating? Just bio-cyber something or others?"

"That, and someone in the military thought it might have serious weapons potential. So, I thought since these bloody lizards have big guns, we might as well get some ourselves. They'll have the Outer Planets completely infested before anyone on Earth realizes how bad it is out there."

"You could try making people aware, you know. Get the word out to the people."

Mags laughed and laughed. "The 'people' want to have me arrested. Fuck that! Do you want to check this place out or what?"

Tarzi swept back his mohawk with one hand and put his black cap back on his head with the other. Today, it sported a patch showing a skull and crossbones, affixed with Velcro. "I even brought tunes," he exclaimed, taking his seat. "The new one from Death By Chainsaw!"

"Rock and roll!" Mags plopped into her seat and got comfortable. She brought the *Queen Anne* up to full power. "Next stop: top secret asteroid bio-lab. Strap in, everybody. Patches, this means you!"

"Mew!"

As they moved into the atmosphere and Earth fell away below them, Tarzi thought he caught a flash of light from the corner of his eye. He looked out the window to see it, but there was nothing. Just the sky, and then suddenly stars.

That Same Day, and Not Far Away.

Hyo-Sonn stood on a rocky outcrop past the edge of the forest. The sound of a river rose one hundred meters from the gorge below. "Are they ready to go, or what?"

"You've got to let them rest for a little bit," said Kala.

"There's no time for that." She stamped her foot.

"Hyo-Sonn, we've been on the go since before sunrise. Some of them haven't eaten since yesterday. Give them a minute, please."

"If we stop, we're as good as dead."

"You know that's not true," said Kala. "Nobody at the Clinic knows which direction we went. Relax."

"Relax? *Relax*? Don't you remember what they did to the last girl who tried to escape?"

"Of course I do. She was my friend, too. Or don't you remember *that*?"

Hyo-Sonn put her face in her hands, rubbing her eyes and forehead. "I can't believe what they did to Sarah." She wiped a tear from her eye. "I can't believe what they did to any of us."

"Sarah's going to be okay. I talked to her. She knows it wasn't her fault."

"Do you know what my parents said when I tried to tell them? They told me to stop lying."

"Mine, too. That's when the fuckers upped my anti-psychotics. They told Mom and Dad it was just a side effect of my mental illness, making up these wild stories. Hallucinations."

"What a nightmare. You know they've called the police by now. They'll send out helicopters soon, put our pictures on the web. We have to get to my cousin's place, Kala. Before everyone in the state is looking for us."

"And then what?"

Hyo-Sonn kicked a rock over the cliff. It clattered down the side of the gorge. "Damn it! I don't know!"

"Come here." Kala put her arms around her friend and held her close. At seventeen, Hyo-Sonn was the oldest of the runaways. Kala, sixteen, was only a few months younger. Together, they had organized the group's escape from the Clinic.

The Clinic's brochures called it a rehabilitation center for troubled teens. In reality, the staff combined intimidation, brainwashing, drugs, and abuse to do whatever they wanted to the young people in their care.

Hyo-Sonn stiffened at the sound of a passing helicopter. "Did you hear that?"

"You're right. We should go. I'll help you get the girls together."

"Kala." Hyo-Sonn took her hand. "Thank you."

They made their way back into the forest. A group of six girls waited in a small clearing, some lying in the grass, some sitting with their backs against trees. Two of them shared the remains of a sandwich, handing out small bites to the girls next to them. They passed around the last water bottle until it was empty.

"Okay," began Hyo-Sonn. "We've made it to the gorge. We just need to go south. We can stick to the edge of the forest, out of sight, and just follow the—"

"Why don't you just admit you don't have a clue what we're doing?"

"Shut up, Suzi. If you want to go back to the Clinic, then just fucking go."

"Listen, you chink bitch, you've been riding my ass all—"

"Fuck you. I'm not even Chinese. I'm Korean."

Suzi pushed her. "A chink's a chink! You wanna *do* something about it?"

Hyo-Sonn cocked her fist, but Kala stepped between them. "Will you two cut it out? Where's Sarah?"

The girls looked around.

"I *told* you to keep an eye on her!"

"I think she had to pee," said one of the girls in the grass.

"You *think?* Which way did she go? Sarah," Kala shouted into the forest. "Sarah!"

Sarah came running into the clearing. At twelve, she was the youngest and smallest of the group. "Kala!" She threw her arms around the older girl, trembling. Welts covered her face where she had run into branches. "Kala, I saw a dragon!"

"Calm down, Sarah. It's okay. You know there's no such thing as dragons. You saw a lizard, maybe? Did you see a snake?"

"No! It was a dragon. I swear. It looked right at me."

"Okay, Sarah. I believe you." She held the girl close again. Kala looked up to Hyo-Sonn and raised her eyebrows in a silent question.

"Oh, for fuck's sake," said Suzi. "Now we're going to play fairy tales? What a bunch of—" She was suddenly knocked to the ground, trapped in a net.

A second net threw Hyo-Sonn to the ground. Her shoulder

smashed into the dirt. She heard screams. Struggling, she rolled her head to one side. She saw more girls taken down, one by one.

Kala grabbed Sarah and ran for the forest, but a net flew through the air and caught them, too. They fell.

Four figures stepped into the clearing. Their guttural laughter desecrated Hyo-Sonn's ears. Their tongues flicked like serpents', but they stood taller than men. She tried to move, but the net tangled her too tightly. Her shoulder throbbed.

One of them poked her with the muzzle of what looked like a gun. It bent over her, inspecting her with eyes devoid of kindness. The stink of its breath, like a decaying corpse, filled her nostrils. For the first time since she was five years old, Hyo-Sonn believed in dragons.

The four dragons slung a body over each shoulder, with Kala and Sarah still bound in a single net. The captors carried the girls roughly through the forest, not caring if their captives smacked into trees or bushes. One by one, they boarded a small spacecraft.

And then, for the first time in their lives, the girls left planet Earth far behind.

Soon, Meteor Mags and Tarzi were inside the laboratory. Patches followed them in, stopping to sniff and rub her face on corners.

"See, that didn't take so long. And we still have a full charge on our pistols."

"Awesome," he said unconvincingly. "Do you think it's safe to smoke in here?"

Mags flipped on the lights. "When is it ever *safe* to smoke?"

"I don't see any vats of oozing chemicals or beakers of flammable beaker stuff. So, screw it." He lit up.

A panel in the wall behind him slid open. The hiss startled him. He drew his pistol instinctively.

A monitor came to life.

He caught Mags' eye. She, too, had drawn a pistol at the sound. Together, they came up slowly to the monitor.

The man on the screen talked on and on in a language neither of them understood. Tarzi did not find him especially dangerous, nor likeable, nor anything at all. Just that he spoke an unfamiliar language.

"Hey, Mags?"

"Yeah?"

"Do you think it's funny that here we are, in a laboratory, on an asteroid drifting in the Belt, and this guy speaks a language neither of us knows?"

"What's so funny about that?" She adjusted her socks. "Just about every language on Earth is spoken somewhere in the Belt. If you include Mars, at least."

"Right." Tarzi took a puff. "But we went to a moon that's been dead for how many thousand years, and we got someone's voice mail in English?"

Mags cocked her head. "You know, you're right." Her tail swished back and forth. "I was so worried about Patches. Maybe they were broadcasting on all known languages?"

"Come on, Auntie. Think about it. Who spoke English ten thousand years ago? And why wouldn't the manual we found be in English, too?"

Other than the monitor in the wall, most every surface looked like stainless steel: clean, smooth, and polished. Sleek cabinets lined the walls and a table stood in the center of the room—all made from the same material. Mags guessed it was plastic, non-conductive, but she hadn't seen anything like it before.

"Remind me to ask them if we ever go back." She smiled ruefully. "Oh, wait. We can't."

Tarzi laughed. "Yeah. Oh, hi there. We sort of flipped a switch the other day and totally destroyed your entire planet, but it was all a big misunderstanding. Really. So, we meant to ask about your language."

"That'll go over great. Hey, let's see if we can find something useful in here, okay?" She scanned the room.

Patches pawed at a cabinet door set flush with the wall. She pressed her paw in several spots around its sealed edge. It slid open and something flew out.

"What was that?"

The blur came to rest like a hummingbird hovering in the air.

"Wow," said Tarzi. "Is that a seahorse?"

Patches jumped on the table, lowering her ears and sniffing at the metallic seahorse floating before them.

"Okay, if this is our big weapons find, I am going to throttle the guy who—hey, look." Mags bent down to pick up a ring from the bottom of the cabinet. She stood up and turned it over in her hand, inspecting it. She saw faint lines etched like circuits into its metallic green surface. "Here, see if this fits you!" She handed it to Tarzi.

"Oh look at that." He admired the ring on his finger. "It's a perfect—" The faint lines glowed green, then brighter. "Uh oh."

The seahorse also lit up with a network of glowing green circuitry. It circled the young man at shoulder height.

"Hey, I think he likes me!"

"Likes you? Tarzi, it's a robot."

"*You're* a fucking robot!"

Mags laughed. "Will you chill?"

"Check this out. You don't see the display, do you?"

"The what?"

"Cool! I thought it was a projection at first, but it's a heads up display. It's like a menu for the seahorse."

"I haven't seen seahorse on the menu since 2016."

"Not a dinner menu!" Tarzi's eyes moved this way and that across a display only he could see. Like the circuits of the seahorse and the ring, it showed glowing green lines. Only, they seemed broken up into menus and sub-menus for—what? "I wonder how you access them."

"They were researching potential weapons here, so maybe this thing has a trigger."

"The ring! Maybe it acts like a controller for the—"

"Easy there!" Her hand gripped his wrist before he could touch the ring to test his theory. "If that *is* the trigger, we don't need it shooting off god-knows-what in this room. Think!"

"Right." But as she let go of his wrist, he said, "So, the infamous space pirate is scared of a little seahorse?"

"I'm scared of people who don't know what they're doing with weapons. But this little guy?" Mags raised her eyebrows and assessed the seahorse. "I don't think he could hurt a fly." She shook her head. "He's kind of cute, though."

She reached out to pet the seahorse. But the instant her hand made contact, a bright green web of lightning wrapped around her. "Gaaah!" Her white curls stood out straight from her head, crackling with green sparks. Rigid, she rose from the floor then fell to the ground. Breaking contact with the seahorse made the web of green lightning vanish.

They looked at each other, wide-eyed, mouths open.

Then Tarzi laughed and laughed. "You should have seen the look on your face!" He made his arms go rigid. He opened his eyes as far as they could go. "Aaaaa," he said, shaking with imaginary shocks.

"Hey!" Her stunned look turned sour as she watched his clowning. "Oh, you are *so* going to pay for that."

"Seriously, though! Mags! Are you alright?"

She picked herself up from the floor and smoothed her skirt. "Alright enough to kick your—oh, my curls!" Her curls and bangs had all fallen straight when the current stopped. "I just had them done!" She searched in her kit for a hair tie.

Patches didn't see anything funny about it at all. She stood on the table hissing at the seahorse. It floated in the air before her, bobbing slightly. She angrily pawed the air.

The seahorse darted back to the cabinets on the wall. One opened in front of him, and he flew in.

Mags and Tarzi could not see what he was doing, as the cabinet was above their eye level, but they could hear him rustling around.

"What's it doing in there?"

It pushed out a stack of dehydrated food in plastic bags that fell to the floor and scattered. The seahorse hovered over one of them and chirped.

Patches looked down from the edge of the tabletop. She sniffed the air, looked at the seahorse, then sniffed again. She jumped down and ripped the plastic bag apart.

"Is that what I think it is?" Mags sniffed the air, too. "I can't believe it. Beef jerky!"

Patches tore off chunks of jerky and chewed them, dropped them on the floor, and chewed them again noisily with her mouth open.

"Now," said Tarzi. "What was that you were saying about this cute little guy and a fly?"

"Ow! Yes, he is definitely a public menace. I take it back."

"Seahorse ain't nobody's bitch!"

"Alright, settle down, G-Money. Let's see what else they have in here."

The crudely drawn map in her kit showed this room and a much larger room. Between them stretched a network of passageways. Supposedly, there was a main walkway, like a bridge, leading directly to the next, more extensive lab. But Mags knew the person she convinced to draw this map had oversimplified everything. What really lay beyond the next door, she could not say.

"I don't see anything else in here," said Tarzi. Imitating Patches' method of pawing around the doors, he discovered how to open them easily. He moved quickly along the walls now. Cabinet doors slid open at his touch.

"Mew." Quite satisfied with her snack and her truce with the shiny floating seahorse, Patches followed behind him. She sniffed around the open doors and peeked inside.

"Okay then. Get your mask on! I'm going to try the next door. Get your little seahorse ready to go."

"His name is Sparky."

"Oh, you've got to be kidding me!"

"What? That's his name."

"You can't give a weaponized cybernetic sea creature a puppy dog name."

"What? You named your cat Patches!"

Mags shrugged and turned up her palms. "What's wrong with

Patches?"

Tarzi threw his hands in the air. "Nothing! That's my *point*."

She sighed. "I'm just glad you aren't calling him The Shocker. Get your mask on! We're doing this."

At the back of the laboratory, a second door led to the next passage. Mags had her hair up now, tied in a bun with a few spikes of bangs framing her cheeks and forehead. She touched the cover of the security panel, and it slid open to reveal an alphanumeric keypad.

Mags fit her modified biohazard mask over her face and secured the straps. It had a pair of filters on the front, like a gasmask, with a headlamp affixed to the forehead. It could accept a small tank of compressed air giving the wearer a thirty-minute supply of breathable atmosphere. With the mask came a handheld meter which fit in her kit and could test the air for chemical and biological contaminants.

She sang as she typed on the keypad. Her fingers moved rhythmically over the keys to the beat of *Black Mask* by The (International) Noise Conspiracy. She started at the fiftieth decimal of pi and worked her way backwards, swaying a little. Her eyebrows furrowed in concentration.

Patches rubbed against her leg and mewed. She loved to hear Mags sing, but the smell of something like fish was exciting her, too. What was it, she wondered, and did it taste as good as it smelled?

Tarzi walked up behind her, activating his headlamp with the touch of a button. "Do you think they could pick a longer access code?"

"It's not too tough. Just the first fifty digits in the decimal of pi. Backwards."

"Wouldn't it be easier to bring it up on the tablet and have me read them to you?"

Mags stopped typing numbers. "Wouldn't it be easier if I didn't lose my place chatting with you?" Her finger paused over a three, then hovered over a five. Then back to the three. "Besides, I memorized the first five hundred after losing a bar bet to Celina in

1993." She settled on the three and went back to typing.

"Mags?"

"*What*, Tarzi?"

"Do you think you could you help me with trig sometime?"

She grinned and typed the last few digits. "As soon as you realize it's just algebra about triangles mapped on a circle, you are going to be dangerous. Have you ever tried memorizing log tables in your trance?"

As the door slid open, Tarzi's light fell on several more layers of the mesh they had sawed through at the front door. "Not more of this stuff," he complained. But layer by layer, like curtains, the mesh slid to one side or the other. "Nice."

Mags turned her light on, too, pointing it towards the dark doorway. "Here goes nothing. Be careful and stay close, you two."

Patches let out a long, plaintive mew. She dashed into darkness beyond the lights from the headlamps.

"Or, just run headlong into danger," said Tarzi.

"Or that. Let's go."

"Tarzi, look at this." In the light of Mags' headlamp, her gloved hand traced smooth curves in the stone walls of the cavern. The circle of Tarzi's light rose from the ground to join hers on the wall. A few meters to the right loomed a sharp drop-off into blackness.

Tarzi placed his left hand on the wall. "Are those carved?" His seahorse faithfully circled in the air around him. The green lines of its circuits glowed in the darkness, faintly illuminating the curves of its metallic surface.

"I don't think so, dear. Look." Mags traced a series of repeating formations. "These are the plates of a trilobite shell. These points on both sides of the plate? Legs. Here is its head. And here, where it ends."

"That's *one* of the buggers? Mags." His light climbed up the wall, all the way to the top, and then up to the jagged ceiling of rock. "The whole wall, it must be hundreds of them."

"Thousands. Tarzi, these went extinct seventy-five million years before the dinosaurs!" Her tail switched back and forth sharply in the darkness.

"Aren't they pre-, what is it, Precambrian?"

"Early Cambrian. Close enough. But what the hell are they doing in the Belt?"

"I don't know, but let's take some." Tarzi pulled his pistol from its holster. He flipped it to "torch." He found the rough point of a small outcrop and slowly sliced it off. The slice of rock fell into his open hand, and he held it in the light. "Oh, nice souvenir."

In the black and grey speckling of the asteroid rock, two distinct trilobite shapes swam past each other, only partially obscured inside the stone. Even darker black minerals had replaced their bodies. With a polish, they would shine like obsidian.

"Pretty," said Mags. "You know, that fossil wouldn't cost much on Earth, but they never get out to the Belt. We might have to come back with proper tools."

"And make millions selling trilobite paperweights to space miners?"

She laughed. "Think bigger, dear! I can think of a few mining tycoons who would spring for a statue carved from this rock."

Patches mewed loudly and rubbed Mags' leg.

"What's the matter, kitty? You just ate!"

Patches jumped onto a small ledge of stone at the bottom of the wall. Lowering her belly and arching her tail, she pinned her ears back. Her paws rhythmically kneaded the stone, first one, then the other, claws outstretched.

She howled and bolted into the darkness.

"Come on, dear. Let's keep going. We can excavate later."

They continued down the rough pathway carved into the rock. Mags kept her light straight ahead, shining a wide circle on the pathway, illuminating the edge of the wall and the edge of the drop-off. Tarzi's light slowly scanned beyond the edge of the drop-off into the abyss. He could not see any bottom to it, though he thought he could make out the wall on the other side.

Mags sniffed several times.

"You smell something?"

"Seafood. It's what Patches is freaking out about."

Patches darted along the edge of the wall through the arc of light, then into darkness behind them. "Mrooowwwl!" She darted back the other way, leaving them behind again.

"Something's alive on this rock," said Mags. "And it's making me—Whoa!"

Tarzi's foot slipped on the rock. His hand shot out to grab her forearm. "Sodding slippery!" But wrapped around his other wrist, he felt the firm grip of Sparky's tail.

"Careful!"

The tail unwrapped and released his arm once he regained his footing. "Got it."

Mags returned her light to the path. "Okay, watch your head. The ceiling is lower right here." She crouched, and Tarzi crouched behind her. They moved forward slowly, staying to the wall on their left.

Her headlamp shone on the path for about a meter in front of them. Tarzi's headlamp mostly illuminated the back of Mags' thighs and her boots, her tail swishing calmly back and forth. Sparky's faint green glow lit up the wall each time he circled around.

The ledge under their feet widened out another meter, then another. But just ahead, the wall came to a jagged end. The low ceiling opened into a much larger cavern.

"It turns out my map isn't as bad as I thought. This must be the land bridge that connects to the main lab." As they pressed on, the doorway at the far side of the bridge came into view. "And there it is."

Tarzi's light moved toward the door, which was recessed a meter deep in an alcove barely wider than he could stretch out his arms. Like the exit door from the first room, it had a security panel. It was the same shiny plastic instead of metal. He raised his light above the door.

"Mags! Look!" The circle of her spotlight drifted up to meet his.

They saw, carved into the stone, an animal shaped like a dolphin but forty meters long, with a thin snout full of daggers. "What kind of fish is *that*?"

"Damn, Tarzi, that's no fish. That's an ichthyosaur!"

"A fish lizard?"

"Literally. A swimming reptile. But look at its skin."

All along the sides of the monstrous reptile carving ran lines like the circuitry on Tarzi's seahorse. Instead of scales, it had smooth plates, like the outlines of Sparky's metal panels. "Is that what they were making here? It's huge!"

"Can you imagine if something that size could generate an electric—"

Patches howled.

Just then, they were slammed and lifted from the ground. The curved edge of a tentacle as thick as a bullet train assaulted them bluntly. Their bodies flew through the air past the edge of the drop-off. They fell into darkness.

Tarzi saw random flashes of the caverns in his headlamp's light before he realized he was falling. He cried out, arms flailing, legs kicking at nothing.

Mags' spine twisted her body around in mid-air before she had a single thought. Instinctually, her joints expanded like a cat's so she could absorb the impact of landing. She heard Tarzi scream. The circle of light from her headlamp swung around in the direction of her fall.

Her eyes brought the bottom of the pit into sharp focus, but she could not believe what she saw. Oval tubes stuck out at all angles from the rocky walls of the pit. They glistened, translucent, a pale green in the falling light. They coated the entire bottom of the pit. Something moved inside them.

Mags hit the bottom feet-first with a loud splat. She sank into gelatinous goo and her fingertips touched the bottom.

Tarzi slammed on his back into the slime beside her.

Her head broke the surface. She tore off her mask and gasped for air. The force of the blow had knocked the wind from her lungs, and the gel had clogged the mask's filters. She took two quick breaths and reached her hand down into the goo to pull Tarzi up.

She tore his mask off so he could breathe.

"Ow! Sod it!"

"Ugh! Here, take your mask. You can still use the light."

As he caught his breath, she ran both hands through her hair. It was filled with gel. Drawing it through her closed hands, she squeezed out as much of the goo as she could. "Gross!"

"Auntie," said Tarzi, shining his light around him. "What in the actual fuck?"

"Look!" Mags shone her light directly onto one of the oval tubes between them. Like the others surrounding it, it stood more than a meter tall. She had damaged it in her landing, and the translucent outer shell was torn open to reveal tentacles. "They're eggs."

"Oh, my god." He stared at the smooth, glistening tentacles, following the orderly rows of suckers along their curves. There, a single eye stared back at him.

Patches howled from the top of the pit. Far above them, her tiny face glowed in the seahorse's light. Her mouth opened to squeeze out another plaintive mew.

"We've got to get out of here," said Mags. "Damn it! I have this goop in my socks now." She scooped a handful of it from her chest and flung it at the wall.

Tarzi slicked back his mohawk and tossed aside more goop. He pulled his cap from the slime. Thick blobs dripped from it. "Disgusting!" He shoved the cap into his pocket and spit to one side.

"Patches," Mags shouted, "Take cover! Hide!"

Patches howled again then bolted out of sight. But the glow from the seahorse began moving down the wall.

"I'll be—check it out, Tarzi."

The seahorse drifted down into the darkness. Holding out his arm, the young man invited it to land like a hawk.

"Don't touch it!"

"Don't worry. He won't shock me." Tarzi's cybernetic friend proved him right. It hovered over his hand and curled its tail around the young man's wrist. "See? He—whoa! Hey!" Tarzi struggled as the seahorse tugged on his wrist. "Cut it out!"

It only tightened its grip and lifted him into the air.

"Tarzi, stop fighting for a second. See if it can pick you up."

"What if it drops me?"

"If it goes nuts, I'll blast it out of the air."

He stopped resisting. "That is so reassuring." Below the seahorse's grip on his right wrist, Tarzi took hold of his arm with his left hand. "Watch my one-handed pull-up." He pulled steadily against the seahorse's grip, breaking his feet free from the eggs and goop with a loud splorch.

"Ten out of ten, great form. Okay, do you think he can get you all the way to the top?"

"What? Oh, sod it. How else are we getting out of here? Come on, Sparky. Take me up!" And with that, the two of them rose into the air.

"Hang on tight!" Mags solemnly watched her nephew. A halo of green light shone around him. Her asteroid exploration kit contained nylon ropes, hooks, spikes, and a small hammer. But climbing out of here covered in this slippery gel presented a problem. She was sure she could handle it. A few bruises, maybe worse, but nothing she couldn't walk away from. But Tarzi? When had he ever climbed vertical cliffs?

She smiled when the light reached the top of the drop-off.

"Made it, Auntie! Yes! I'll send him down for you."

Again the green light grew larger and larger as the seahorse descended into the pit. Mags held her wrist up to it. The seahorse's tail uncurled, wrapped around her wrist, and tugged. Her feet rose a centimeter from the floor of the pit, two centimeters, and then BAM. She fell back to solid ground.

"Come on, buddy. Try harder than that."

The seahorse pulled. Again, Mags rose into the air one centimeter, then two, but dropped to solid ground.

"Tarzi! Can't you make it go any harder!"

"What's wrong?"

"It keeps picking me up and then setting me down."

"Maybe you're too heavy."

"Fuck you!"

"Sorry, Auntie. I just meant—"

"I bloody well know what you meant! Now let me think."

"Oh, holy shit! Mags!"

"What?!"

Tarzi scrambled away from the edge of the drop-off and out of her sight. Three flashes of laser light burst from his pistol. "It's huge! Whatever hit us, it's still in here!"

A massive tentacle appeared at the edge of the pit. It snaked down the wall faster than the eye could follow. Mags drew her pistol, disarming the safety, but it was too late. The tentacle came right towards her and wrapped her up. Suckers gripped her flesh. They tore the pistol from her clenched hand as the cold and slimy thing pulled her out of the pit, past the edge, and up into the air above Tarzi's head.

Then she saw the horrifying thing that lived on the other side on the rocky bridge. From the depths of another pit, an enormous head swelled up. Its tentacles waved in the light of her lamp. A beak that could cut a school bus in half clacked angrily. She screamed.

The tentacle brought her up to a pair of eyes set in a gelatinous globe of a head. The pupils focused on her, and her light shined into their caverns.

With a heart-wrenching howl, a calico blur shot through the air. Patches landed on the tentacle which gripped Mags. She ripped into it with her claws. She tore a chunk free with her teeth.

Then Patches felt something she had never felt before, a powerful presence for which she had no words. It pulled at her mind like a magnet. She stopped her attack to look into the eyes of this giant thing which smelled like fish but was not. Then Patches went limp. A second later, so did Mags.

"Mags!" Tarzi shouted. He aimed his pistol at the swollen globe of the monster's head, knowing the tentacles had crushed his friends and killed them. In his rage and sadness, he fired.

But Tarzi could not have been more wrong.

A great tableau unfolded before Mags, like a scroll containing images from the life of the octopus. The images came to life. Tentacles undulated. Figures in lab coats conducted experiments. The ocean surf splashed and kissed her face. Then she was drawn in.

She swam through this projection of the life of the octopus, now all around her. The cold pressure of the sea surrounded her. Down she dove. Her arms and legs flexed, now boneless and lined with suckers.

A light suddenly pierced the waves above. Mags looked up into its glow. Scores of baby octopuses and small fish interrupted the beam, casting shadows below them. She reached out a tentacle to touch the newborn octopuses.

A hose snaked into the water, coming straight for her. Mags propelled herself out of the way, but the sea creatures were not so lucky. The hose sucked them up, not choosing any ones in particular, vacuuming up anything in its path.

Then a calico torpedo plunged into the sea. Mags saw Patches' body deformed like hers, reshaped like an octopus, shooting down from the surface of the water. Patches attacked the hose violently. She wrapped herself around it, trying to dig in her claws. But she had no claws. She tried to kick her back legs and shred the hose, but she had no legs. Only tentacles.

Mags thrust forward to join Patches in the rebellion. But when her strange limbs touched her cat, the hose sucked them into its pull. Up, up, up it took them before retreating from the sea. A white light obliterated everything.

"Patches? Patches!"

The indestructible calico heard Mags' voice, but not from any particular direction. All around her, the impenetrable white light shone with it.

"Patches! Where are you?" Mags heard her from everywhere all at once. "Patches!" Again, the mewing. She tried to close her eyes and concentrate, but she had no eyes. She tried to touch her hands to her face, but she had no hands, nor any body at all.

Somehow she could look into the light in any direction, but she could not see anything, not even herself. "Bloody hell," she said with no mouth. And then she was born.

Patches arrived at the birth of Meteor Mags and relived her entire life in a flash. She saw Mollie hold her new baby for the first time. She lived through the uprising in Spain, and the terrible days in Barcelona. Patches held Mollie in her arms as she died from gunshot wounds. She met Celina and sailed to the United States. She danced.

Patches joined Margareta in preparation for the invasion of Normandy, and later met John Coltrane. She witnessed the development of the GravGens at La Plaza Margareta and rode a motorcycle on Gramma's last night on Earth. Patches joined Mags in her quest to get off-world, her return to a life of smuggling, and the building of her club on Vesta 4.

Then a kitten was born.

As the calico relived her own life, Mags lived it with her too. They witnessed the tragic train wreck etched upon Patches' mind as her first memory. From her vantage point, Mags could see the truth behind this awful wreck, a truth not even Patches understood.

But Patches suddenly did understand, and Mags felt her understand. Then both of them realized what was happening to them.

"Kitten, we're inside each other's minds. Do you feel it?"

Patches mewed and imagined herself in Mags' arms. Purring, she licked Mags' nose and nuzzled her.

"My baby kitty."

Together, they watched Patches' life unfold from the inside. Patches learned how Mags had become trapped in the storage room in the spaceport on the day they met, and together they purred as they relived their first meeting.

As the life they had lived together replayed before their eyes, they felt a rush of understanding. Everything they had ever known, everything they had ever felt, everything they had ever sensed or touched or deduced—all of it was laid bare before them, shared completely.

Their minds reeled, flooded with information, flooded with physical sensations and emotional memories. Overcome, they surrendered to the rush. And then, as the experience brought them right up to that very moment in their lives, the bright light returned. Like a sun going nova, it consumed everything.

Stunned, Mags and Patches awoke in a glass test tube. Their tiny bodies floated in a briny liquid. Beside them swam a single baby octopus.

"We're inside its mind, too." Despite the physicality of the experience of swimming inside this test tube, Mags could mentally feel Patches close to her, as if her arms still held her kitten. This comforted her.

Forceps clamped the baby octopus. Operated by giant hands, a syringe pierced the infant's skin.

The octopus writhed in pain. Released into the water, it struggled in vain to find shelter. Only relentless, transparent walls met its touch.

The hands, gloved in white, lifted the tube and set it in a chamber. The chamber grew dark when its door slammed shut. Then they felt the heat, and they felt the octopus feel the heat, and a strange glow enveloped them.

"The bastards are radiating us! Oh, this poor little thing." The three of them floated in the green light as their bodies burned, cooking like eggs in a microwave oven. Their DNA broke apart and reassembled in new mutations. Mags screamed.

Patches clawed at the walls of the tube to no avail. Her fear and the octopus' fear swept over Mags, whose heart ached in her chest.

She opened her arms to hold the octopus the way she held Patches in her mind, to establish the same mental union which felt like a comforting hug to both of them.

The baby octopus swam to her and wrapped around her. Mags cradled it with Patches, who nuzzled the terrified sea creature.

Then they were all caught up in the white light once again.

★ o•♥•o ★

"Tarzi. Tarzi, stop."

He heard Meteor Mags' voice and looked around.

"Tarzi, stop shooting."

"Auntie? Is that you?"

"Yes, it's me! Now will you please listen?"

"Where are you?"

"I'm—it's hard to explain right now."

"How can I hear you?"

"I'm speaking right into your mind, Tarzi. Now please. Just relax for a minute. Everything will be fine."

He had fired his laser pistol at the octopus, shooting at its central mass. He had not fatally wounded the octopus, but gouts of green blood now oozed from the wounds he had inflicted. "Mags! You're freaking me out. What's that thing doing to you? I'll fucking kill it, I swear!"

"Dude, calm your tits! We're just—we're just talking. I'll be right down, I promise."

He lowered his pistol, but kept the safety off just in case. "Okay. It's cool. I'm cool. It's all cool."

"Sooo cool, dear. Be right back."

Tarzi leaned against the rough-hewn wall to his back. Without taking his eyes from the octopus, he fished in his pockets for a pack of smokes. As he lit up and puffed, Tarzi brought up the display for his seahorse again. He slowed his breathing, calmed his mind, and imagined Swans in concert. The crushing beats and the pulsing drone grew farther and farther apart as he entered his trance. He studied the seahorse's menu in detail.

Before his cigarette had burned halfway down, he realized the full extent of what his new pet could do.

 ★ o•♥•o ★

In their quest to create cybernetic lifeforms, the researchers in the asteroid lab ran into several problems. The octopus which held

Meteor Mags and Patches in its grip formed the first stage of their solution.

Proteins form the basic building blocks of cellular life, so the researchers needed organic lifeforms which could merge with their inorganic cellular technology to create weaponized, metallic life. The researchers found no existing, complex lifeforms could achieve this union. However, their studies on bacteria showed that genetically altering successive generations could result in an animal whose biology was up to the task.

As Mags and Patches relived each moment of the octopus' life, they learned this as the octopus had learned it. For the researchers had not considered the implications of working with octopuses. Among Earth's most intelligent and adaptive animals, octopuses already possessed impressive brains. Aside from one central brain resembling a mammal's, an octopus had a network of neurons distributed throughout its tentacles. This allowed each tentacle to act independently. When grown to the size of the mutant octopus in the lab, that networked brain became a force to be reckoned with.

The electrical field generated by that brain now gave the octopus a reach and ability beyond anything which had ever existed. As it grew in its isolation tank, the octopus became aware of the researchers' minds. Quietly, unnoticed, it observed them. In time, the octopus grew to understand not only their language but their intent. Mags and Patches, from their vantage point inside the mind of the octopus, at last understood that intent as well.

Mags whispered, "They're going to kill her babies."

Though she had never become pregnant, Patches understood the primal bond the octopus felt with its young. She felt the violation as the researchers forcibly impregnated the octopus with spermatophores of their own creation. These cells, engineered nowhere in the universe but in this asteroid lab, contained a synthetic form of haploid DNA. The resulting babies would generate the living tissues which could be harvested to create the third and final cybernetic generation of sea creatures. That the second generation infants would die in this process meant nothing to the researchers. But it meant everything to the octopus.

During the few weeks in which her fertilized cells grew into eggs, the octopus decided her course of action. Reaching out with sheer mental force, her massive brain subverted the researchers' wills. Intelligent though they were, their tiny mammalian minds were no match for hers. The octopus seized control of their bodies, forcing them to open first the door to the caverns outside their lab, and then to destroy the glass barrier of her gigantic isolation tank.

The water in her tank burst into a flood, pouring out of the laboratory and into the caverns beyond. The octopus flowed out into the caverns with it. Her flexible body squeezed through the doorway. The shock of submersion nearly freed the minds of the researchers from her spell. But the octopus, having absorbed what they knew about anatomy, used their knowledge against them.

As Mags and Patches experienced this escape, they felt the mother octopus' ruthless hatred. They joined her great mind in shutting down the researchers' respiratory and muscular functions. They reveled in her rage as the researchers drowned, powerless beneath the waters. Then they shared her joy as she laid hundreds of eggs in the moistened caverns.

But this joy soon turned to disappointment. Though her mutations had given her and her potential offspring the ability to survive on limited amounts of water, the eggs required full submersion to hatch. The octopus had not realized this, for neither had the researchers. And so, the mother octopus took refuge in the largest of the pits, where the most water had gathered, and she bided her time with an unearthly patience. Her mind reached out to her hundreds of unhatched offspring, soothing them, calming them as they grew inside their translucent shells. She waited in this communion for years.

As their reliving of the octopus' life brought them right up to the present moment, both Mags and Patches knew what needed to be done. "You need water, dear," Mags told the octopus. "Your babies need it to hatch."

Patches visualized the enormous tanks which lie beyond the doorway where Tarzi now stood, picturing them in her mind so the octopus could see them. Mags felt something she had never felt before, and she realized Patches was communicating with the octopus nonverbally. Patches' feline imagination pictured her and Mags, and then showed them releasing the waters into the caverns. Her mind drew a picture of the eggs hatching.

Though her body remained captive in the tentacle, Mags felt a glowing pride. Look at my little kitty, she thought, solving this problem on her own.

As Patches and the octopus conversed in their wordless, animal way, Mags reached out with her own mind to talk to Tarzi, and to calm him. Then she returned her attention to the animals' conversation.

The octopus gave the combination to the lab's door. It had slammed shut shortly after her escape due to the lab's security systems, but she had gleaned the code from the researchers' minds before she killed them. She could not use it, for her tentacles were too large to operate the keypad. But now, the code numbers floated in sequence across the canvas of Mags' mind. Then slowly, gently, the monster set them down on the bridge.

Mags scooped up Patches in her arms. "Oh, my little kitten." Patches nuzzled her and licked her nose several times, purring.

"Auntie! Patches!" Tarzi ran to them. "Are you okay?"

Mags threw an arm around him, and the three of them embraced. "Tarzi, you are never going to believe what's on the other side of that door!" His eyes grew wide with disbelief as she told him all about it. "Now come with me," she said firmly. "Patches and I made a promise, and we intend to keep it."

"Just look at these poor little blighters." Mags stood before one of dozens of giant salt-water tanks. Transparent tubes networked with an array of circuitry, they towered a half dozen meters into the air. They ranged in diameter from one to five meters. Only one of the tanks stood shattered and empty. "They must have starved to death."

The bottom of each remaining tank held nothing but skeletons, the flesh having dissolved into the water long ago. "What an awful way to go out." Tarzi shook his head. "But I don't get it. I thought they were supposed to be cybernetic. These look like regular old bones."

"Because that's all they are. The eggheads found out they needed to create a couple generations of mutated animals first, so they could cull the modified tissues for the cyborgs. We're looking at the remains of those early generations."

"Fuck. Do you think that's how Sparky was created? By mutating and then murdering some poor seahorses?"

Mags sighed. "I wish I could tell you otherwise, but that's the bloody truth."

Sparky hovered, and if he was capable of feeling anything for the dead creatures in the tanks, he showed no sign.

Mags placed her hand on the young man's shoulder. "Don't be sad, dear. What's done is done, and the bastards who did this got what was coming to them." She spat on the floor. "Animal experimentation makes me fucking sick. But at least these tanks can serve one final purpose." She stormed off. "First, come take a look at this."

The smuggler and her cat walked through the laboratory as if they had been there before. And, because of all they had learned in their experience within the octopus' mind, they had. Mags stepped over the skeletal remains of one of the researchers. Patches ran ahead to a cabinet on the far wall. She rubbed her face on its corner and curled her tail around it.

Tarzi followed. "God, this place is huge. They must have carved it right out of the rock." His voice echoed in the cavernous space, from the manmade surface below his feet to the stony walls and ceilings. He stepped over the skeleton of another researcher. The skull and hand bones protruded from a dirty white lab coat.

"Hand me your pistol, dear. Mine's down in that sodding pit now." Setting it to "torch," she sliced off the padlock from the cabinet. The lock clunked loudly on the floor.

Patches scampered away, then returned to poke her nose

impatiently at the cabinet's double doors.

Mags opened them up. "You still reading that Dobzhansky book, dear?"

"Theo is the man! I read it like four times already." He took the pistol and holstered it.

"My budding evolutionist. You're gonna love this." She grabbed the handle at the top of a black box taller than she was. "Here, give me a hand, will you?"

"Whatever you say, Auntie." Tarzi clapped his hands together several times.

"No, you idiot. Help me with this goddamn thing!"

He stood beside her, placing his hands on the black box. The four corners facing them had wheels. Together, they strained against the weight as she pulled the top forward and lowered it to the floor. The box slid out of the cabinet. It was as wide as a pair of coffins. Mags wheeled it back and lifted open its lid.

"What's all this, then?" Tarzi saw microscopes, and what appeared to be a computer, and more equipment he could only guess at.

"It's a portable genetics lab."

"No shit?"

"No shit, little man. The researchers used it in their field work, collecting specimens from earth and so on. You could sequence the genome of just about anything with these tools. Plus imaging equipment, miniature electron microscopes, all kinds of fun stuff."

"I can't believe you know all this without even looking at it. Do you know how it works?"

"Let's just say I got a major crash course in genetics a few minutes ago. And you know what's really fucked up?"

"What?"

"So did Patches."

"You're kidding."

"No, I'm not. Of course, I don't think she understands it all. I don't even understand it all. It's a little fuzzy, and frankly it's giving me a bloody headache just thinking about it. I guess you can't just dump a bunch of information into a brain and have it make immediate sense. Now be a dear and give your auntie a square, will you?"

Tarzi presented his pack of smokes and took out one for each of them. "What do you think she'll *do* with all that information?" He held out a flame.

Mags touched her cigarette to the light until it glowed red. "Such a gentleman." She blew a series of three smoke rings. "You mean Patches?"

"Yeah." Tarzi lit up. "I mean, hell. I don't know what I mean. Can she talk now or something?"

"I've told you before. Patches has *always* talked. You just don't understand cat." She took another puff. "But how much of my mind, the octo's mind, and the minds of all the researchers the octo had scanned—she's always been a smart kitty, but that's a lot to process. I think we'll just have to wait and see."

Patches rubbed against Tarzi's leg and mewed. He knelt on the floor to scratch the side of her face.

"See? Same old Patches," Mags lied.

"Yep. Same old Patches. Just—indestructible. And a genetics expert."

"And maybe that. Okay, back to business." She pushed the black box across the shiny plastic floor. "Our idiot mapmaker didn't know about it, but there's an elevator back here. It leads right up to the surface. We can take our booty up that way."

"Argh," said Tarzi. "Our godless gains." He and Patches followed her through the cavern. "So that's it? A bunch of dead fish, a psychic octopus, and a weaponized seahorse?"

"Oh, no," said Mags. "Your little friend wasn't the only finished project here. Do you see that cabinet up ahead? Torch the locks off it. And get some fresh filters in your mask!" She rolled the black box to the far end of the cavern while Tarzi got to work.

She returned from the elevator to find him struggling with another black box. "Dude, don't give yourself a hernia! Teamwork, little man. Let me help you."

Tarzi had torched the locks off two more cabinets. "These things are even heavier than the last one. What the hell is in them?"

"Set her down, and I'll show you." Mags opened the lid. Inside, a trio of eels lay in molded plastic. Their sleek, metallic surfaces glistened in the laboratory's light. A meter long, each showed a ferocious array of teeth, soulless red eyes, and paneled skin like Sparky's. "Not as big as that ichthyosaur carving out front, but still pretty bad-ass, don't you think?"

"Look at those faces! I don't know whether to scream or shit my pants."

"I'd advise against the latter, dear. We've got a long way to go before we're home. Here, help me with the next one."

They pulled the second box out of the cabinet and proceeded to the next one. It held another black box, but the second half of the cabinet held a rack of full-body suits.

"That looks like the mesh we sawed through."

"That's because it is. Remember what I told you about Faraday cages and mesh?"

"Yeah. None of the juice can get through, right?"

"Right. These are Faraday suits. They go with these cyborgs we're plundering."

"Of course," Tarzi realized. "It wouldn't do any good to have a weapon like Sparky unless you were safe from all the juice he's kicking out, would it?"

She patted the young man's shoulder. "Damn right. And look at this." Mags showed him the inside and outside of the helmet on one of the suits. "Whoever made them figured out a way to communicate from inside."

"Wouldn't a suit that can block electricity block out radio waves, too?"

"Exactly. I'm guessing they have an analog system here. The piece on the inside converts the microphone signal to a pressure wave, which is picked up by the piece on the outside, and then sent as a radio signal."

"So if you had a platoon of soldiers wearing these in combat, they could still talk to each other."

"Mhm." Mags admired the technology. "Throw them on top of

this case so we can wheel the whole lot of them to the elevator." She flipped through the rack quickly. "I just hope they made one in my size."

In the elevator to the surface, Tarzi asked, "You said something about a promise?"

"I did. That octopus out there needs water to hatch her babies. And we're going to give it to her."

"What's the plan then? We blow the tanks?"

"I've got enough explosives in the *Queen Anne* to do it. But we also need to turn on the water pumps from under the surface. Those tanks aren't all the water on this rock. The eggheads had a whole system to clean the water for the tanks, not to mention their own personal use, and there's a subterranean reservoir linked to those tanks. We need to open that door, open the tanks, pump the water out, and get the hell out before it drowns us."

The elevator stopped at the surface.

"It's all computerized, isn't it? The whole system?"

"As far as I can tell, thanks to the octopus. The GravGens should be on their own system, though, as usual. What are you thinking?"

"I studied Sparky's menu. And I have an idea. We wouldn't need to blow up anything at all. And we could do it from a distance."

"You, my dear, are one stand-up criminal. You think your little seahorse can override the system?"

"I bet he can!"

"Go for it. Let's see what these things are capable of. No one had a chance to get them out of the lab and test them before that sodding kraken killed everyone."

"And Plan B is explosives."

"Agreed! Put your mask on, wheel these crates out the door, and we'll bring the *Queen Anne* around to pick them up when we're done."

Moments later, they stood before the lab's central control panel. "Patches says she wants to watch." Patches lay comfortably on Mags' left arm, held to her chest as the smuggler rubbed one fuzzy ear and then the other.

"She probably can't be hurt, but you and me might want to get back to the elevator door." Sparky hovered over his shoulder. Tarzi tapped his ring and turned it slightly, tapping it some more.

"You're not going to fry us, too, are you?"

"Ha! I bloody well hope not. Stand back!"

The seahorse lowered onto the control panel. A web of green lightning gathered around his body. Crackling tendrils of electricity reached into the panel. The bones and decay in the bottom of the tanks bubbled and stirred.

"He's overriding the pumps." The tanks creaked. The water pressure inside steadily increased, straining at the glass and metal bonds.

Patches' ears twitched. "Mew!" She leapt down from Mags' arms and ran for the elevator.

"Good idea!" Water sprayed from the seams around the bases of the tanks. A pipe burst overhead, shooting a stream of cold water into the cavern. "Tell him to blow the doors and let's get the fuck out!" Mags took off after Patches.

"On it," called Tarzi. "Just—one second." He tapped his ring again. His eyes darted across the menus only he could see. Water pooled around his feet. "Oh, shit. Maybe this wasn't such a good idea."

"Tarzi!" Mags called back to him. "Are you trying to electrocute yourself? Let's go, go, go!"

"Come on, Sparky. Blow the damn doors already!"

Suddenly, the web of electricity grew to a sphere. It engulfed the entire control panel. Tarzi fell back into the water. He scrambled backwards on his hands and feet. His muscles spasmed as a series of shocks racked his body. The door to the outside cavern slid open.

Tarzi pulled himself to his feet and sprinted for the elevator. The lightning sphere grew in size, until it was several meters across. Sparky hovered calmly in the middle of it, feeding electricity into the system. Sparks crackled on the water and all along the metal circuitry of the tanks. The cavern groaned under the increasing pressure.

Tarzi ran like hell.

Mags stood at the elevator door, holding it open for him, with Patches standing behind her. Their faces flickered in the green glow of lightning that filled the cavern.

Then the tanks exploded. A deluge erupted into the laboratory. Torrents of water poured through the small door to the cavern where the octopus waited.

A wave rose behind Tarzi as he ran. Mags held out her hand. "Come on, come on, come on!"

The wave caught up with him and threw him down. The force propelled him across the floor and towards the elevator. Tarzi screamed.

Patches leapt into Mags' arms. The wave smashed the young man into the back wall of the elevator. Holding Patches with one arm, Mags reached down to pull him up.

He sputtered, finding his footing. "Sparky!" Water rose in the elevator.

Mags held her finger over the button to close the door. "Here he comes!" The seahorse zipped across the waves, speeding towards the elevator, and slipped inside.

"What the hell are you trying to do?" Mags yelled at the seahorse. "Drown us all?"

Sparky chirped happily and hovered over the young man's shoulder. The doors closed. Tarzi shivered as he stood up to his chest in the cold water trapped in the elevator with them. Patches meowed unhappily, climbing onto Mags' shoulder.

But as the elevator rose to the asteroid's surface, a strange feeling of elation came over each of them. The mother octopus reached out with her mind to show them what transpired in the caverns below.

Submerged in water now, hundreds of octopus eggs began to hatch. Tentacles emerged from translucent shells to wave in the water. The baby octopuses pushed aside their shells and swam up, up, up.

Floating in the water-filled cavern, their mother greeted them.

The babies gathered around her, their tentacles playfully touching her. She swished the water around them. She touched their minds, one by one, feeling their joy and newfound freedom.

The elevator came to a stop. The door opened to the asteroid's surface and water spilled out onto the rock, taking the trio with it.

Patches leapt clear.

Mags scrambled to her feet and shook her head.

Tarzi grabbed her arm. "Is that what it was like, being in her mind?"

"That was just a little taste. I think it was her version of a thank-you note!"

Patches shook the water from her fur. She purred with satisfaction.

TIME TO GET KRAKEN!

PART TWO: THE LIBERATION

The dragon leaned over the top of the pen. Its tongue flicked through the metal bars, tasting the captive scents.

Kala held the trembling Sarah tightly. The dragon's breath turned her stomach.

"Jesus, what are these fucking things?" Suzi huddled against the back of the pen. No one could answer her.

Once clear of Earth, the ship's crew charted a course for their rendezvous with a much larger ship on the edge of the Belt. They spoke to each other in a growling, hissing language punctuated by rasping shrieks like giant grackles. The girls could not understand a word of it. Perhaps that was for the best, for the current topic of dragon discussion centered on how angry Major Dekarna might be if they ate some of the captive cargo before the rendezvous.

Beside the pen, a wall of smaller cages held more trapped animals from the forest: rabbits, foxes, squirrels, stray dogs and cats. The dragons' breeding stock of live mammals had grown weak from generations of inbreeding in their travels across the vast desolation of space to our solar system. Fresh genes, they hoped, would strengthen their farms. And new tastes from Earth would always be a boon for their kitchens.

Hyo-Sonn listened to the pitiful cries and chatter of the animals next to her. She held her hands to her ears to block the noise, but it made no difference. She felt on her neck the dragon's breath, as warm as a fresh pile of dung. The dragon's tongue flicked across her face. She screamed and pressed her body to the floor. Then the dragon spoke.

"Mammals," it growled.

"Fuck me, they can talk?"

"Suzi, shut up!" Hyo-Sonn looked up into the dragon's face. A pupil expanded and contracted as its eye's yellow orb swiveled back and forth, taking in the sight of her fear.

"Hurr hurr hurr." The dragon laughed in its laconic, reptilian fashion. It waved one of its comrades over to the cage.

The second dragon brought a pole a meter long with a spiked

hook on the end. He made more unintelligible noises to the first dragon. Had Suzi understood their language, she would not have been pleased to know the beast remarked on how much energy she had. The two dragons chirped back and forth about whether it would be better to save the energetic one for breeding or to eat her right away.

The second dragon opened a door on the top of the pen. All nine girls scrambled away from the opening. The first dragon took his weapon, a pronged staff, and ran it along the bars of the pen. Sparks flew where it scraped against the metal bars. Shocks racked the girls' bodies everywhere they touched the pen. The reptile laughed again. "You," it said, pointing to Suzi. "We save for later."

But the girl next to Suzi was not so fortunate. As if spearing a fish, the second dragon thrust the spiked pole into the cage. It impaled the girl next to Suzi, entering into her soft abdomen and hooking on her ribcage. She struggled helplessly as the dragon pulled her toward the opening.

"Let her go," Hyo-Sonn shouted. Tears soaked her face.

The first dragon shoved his weapon between the bars and delivered a shock unlike anything Hyo-Sonn had ever felt. Her muscles spasmed. She flailed like a fish on land.

The girl on the hook tried to resist, but life grew rapidly dim in her eyes. Blood spilled from her wound and the corners of her mouth. As the dragon yanked her through the narrow opening, her neck and limbs broke in horrible angles. The pen's door slammed shut.

The dragon's eyes grew wide with pleasure. He pulled her body from the hook to dangle like a broken trophy in its hands. With claws wrapped around her neck and head, he took a firm grip.

The other dragon grabbed her arm. The two monsters pulled her limbs off her body. Other members of the crew watched the display with delight, encouraging them to feast.

The girls in the pen screamed. Hot blood splattered across Hyo-Sonn's face and arms. The dragons tore off chunks of the broken girl's skin and muscle and gulped them down. They crunched her bones, flicking their forked tongues between mouthfuls. They moved on to her internal organs.

Sarah closed her eyes. Even the horrors visited upon her in the Clinic could not compare to what happened just outside the cage. Her mind recoiled at the thought, reaching instead for something to comfort her.

She thought of her favorite song, the song she would sing quietly to herself when the Clinic's staff would have their way with her. She sang the verses in her mind over and over again until they drowned out the awful things. Sarah retreated into the song until she could hear the screams and the tearing flesh no longer. She imagined the singer, brave and strong, someone whom no one would dare make suffer in the ways Sarah had suffered. She held this image in her mind until it glowed with a white light that outshined everything.

Then, in some way Sarah could not have explained, she felt someone else listening.

"Oh, god, that's so much better." Tarzi emerged from the shower room aboard the *Queen Anne* wearing a pair of sweat shorts, scruffing the water out of his mohawk with a towel. He tossed his freshly cleaned cap on his bunk. It landed next to Sparky, who lay motionless beside the pillow where Tarzi had set his ring.

Meteor Mags sat on the edge of her bunk next to Patches. She wore a towel wrapped around her body and another like a turban around her head. "No kidding. I think I horked up a gallon of snot before I got that octopus goo out of me."

"That's just a lovely image, Mags. Thanks for that."

Mags had her portable keyboard set up on its stand by her bedside. A melody played on the ship's speakers. She harmonized it with a handful of chords, trying a few different voicings.

"Is that song what I think it is?"

"As long as you think it's *Invincible* by Kelly Clarkson, then yeah."

"Get the fuck out, Auntie. How can you even listen to that over-produced, pop bullshit? If there was any more reverb on that track, I'd have to vomit."

"Shut the fuck up! Patches loves this song!"

Patches stretched out alongside Mags' thigh and kneaded the blanket, opening and shutting her eyes slowly. Though Patches was no longer sharing her mind directly with her pirate friend, she felt closer than ever before. Patches had always felt a great bond with her unruly companion, but this was something more. She did not know if it would wear off, or last forever, but she could feel Mags' love for her the way a planet feels light from a star. Patches basked in it.

"She would, wouldn't she?" Tarzi plopped down on the edge of his bunk. "I think Clutch's *Immortal* would be a better pick for her, though."

"Word. But you just need to hear the song itself instead of thinking about how it was produced."

Tarzi scoffed. "She should have had Steve Albini produce that album. It would have been a million times better."

"Or Rick Rubin."

"Come on, now."

"What?" Mags threw her hands in the air. "Hello, dill-weed! That guy even made Def Leppard sound like a real rock band on *High'N'Dry*."

"That was Mutt Lange, dumb-ass. Rubin did that Cult album you like."

"Whatever! And don't even start with that 'Rick Rubin ruined The (International) Noise Conspiracy' crap again. *Armed Love* is the best album ever!"

"I don't know," said Tarzi. "I liked their earlier stuff way better. *A New Morning* all the way." He made the sign of the devil.

"I can't fault you for that pick. But just listen to this song, okay? And forget you ever heard it another way before."

He resigned himself to his fate and listened.

Mags touched the keys. In response, a grand piano played over the speakers. She sang.

Tarzi's incredulous look melted away. His lips slowly spread into a smile. Patches purred like it was going out of style, flexing her paws happily. Mags closed her eyes, swaying as her hands moved over the chords. But halfway through the chorus, she stopped.

"Did you hear that?" She opened her eyes and looked around.

"Hear what?"

"I heard somebody singing."

"All I hear is you, Auntie. And it sounds great. I take back what I said about—"

She stood. "No, seriously. You don't hear that?" She stared out the window. "There it is again."

"There's what again? I think that octopus addled your brains. There's nobody here but us."

She whirled around to face him. "Tarzi! That's not just any song. That's *my* song. From the Psycho 78s album! And someone else is singing it."

He ran his hands over his damp mohawk. Mags seemed completely serious, but he heard nothing unusual. Through the window of the *Queen Anne*, he saw nothing but stars, the occasional asteroid, and distant nebula.

"Someone else is out here, little man." She took her seat at the ship's command console. "And we're going to find out who it is."

Tarzi stood behind her and peered over her shoulder at the monitors. "But look. Not a thing on radar. We're a gazillion miles from any—oh, what's that, then?"

A blip flashed on the screen.

"See? I told you! Why do you always gotta act like your auntie is a crazy person?"

"I don't know. Maybe because everywhere we go, we either almost die or rack up a massive body count for no reason thanks to your infamous temper?"

"Hahaha, fuck you." She touched a screen. It zoomed out to a wider field of view. "Look at this. That ship's on a course for this blip way up here. Does that radiation signature look familiar to you?"

Tarzi's smile turned into a grim mask. "It sure does. That's not one of ours. That's a lizard ship."

Mags raised an eyebrow into a wicked arch. "You learn fast, dear. Now get suited up. This ride isn't over yet." She marched back to the armory, flinging her towel on the bed. "We might even get to play with our new toys."

The Outer Planets.

"Commander." Major Dekarna stood at attention with her helmet in her hand. Always loyal to her commander, she had taken advantage of her leave to visit Cragg, now under house arrest for the loss of his ship in the ill-fated attack on the *Queen Anne*.

"Major," hissed Commander Cragg. He sucked the marrow from some hapless mammal's femur, then tossed the remains on the pile in the corner. "Can you believe this insult? The 'great empire' can't even provide live food here." He seethed. "Come sit, Major."

The dragons spoke in their own tongue. Dekarna looked around the room. "Nothing about this treatment befits a commander of our forces. 'Insulting' is putting it mildly." Narrow windows let in slats of light from the surrounding moons. The light grazed Cragg at his unimpressive table before falling on concrete walls devoid of any decoration. The single object which had decorated the wall, a picture of the dragons' supreme leader, lay in fragments on the floor. The dead skin on the ground showed Cragg had been sequestered here long enough to shed. "Has the council given any word on when they will issue a decision?"

"Ha!" He slammed his fist on the table and rose to his feet. "Any time they find it convenient. The whole proceeding is an exercise in administrative nonsense, Major. The case is simple. The smuggler used unexpected weapons against us in a council-sanctioned military maneuver. Our ship was destroyed. This is to be expected in a war." Cragg paced back and forth. "But in the end, they will reinstate my command. They have no choice. They merely have to put on a show first to please the accountants who would rather tally expenses than pursue victory at all costs."

Dekarna's tail lashed the rancid light. "Your command has *never* been in question, sir."

His lips peeled back in a gesture that, in some species, could be called a smile. "My faithful Major. Have you brought me good news?"

"Indeed. The smuggler has no support on Earth. Not a single authority would lift a finger if we attacked her base. We risk no unnecessary conflict."

"And her base is the asteroid, Vesta 4?"

"Yes, sir. The politicians say her presence in the Belt is utterly uncondoned. Her crimes are beyond number. Frankly, our contacts would welcome the opportunity to be rid of her and begin mining that rock without her interference."

"As long as they think that will happen, then." Cragg leered, clenching and unclenching his talons. "The simpletons. So easy to manipulate. What do they *think* will happen once we have unimpeded access to Mars and the Belt?"

Dekarna enjoyed a rare chuckle. "Money, most likely. More money and power for those who already have money and power. Such is the concern of these primates."

"Fools." He pulled another lifeless mammal from his bowl, gesturing for her to do the same. His teeth leisurely tore chunks of dead meat from its face and neck. "And what of our collection missions from Earth?"

"They continue without any interference from Earth's military forces. The clearance codes from our political contacts remain intact. We expect to have viable breeding populations established in a matter of months." Dekarna shook her head in disgust. "Tell me, Commander. What sort of lifeform willingly sells its own kind into slavery and death? It seems almost beneath us to make these arrangements with them."

"Ah, Major." He reared back and laughed with a sound like children dying in a fire. The noise chilled even Dekarna's calloused soul. "The kind we *made*, damn it!" Cragg slapped his meal on the table. He walked over to the window slits. Moonlight fell upon his face and wished to die there. "Listen to me, Major, and I will tell you a piece of history they omitted from your training at the academy."

She had accepted the offer of food, as was the dragons' custom. But now she set the quadruped's remains on the table to fix her attention on her commander.

"Many millions of years ago," he began, "our tribe was the only one to escape the great dying on Earth. This much is known to any cadet. We boarded our ships and escaped the meteoric death which forever brought an end to the reign of reptiles on that green, delicious planet.

"And so we took to the stars, and we found a new home. But no system in the nearby universe could match the abundance of food and perfect weather of our birth planet. In time, though its atmosphere cooled, it also cleansed itself of poisons, and the climate began to stabilize.

"We watched as the mammals evolved, coming out of the trees, walking upright, discovering tools. Eventually, they dared what we had dared: to free themselves from the bonds of gravity and explore the surrounding planets. This happened before we would have liked, for it came at the same time their planet's ice age began to recede and the climate once again began to warm to something better suited for our species."

This much, Dekarna knew from textbooks.

"But what they decline to teach in the academy is this. Many centuries ago, the council sent an advance team to steer the course of human evolution in a direction more suited to our return. That team determined a simple extermination of the primates would gain us nothing. It would be far better to train them, to make them accomplices in their own enslavement at our hands. This plan, you see, would guarantee us an endless supply of food, not only upon our arrival in this system, but in our eventual reclamation of our birth planet."

Cragg turned away from the window to face his second-in-command. "I was *on* that team, Major. And it took only the slightest manipulation to turn the primates into their own worst enemies. Through our agencies, we taught them slavery on a massive scale. It may seem inconceivable to you now, but they crossed entire oceans in primitive, wooden ships for the express purpose of making their own kindred into chattel. Their willingness to disregard their own species would have been disgusting had it not served our plan so undeniably well. But then, Dekarna, my team confronted an unexpected complication.

"We encountered a pirate, a truly despicable villain of the sea. And, as her kind was known for the capture and sale of human lives as well as trade goods, we thought nothing of enlisting her services to carry human cargo. This one, however, steadfastly refused to do business with the agencies we had established through the humans.

"My team located her in her island fortress with the intent to slay her and remove her as an obstacle. The force I sent to deal with her nearly succeeded. In the night, as she and her mate lay together, they took his life. But I am ashamed to admit, she outwitted my force, and the soldiers dispatched to end her life instead met with death themselves.

"That was not satisfaction enough for this pirate. Not even close. In her lust for vengeance, she pursued the rest of us. Even with a cub gestating in her belly, she dared to fight us all. And she destroyed my entire team. All of them, save me. Sorely wounded, I retired from that planet. But I vowed to return. And I tell you this, Major. I will not rest until she is in her grave."

Dekarna could feel the blood pulsing in her temples. Her pupils had grown wide as the commander relayed this tale to her. She sat in shock, a mere statue of herself. Then she found her voice. "Do you mean to tell me, sir, that this pirate is still alive?"

"No, my loyal Major. But her *blood* lives on. The descendant of her cub is none other than the smuggler, Meteor Mags. *This* is why we will destroy her, without mercy."

Then Cragg laid out his plan for the attack on Vesta 4.

★ ○•♥•○ ★

"Okay, I plotted their trajectories," said Meteor Mags. "Now we pull way out of radar range and wait." Her fingers moved over the console as she programmed a new flight path.

"Why don't we just intercept them and blast them out of the sky right now?"

"And kill whoever is on there singing? I don't think so. We'll swoop down on their rendezvous, come out shooting, and force them to board the main ship. We can take them in the landing bay."

"You want to board the *bigger* ship? Are you nuts?"

"It's been said before. You handle the flying, and I'll handle the cannons. We'll drive them right into the belly of the beast."

Tarzi touched his fingertips to his temple, shaking his head. "You're bloody serious. At least tell me how we 'swoop down' on a ship when we aren't even in radar range."

"We still don't know what kind of propulsion system the lizards use, but how do you think we get around the System so fast?" Mags picked up a pack of cigarettes and offered one to him. "You see, within any inertial frame of reference, it's impossible to tell if the acceleration is caused by motion or by gravitational force, got it?"

He took the cigarette. "If we have one more science lesson today, my head is gonna explode."

"Let's just stick with the short answer then, dear. It's a side-effect of the GravGens. By pumping out our own gravity, we trick the fabric of space-time into letting us go faster than we could ever go by just burning fuel. I wouldn't call the speed 'relativistic', but it's a damn sight faster than any jet plane."

"So instead of taking years to get from planet to planet, we can zip around on weekends."

"Precisely. Here, trade seats with me."

Tarzi took her place at the console. "Okay. Top ten drum fills of all time."

"Easy. The end of Slayer's *Gemini*."

"Bringing out the big guns first. I'll go with John Bonham in *Good Times, Bad Times*."

"Yeah, but which fill?"

"All of them!"

"Agreed. And those tasty bass fills by John Paul Jones. That whole song is genius."

"Top that!"

"Hmmm... The end of *Burning from Inside* from Revolution Mother's 2023 concert at the first moon base."

"Best reunion show of all time!" Tarzi held up his palm.

Mags slapped it with a hearty high-five. "I was there, you know."

"What?"

"Yeah, me and Celina danced at that one. Low-grav pole dancing, you gotta love it. And you wouldn't *believe* the after-party."

"How come you never told me?"

Patches made a raspy mew at Mags' feet.

"Awww, kitty. What's wrong? Come on up." Mags patted her lap, but Patches whined. Mags scooped her up and pet her. They rubbed their cheeks alongside each other. "I know, baby. I know."

"What's wrong with Patches? Did we leave out her favorite drum fill?"

"She does love that one at the end of *Window Paine* by Smashing Pumpkins. But that's not it." She sighed. "I know it sounds weird, but I can sense Patches in a different way right now. I can, like, *feel* her thinking. Not read her mind or anything. But ever since that octopus set us down, I can tell she's been having some heavy thoughts. Tarzi, did you ever think about what it means for her to be indestructible?"

"Not really. I mean, it's pretty awesome, isn't it? She can't get hurt. She doesn't have to worry about getting shot or blown up or blasted into space. Hell, for all I know, she can't even die. It's like a dream come true."

Mags rubbed Patches' ears. "Yeah, but think about that for a minute. I've lived a long-ass time, and I can tell you outliving all your friends and family is no special treat. It's kind of depressing, actually. But that's nothing. I'll die, someday, just like everybody else. But if Patches really is immortal, she'll outlive the whole bloody universe!"

Tarzi took a drag on his cigarette and frowned. "Whoa. That *is* heavy."

"We're having the time of our lives now, but what about when all the stars burn out in billions of years? She's just going to float around in a void all by herself?" Mags wiped a tear from the corner of her eye. "It's all my fault, too."

"Oh, Auntie. It's not your fault the stars won't last forever."

"No." She sniffed. "But if she hadn't been exposed to everything I know about astronomy and physics, it probably wouldn't have crossed her mind. Not yet, at least. Poor little kitten."

They sat in silence for a minute. Tarzi leaned over to scratch the side of Patches' face. "Don't you worry, Patches. We'll figure something out. You know we love you." She purred softly, rubbing on his hand. "And until then, we can take out our goddamn frustrations by exterminating these sodding reptiles. Coming up on the coordinates now, Mags!"

"Good. Let's focus on something happy." A grim smile formed on the smuggler's lips. "Something like absolute vengeance."

The *Queen Anne* easily outweighed the dragon's jump ship, doubling both its size and cannons. As it approached the coordinates she had programmed, Mags reached over to turn on the radio.

"—are now tuned in to the Puma Broadcasting Network," came the DJ's voice. "That was Joe Bonamassa with *Oh, Beautiful*. Up next, *Rebel Girl* by Bikini Kill, L7 with *Fast and Frightening*, and a whole lot more sonic anarchy for your earholes. Long live the resistance!"

Mags turned it up. "Tarzi," she said. "This is just between you and me, but if I *were* ever going to hook up with some dude, this DJ would be at the top of my list."

"He's got great fucking taste in music." He gripped the ship's control wheel. "There they are!"

"Pull back on the speed!"

Tarzi decelerated. The stars around them slowed from blurs into crystal-clear pinpoints of light.

"I've got a lock! Pull to starboard!" Mags ran her fingers over the touch-screen controlling the cannons.

"Auntie, will you please shit-can the nautical terms?!"

"Pull right, goddamnit!"

The dragons' small jump ship came into the center of the window on the *Queen Anne*. Then Mags and Tarzi set eyes on the larger ship it intended to rendezvous with.

"Jesus sodding christ," he exclaimed. "That thing's huge!"

She fired the cannons. The music pummeled her ears. "Bring her around!"

Tarzi steered the *Queen Anne* to face both the ships. The dragon's jump ship attempted to evade the cannon blasts by pulling away from the larger one. Bright lights from the larger ship's open landing bay glowed in the dark void of space. Mags fired the cannons into the smaller ship's path.

Hundreds of years ago, her great-grandmother Mad Dog had commanded ships with similar cannons. But those were only iron and gunpowder. Now, Mags' cannons ripped through the void with lasers powerful enough to eviscerate a battleship.

The jump ship pulled away from the barrage and back toward the larger ship.

"Get us behind the jump ship, Tarzi! Come on!"

He pulled the wheel, cranked it around, and pushed it forward. The *Queen Anne* swooped into position on the opposite side of the jump ship from the larger one. Mags fired again and again.

"Nice flying, ace! Now the big ship can't fire on us without killing their own." She adjusted the guns and began a fresh cannonade. The jump ship returned fire.

Tarzi pressed the wheel forward. The *Queen Anne* dove below the laser blasts. Their light blazed only meters away through the void. Mags blasted away, taking care to miss the jump ship but leave it no escape route.

"There they go, little man! Right into the bay! Pour it on!"

He accelerated, swinging the ship into position after its target. Mags punched laser blast after laser blast into a web around the smaller ship.

"They're taking it in," she cried out. "Get up on them right fucking now!"

Tarzi forced the *Queen Anne* into a dive. "Right behind them!"

As the smaller ship entered the landing bay, the *Queen Anne* came up right on its tail.

"Ram the bastards!"

"What?!"

"Ram them! Drive them to the wall!"

Tarzi pressed the wheel forward again. The *Queen Anne* smashed into the jump ship. Their hulls sparked against each other. The force drove the smaller ship forward, crunching its nose into the deck. It scraped along the floor of the landing bay, tearing up strips of metal as it went.

He whipped the wheel around and pulled back on the speed. The *Queen Anne* turned to the side and skidded. It followed the jump ship and pounded against it.

The door to the landing bay slammed shut behind them. Mags and Tarzi shook violently in their seats as the two ships crashed against each other, pinning the smaller ship to the far wall.

Mags tore off her safety belts and bolted for the door. "Tarzi! Open her up!" She grabbed the shotgun and bandolier she had set by the door. She already had her pair of Desert Eagles holstered and ready to go with clips full of hollow-point shells. "If anything reptilian comes through this door, kill the fuck out of it!"

Mags leapt through the open door, and Patches followed right behind her. Their feet slammed onto the deck of the landing bay together. Mags ran for the jump ship, chambering a round.

Things might have gone differently that day if the dragons had stayed locked in their ship and waited for reinforcements. But they simply could not pass up a fight with this troublesome mammal. They flung open the jump ship's door, ready to kill their attackers.

Mags swung the shotgun up to her shoulder. Patches sped by her. The little calico jumped onto the open ramp of the door to the dragons' ship. Mags fired. A three-inch slug ripped into the first dragon at the doorway. Another round entered his chest, and he fell backward into the soldier behind him. Mags swept her shotgun to the dragon beside him and fired again. Three slugs punched fatal holes in his torso.

Patches ran forward to the console. Her legs propelled her into the air, where she landed on the pilot's neck.

The pilot roared, reaching up to grab the cat. Patches' teeth pierced the glove of her body armor. They went all the way to the bone. The pilot flung her arm forward, smashing Patches into the console. The force of the blow dislodged the angry cat, but she took chunks of the pilot's skin with her.

Mags stormed the doorway. With no idea how many awaited her inside, she jumped onto the door.

A dragon kicked her in the stomach and sent her flying backwards. He aimed the gun which had fired nets to capture the girls earlier.

Mags twisted in mid-air like a cat and landed on her feet. Her tail sliced the air angrily. She ducked, and the net passed over her head. "Come on, then, bastards!" She brought the shotgun up again and put two slugs into him. Now she could hear screaming from inside the ship.

Patches shook her head to clear it. Howling, she assaulted the co-pilot. Claws raked his face. The pilot swung her fist to strike Patches but punched the co-pilot in the snout instead.

The co-pilot roared. His talons snapped shut around Patches. He pulled her to his mouth. His jaws clamped down. But instead of releasing mammalian blood into his mouth, his teeth cracked and splintered.

Patches sank her teeth into his tongue. He screamed. Patches whipped her head to the side, tore his tongue out, and dug her claws into his soft tissues.

The pilot had never seen such a demonic mammal in her life. It would be the last thing she ever saw. Flinging herself through the doorway and into the ship, Mags drew one of her Desert Eagles and pumped five hollow-point rounds into the pilot's back. The dragon's head bludgeoned the console.

Mags swung the pistol towards the co-pilot, but a fist caught her in the side of her head. The blow sent her flying into the pen of captive girls, where she fell to the floor.

The dragon who had punched her swung his electric staff at her like a hatchet. She rolled to the side, and the staff sparked as it smacked into the floor. Lying on her back, Mags fired into his center of mass. As he lunged at her, the bullets ripped through his body armor to spray his blood and pieces of his organs across the cabin.

But his momentum carried him forward. Bright, electric arcs from his rod cast angular shadows on the cabin's walls. Mags pushed herself up to meet his charge. She rammed into him from underneath, and flung him to the side.

His rod, still active, wedged itself into the bars of the animal cages beside the girls' pen. The electricity leapt into the cages. The mammals thrashed behind bars, their flesh cooking, their hair catching fire. The animals' cries pierced Mags' soul.

She aimed her pistol at the dragon and pumped round after round into it until the clip was empty. At last, its hand released the controls on the rod, and the electricity faded away.

"Motherfucker!" Mags yelled at the lifeless beast.

The remaining dragon had his hands full with Patches. She tore at his eyes. Blinded, he grabbed at her.

Mags holstered her pistol. "Patches," she shouted. "Get the fuck down!" Mags brought her shotgun up with both hands. She blasted the dragon in the side with the last round in it. The slug tore into his lungs. He spewed blood from his mouth all over Patches, who leapt to the floor.

Mags walked up to the co-pilot and shot him five times in the face with her second Desert Eagle. "Punk-ass bitch!" She kicked him in the shoulder. His body fell over the side of his chair and crumpled on the floor. "Don't you ever touch my fucking cat!"

Patches rubbed against her boot, leaving a bloody smear. Then she dashed over to the pen.

Klaxons blared throughout the larger ship, and Mags knew

trouble was on its way. But through the sirens, she heard her name.

"Meteor Mags!" Sarah's tiny hands gripped the bars of the pen. She pressed her face to them. "I can't believe you're here!"

Sarah's smile warmed the pirate's heart like a desert sunrise. Mags recognized her voice immediately. She knelt down before the pen. "Believe it, darling. I heard you singing. I don't know how, but I did."

"They left me in a cage to die," whispered the little girl, quoting Mags' song.

Mags covered Sarah's hand with her own. "None could hear my screams." She squeezed the girl's hand. "But I heard you. What's your name?"

"Sarah. And this is Kala, and Hyo-Sonn, and Suzi, and—"

"Let's save the introductions for later. More of those lizards are on the way. Let's get you out of there. Stand back now, dear. All of you."

The girls in the pen moved to the back. Mags produced a small laser torch and began slicing through the bars.

Kala took Sarah's hand. "What did she mean? She heard you singing?"

"I never thought she'd really come," said Sarah. "But she did." She hugged her friend.

Mags worked quickly, but she stole glances at the girls. They all wore the same outfit, some kind of bland uniform she would expect to see in a hospital. It looked like they had been dragged through dirt. Mags noticed the blood splatters, but none of them seemed hurt. Just scared. They reminded her of girls she had known in Spain more than ninety years before, and the refugees after World War II. She smelled the fresh pool of blood on the ground outside the cage. It was not merely dragon blood. Mags could only guess what horror they had been forced to witness on board this ship.

As the bars fell to the deck, Hyo-Sonn stepped through first. She held out her hand to help the next girl. Suzi reached out, hesitantly at first, and then took a firm grip. She joined Hyo-Sonn in helping the other girls to their feet.

"Hyo-Sonn," she said. "I just wanted to say—sorry for what I called you. I was just—" She met Hyo-Sonn's eyes briefly then looked away.

Hyo-Sonn smiled. "Me too, Suzi. Me too. Let's just get the hell out of here."

"Great idea," said Mags. "Follow me." She led the way, running out the jump ship's door with the girls close behind. Patches raced by her and up into the *Queen Anne*.

Across the expanse of the landing bay, double doors slid open. Dragons charged through. In the doorway of the *Queen Anne*, Tarzi blasted away with a laser rifle into the mass of attackers. "Get in," he shouted over the klaxons.

Mags and her entourage wasted no time doing just that. The door snapped shut behind them. Laser shot peppered the hull. The pirate headed straight for the armory and pulled the largest Faraday suit from the pile. "Tarzi, get ready to take her up!"

"Up? Don't you mean out?"

"Up. As in, lift her off the deck by a good five or six meters! We're not ready to leave just yet." She squeezed her ample curves and her tail into a suit clearly made for a man, tugging here and adjusting there. "And get your seahorse ready for a repeat performance. Only this time, we're taking out this whole fucking ship!"

"Christ, Auntie!" He slipped the ring on his finger. Sparky rose from the pillow and glowed, circling obediently around the young man. "I don't know if he's got enough power for that."

"That's why we're giving him a boost." Mags wrapped a holster around her waist and picked up fresh clips for her Desert Eagles. She strapped a knife to her thigh and loaded eight more shells into her shotgun. "Me and those goddamn lizards are going to make a circuit with all the juice he can handle. Listen for me on the ship's radio, okay?" Mags pulled the helmet of the Faraday suit over her head and sealed it. "Testing, testing. Can you hear me, Tarzi?"

He dialed in the ship's receiver, locking on her frequency. Her voice came over the speakers. "Loud and clear."

"You send Sparky out after me, close the door, and take the

Queen Anne into the air. When I give you the word, you tell that little seahorse to turn the juice all the way up, and don't stop for anything! Got it?"

"Got it!"

Hyo-Sonn put her hand on the smuggler's arm. "Mags," she said. "Be careful."

Mags smiled inside her mask. "Don't you worry about me, dear." She put her hand on Hyo-Sonn's cheek. "I'll be just fine!"

But in her mind, Mags said a silent prayer. "Great-gramma. If you were ever looking out for me, please look out for me now."

Mags leapt out, with Sparky right behind her. She rolled to avoid the hail of laser fire. She came to her feet face-to-face with the oncoming horde. Behind her, the *Queen Anne* rose from the deck.

Meteor Mags had often fought for peace: peace for herself; peace for the young women in her care in Spain, at La Plaza Margareta, and on Vesta 4; peace for those close to her, like her nephew and Celina and her grandmother.

But Mags had a secret, passionate love beyond all of that. Mags loved war. And though she hated her enemies with every fiber of her soul, she could not help but love them just as deeply.

As she tore into the dragons with unmatched rage, she loved each and every one of them. She loved them for being unequivocally evil. She loved them for threatening Tarzi, Patches, and the girls. She loved the way they fought her, and she reveled in the way they died at her hands. Their blood splatters on her suit were an ecstasy. Their screams of rage sounded in her ears like the sweetest orchestra imaginable.

For Mags was no ordinary human. The same freak forces of genetics that had formed her tail, her sensitive ears, her eyes that penetrated darkness, her bones and muscles that met danger like a cat's—those same forces had made her into something none of her friends could ever fully understand.

Though she had enjoyed unheard-of quantities of intoxicants in her long and colorful life, Mags' one true drug of choice was the adrenaline that pumped through her veins and organs in battle. It flooded her brain. It flooded her tissues. It gave her the highest high of anything. She could not help but love it.

As the shotgun kicked in her hands and the slugs tore gaping holes in the dragons and their armor, Mags smiled wickedly inside her mask. Teeth bared, eyebrows arched, her lips glistening wet with hatred, she felt truly alive. When one of the dragons closed in on her, she pulled her knife and plunged it into his neck again and again. She rejoiced in its rancid sprays of blood.

She spun and kicked the beast in its belly. It flew backwards. She whipped around and continued blasting the shotgun. In her heart, Mags wished they would never stop coming. She wished she could kill until she could live to kill no more. Let them come. Let them *all* come. Let their unquenchable fire burn before her eyes forever.

Then the mass of dragons overcame her, and she knew it was time. "Tarzi," she cried. "Time to turn on the juice, motherfucker!"

A dragon slammed into her. It crushed her to the deck. Her fingers clamped around its electric staff.

Another dragon clambered on top of her and thrust its staff. She parried the strike with her free hand. Her arm whipped around the weapon like a python catching a rodent. She pulled.

The first dragon's teeth snapped with the force of a steel trap a centimeter from her face. Mags kicked the sole of her boot into its chest, not releasing her grip on its weapon.

Then she strained. Her muscles felt like they would rip the tendons right off her bones, but she only pulled harder. The tips of the two weapons came closer together, lovers who despised each other but could not resist touching anyway. "Tarzi," she shouted again.

In response, a ball of green lightning appeared above the thrashing bodies pressing her to the floor. The flash constricted Mags' pupils to pinpoints. A sphere of electromagnetic whips, it burned and tore the air around her, ripping electrons from their atoms like a hurricane tears trees from the ground. Mags let loose an ungodly yell like continents crashing into each other. In her grip, the dragons' electric weapons at last came together.

94

Sensing the completed circuit, Sparky's lightning stretched out its fingers to the weapons. Sparky crackled with energy in the middle of the electric ball. His little tail flexed. The current surged. Bolts of electricity exploded from the connection. They leapt from dragon to dragon, igniting the power sources in their laser rifles, setting them off like a chain of firecrackers, connecting each electric staff to the next in one giant circuit.

The dragons on Mags burned. Smoke poured out of their body armor as their skin cooked. She thrived on the awful sounds they made, and she kicked them away.

Their hands still clenched the rods. Mags smashed her heel into their faces; first one, then the other. Their bodies jerked like a madman's puppets on strings of current. A terrible, stark light filled the landing bay: flickering, crackling, coruscating light. The rods jerked free from their hands.

Mags kept the rods pressed together. She found her footing and raised the weapons above her head, crossing them like two sides of a brutal triangle. Electricity wrapped around her from head to toe. Then she screamed and screamed and screamed.

Sparky's ball of lightning grew larger. It spread from the dozens of dragons near Mags to the rest of the gathered soldiers. It devoured them all, one by one. Hundreds of reptiles danced helplessly to its merciless demand. The bolts of energy leapt from one to the next, destroying them.

Next, the lightning bolts permeated the ship itself. Every circuit they met only amplified their power. Lights exploded in their fixtures, beginning in the bay and then throughout the rest of the ship. The communications system gave up its ghosts. Resistors melted. Transistors fused from one end of the ship to the other.

Sparky's green glow turned a fiery red. His metal panels burned with electric heat. Every dragon in contact with the ship's surfaces incinerated where it stood. They twisted and spasmed out of control. Lightning blazed, and the brilliant red seahorse flexed its tail. In the center of the unimaginable heat, Sparky poured out amp after amp after amp. A ball of light formed at its core, surrounded it, and finally burst.

The force knocked Mags to the deck. Then she saw nothing.

The *Queen Anne* hovered in darkness save for the glow from its engines. Tarzi activated the lights along her side and set her down gently onto the deck of the landing bay. "Everybody, just keep calm!" He lowered the door and looked out.

Meteor Mags' body lay sprawled atop a pile of blackened reptile corpses. Tendrils of smoke drifted up from them, twisting and turning in the ship's stark lights. The young man ran out to her, with Patches right beside him. A few of the girls cautiously watched from the doorway.

"Mags! Auntie!" Tarzi feared the worst.

Then her body rolled to the side. She pushed herself up into a crouch and held out her arm to him.

Tarzi took her hand, helping her rise to her feet. "Are you alright? Say something!"

Suddenly she gripped his shoulders. A painful howl came from inside the Faraday suit. She flung her hands to her head and screamed. Grasping the sides of her head, she turned away and thrashed violently. Her high-pitched yells, like the death noises of a wounded animal, chilled Tarzi to the bone.

"Oh, my god! Mags! Mags, what is it?"

She ripped open the helmet of the Faraday suit and flung her arms into the air. Like a magician, she announced, "Ta-da!" Mags laughed and laughed. "Holy shit, you should have seen the look on your face!"

"Auntie, what the—"

"Laugh at me for getting shocked, will you? Ahahahaha! I warned you I'd get you back for that!"

He snorted and could not keep from laughing, too. He threw his arms around her. "Goddamnit, Auntie. You are so fucked up sometimes!"

Mags held him tightly as they shook with laughter. She leaned back and looked into his eyes. "You did great, Tarzi. Just perfect.

And so did your little sea—oh, no. Where's Sparky?"

They tore away from each other.

"Sparky!" Tarzi touched his ring, but none of the menus came up. "Sparky!"

They quickly looked around, but Patches found it first. Mags crouched down next to her on the deck. At her feet lay the fractured remains of Tarzi's pet. Fragments of his tail and fins still glowed red with heat. Half of his head lay there, broken, with burnt wires protruding from the cybernetic skull. Nothing was left of him but scrap metal.

Tarzi knelt beside her. "Oh, no. No." He tried to pick up the pieces, but they burned his fingers.

"Here. Let me do it, dear." With her hands protected by her mesh suit, Mags scooped the seahorse fragments into a pile. "Hand me your cap." She placed the pieces into his hat and handed it back.

The young man wiped his eyes. Then he quietly walked back to the ship. Mags and Patches followed.

Aboard the *Queen Anne*, the pirate instructed everyone to take a seat. She turned the ship's cannons on the landing bay's exit door and opened fire. She punched holes in it until she had enough room to fly through, and then they began their journey home to Vesta 4.

Hyo-Sonn and Kala took charge of finding something for the girls to eat and making sure everyone was okay. Patches followed the two of them around, sensing how upset some of their friends were. None of them could resist petting Patches when she mewed at them, and even the saddest of them was cheered up by the carefree little calico sprawling next to them for belly rubs.

All of them, that is, except Tarzi. He had gladly given up his bed so they could sit. In the armory at the back of the ship, he sat alone on a bench, staring at the floor. His cap held Sparky's fragments.

Eventually, Hyo-Sonn approached him with a bottle of water. "Would you like something to drink?"

He looked up without smiling, but he took the bottle of water.

"Thanks," he said quietly.

"My name's Hyo-Sonn. I'm sorry about your friend."

Tarzi said nothing, returning his gaze to the floor.

"I lost a friend today, too," said the young woman.

Tarzi looked up at her again. He scooted over to make room for her on the bench. "Here. Have a seat."

They sat in silence, thinking over the day's events. But the silence did not last very long. Sarah had taken a seat by Mags, and the two of them pounded noisily on the keyboard. Mags yelled something about Kennedy's head and concrete. Sarah laughed loudly and smacked the keys.

"What the hell is she doing?" Hyo-Sonn asked.

Tarzi's somber frown relaxed into a grin. "It's just a Misfits song."

"A what?"

"It's uh—It's a song about a political assassination. It's called *Bullet*."

"And she's singing it to a little girl?"

Tarzi laughed and shook his head. "That's Auntie for you. She believes rage is a path to liberation. Or something."

"Is she really your aunt? She seems kind of—mentally unstable maybe?"

Tarzi found this hysterical. His sides shook. "Are you calling my auntie crazy?"

She looked away, embarrassed.

"She *is* kind of crazy," he said. "She's violent, reckless, hot-tempered, and downright homicidal sometimes. But you know what? She's way more fun than anyone I ever met before. And she's got great taste in music. And if Mags likes you at all, she would storm the gates of hell if she thought you needed help." He turned up his palms and shrugged. "That's just how she is."

Hyo-Sonn assessed the young man with her eyes. "Sarah certainly likes her. It's nice to hear her laugh, after what we've been through."

Tarzi thought of something. "Do you like fossils?"

"I do! I used to have a little collection of them from the creek by my parents' house."

"Really? I have a gift for you then. Something Mags and I picked up earlier today." He reached into his pants pocket and pulled out the pair of trilobites he had cut free from the asteroid rock. He gave it to her.

"Wow." She took the rock in her hand. She ran her fingers over the ridges in the shells of the two trilobites, forever swimming, locked in stone. "It's beautiful. Where did you get this?"

"Can I tell you about it?"

The two of them talked all the way back to Vesta 4.

Two days later, Meteor Mags awoke from a dream. She had been prowling through the dense underbrush in a forest on Earth. Fragments of sunlight and shadow formed a quilt around her. Her calico fur blended seamlessly with the quilted forest. A bird captured her focus. She stalked it slowly, picking up one paw at a time, setting it down with silent determination. Then something startled the bird. Its wings beat the air like thunder and took it out of sight into the branches overhead. There the dream ended, and she opened her eyes.

Mags yawned. She raised her paw to her face and licked it. Then she held it out before her, studying it, as if she had never seen it before. She suddenly sat up.

"What in the hell?"

She walked into her loo and flicked the light on. Her reflection in the mirror showed nothing unusual. Skin and star tattoos covered her, not calico fur. She pressed a hand, not a paw, to the mirror. "Maggie," she said to her reflection. "Get a grip, you old sod!" She washed her face and brushed her long, white hair.

She felt like she had slept for days. It was normal for her to need extra sleep after an especially intense adrenaline rush. But she could not recall ever waking up confused about who she was. She set her brush down and walked to the window. Out there, on a rocky slope of Vesta 4 behind the club, her nephew and her calico cat sat by a sculpture in the dark. She decided to join them.

"Morning, little man. What are you two up to out here?"

Tarzi sat cross-legged on the ground, scratching Patches' face. "We're waiting for the sun to come up. You've been out for like a day and a half. Are you okay?"

"I guess so. I feel fine, but I just woke up thinking I was Patches for a minute! It kind of freaked me out."

"Weird."

She noticed the lack of Tarzi's typically enthusiastic tone. "Totally weird. What have you got here?" She waved her hand at the sculpture.

"Just something I sketched that night we got back, after everyone had gone to bed. The guys helped me make it in the machine shop."

"Fuzzlow's about as handy with tools as he is with a microphone, isn't he?"

The base of the sculpture stood a meter tall, bolted into the rock, a metal obelisk with the top sliced off to form a flat plane. Above it floated a metal sphere with rings like a planet, slowly spinning. Mags admired the handiwork.

"Fuzzlow came up with the idea of installing magnets to make the planet float. We buried—" The young man sighed. "We buried what was left of Sparky under it."

Mags knelt beside him. She put her hand on his shoulder. "I'm sorry, Tarzi."

He sniffed. They sat together quietly for a moment. Then the sun broke the asteroid's horizon, casting long shadows across its rough terrain. Fingers of light crept over Vesta 4. When the light reached the sculpture, its metal surface glowed red, just as Tarzi's seahorse had in its final moments. A small hologram of Sparky appeared, circling the sphere. It, too, glowed red in the morning light.

Tarzi stood and cleared his throat. "I wanted to read something I wrote for him." He took a folded piece of paper from his pocket and opened it. Patches bumped against his leg. Mags stood, too, bowing her head in respect. She listened as the young man spoke.

Red metal at dawn
pounded smooth by solar hammers:
a monument to your sacrifice.

No star will shine as bright without you now
but all of them shine brighter
in the eyes of those you freed.

Let us not waste this gift.
Let us remember the price
with which you bought our lives.

Red metal at dawn:
We weather the storm
and still we press on.

Mags put her arm around him. "You wrote that, dear?"

"Patches helped."

The bushy calico looked up and blinked. She licked her paw, rubbed it over her ear, and licked it again.

Mags chuckled softly. "I'm sure she did."

"What do you think?"

"I think it's a fine poem, Tarzi, and a fine memorial." She patted him on the back. "You did good, little man. It's good to remember your friends, and to honor them."

He smiled.

"You know," she said, "I've been thinking about what you said back at the lab."

"About helping me with trig?"

"Silly, you know I'll help you with that anytime. I mean about getting someone's ten-thousand-year-old voice mail in English."

"Oh! Yeah, it just seems—impossible. But after what we've seen, who knows? Prehistoric fossils in space? Giant octopuses that can read your mind? I don't even know *what* to think anymore."

"I think you were right. It *was* impossible. Because that message should have been in whatever language the manual was in, you know? It's that simple. Octopus I can believe. I was there. I was in its mind. But this?" She looked into space and sighed. "So, there's only one thing I can think of."

"What's that?"

"Something Great-gramma said to me once, the first time she ever appeared to me."

"You mean that time with the gravity thing?"

"No, no. That wasn't the first time she came to me. This was long before then, back in 1938."

"Damn, Mags! Just how old are you, anyway?"

"Tarzi, I'll be a hundred and six years old this November. And you'd better not miss the party!"

"A hundred and—wait. When's the party?"

"Don't worry, dear. I'll come pick you up! Anyway, the first time Great-gramma came to me, she told me something. She said she would always be watching over me. And sometimes I can feel her, even when I can't see her or talk to her. I just know she's with me, watching out for me."

"And you think she had something to do with the message we got from the Ghost Moon?"

"What I think is, that message was never in English at all. I think she just made it so we heard it that way. So we could save Patches."

"Mags, I don't get it. I thought Mad Dog was dead. Are you saying she's a ghost? Or that she isn't dead at all?"

"I'm not sure how to say it, really. It's like she's gone, but she isn't. Tarzi, I think it's time I told you what happened to Mama."

And there, at Tarzi's memorial to his departed pet, Meteor Mags told him all about it.

9

The Curtain of Fire

I would rather be ashes than dust.
I would rather my spark burn out in a brilliant blaze.

I would rather be a superb meteor,
Every atom of me in magnificent glow,
Than a sleepy and permanent planet.

I shall not waste my days trying to prolong them.
I shall use my time.

—Attributed to Jack London by Ernest Hopkins;
San Francisco Bulletin, 1916.

PROLOGUE: THE GIRL WITH A TAIL

February 1938: USA.

Bertrand stared at the girl dancing on his stage. He raised his hand, as if to pose a question. But he could not find the words.

Meteor Mags wore some of Celina's clothes, and they were a little too big. She explored the stage, smiling, doing a few dances her mother taught her.

"Celina, does your friend have a—wait. How old is she?"

Celina, seventeen years old at the time, replied, "She's eighteen, same as me."

"Oh, bullshit. Listen, I love your mom and pops, but don't bullshit me. I've been in the club business sin—"

"Since before I was born. I *know*, Uncle Randy." She took a sip from a bottled beer. "Go, Mags! Go!"

Mags smiled and waved back.

Bertrand rolled his eyes. "Puh-*lease* don't call me that in front of the customers!"

"Please don't call me on my bullshit, when you know damn well it's the right answer if vice pays a visit. *Bert*." Celina unsnapped her purse, which she had sitting on the high-top table between them. "Don't get so cross. I brought you a prezzy."

He lifted his chin and eyed her purse skeptically.

She knew better than to play the "close your eyes" game with him. Bert was a decent man, but he could be no fun at all if you teased him too much. He had extremely profitable arrangements with Celina's parents, acting as a distribution point for smuggled goods into the States, and he deserved a certain level of respect.

His eyes lit up when she opened her cigarette case. "A-ha! You've come to do more than give me a hard time." He took a cigarette and produced a lighter, but he lit Celina's first.

She nodded her thanks. "Bert, she doesn't even *want* to dance here. We talked about it. So don't you worry about how old she is or isn't."

He took a long drag, inhaling some of the smoke through his

nose. He breathed it out. "Does your friend have a tail?"

She glanced over her shoulder at Mags, as if she had never noticed. "You little ripper! I think she does!"

Bertrand shook his head. "It's an amazing costume. I mean, your clothes don't fit her, but she's what? Thirteen? Fourteen? She'll fill out someday. But the tail is—the tail is so *lifelike*. How does she do that?"

"Well," said Celina, "it appears to be attached to her spine. Imagine that."

Bertrand set his hand palm-down on the table. He leaned in and said, "Attached?" His looked back and forth from one of her eyes to another. "She can take it off, right?"

"Take it off? I *told* you she doesn't want to dance here, Bert."

"Not her clothes, goddamnit! The tail!"

"Shhh!" Celina put her finger to her lips. "Bert," she spoke slowly. "My friend. Has. A tail."

He rubbed his chin and then his mouth and then his whole face. He made a fist and released it like he set something free. "Okay. Okay. I get it." He watched Mags for a moment more. "Is she doing some kinda flamingo?"

Celina laughed and shook her head. "Fla*menco*. It's all the rage in Spain, from what she tells me. Don't see much of that down under."

"No. No, you don't." His eyes studied the girl on stage like a surgeon studies anatomy. He had become jaded by constant exposure to naked bodies of all shapes and sizes in his club, male and female, young and old. But this girl in her ill-fitting skirt and her clumsy shirt, dancing barefoot on his stage and swishing her tail back and forth? This was unlike anything he had ever seen. *Imagine what she'll be like when she grows up*, he thought.

"So, you don't mind if she stays in my room? She speaks fair English, but a lot of stuff seems to go over her head. I worry about her on her own."

"Celina, I can't even understand half of what you call English."

"Don't be such a knocker!"

"See what I mean?" He sighed. "As long as she can pull her own weight in the kitchen, I guess the extra bed is no biggie. And I'll put her on a cleaning crew that comes through when we're closed. She just can't—we can't have her out here when the club is open, Celina." He leaned in again. "Listen. If people see a girl with a tail in here, this place will turn into a shithouse riot. I guarantee it. And I mean in minutes. *Seconds.* You gotta find a way to—cover her up or something."

"Bert, she isn't some kind of freak!" Her eyes misted over.

"Aw, Celina, I didn't mean it like that. Hey." He placed his hand on her shoulder. "*Hey.* This is your Uncle Randy talking to you, okay?"

She smiled. "Okay."

"And all I am saying is to put some pants on her, and put the tail down the pants leg, or strap it to her leg, or *something.* Put her in boy clothes. People will absolutely lose their shit when they see her, and she's too damn young."

"Your brilliant plan is to have a 'boy' bunking with me?"

He lowered his face into his hands. Then he sat up. "Look, we'll figure something out. Are you *sure* she doesn't want to dance here? She seems to like the stage."

"Bert, after what this little sheila has been through, this hotel is like a World's Fair exhibit." Celina exhaled, shaking her head. "You can't even imagine."

"Her mother died, you said?"

"I did. And I don't think I've heard the half of it. All of Europe's going to bloody hell right now."

"It sure is. I'm glad we're not involved."

"So am I," said Celina, watching her new friend. "So am I."

PART ONE: VIVAN LAS ANARQUISTAS

1936: Spain.

Mags held her mother's hand. She threw another piece of wood onto the fire. The church blazed before them in the night. Flames sparkled in the child's eyes.

Her mother, Mollie, smiled with wicked satisfaction. "It's beautiful, isn't it, Maggie?"

"Yes, Mama. But why do we have to burn it down? Maybe people could live here. Or make a home."

"As Durruti likes to say, 'The only church that illumines is a burning church.' Do you know what that means, Maggie?"

Mags lifted her eyes away from the inferno to look up at her mother. "It doesn't make light until we set it on fire?"

Mollie laughed softly. "That's true, too, dear. But it also means illumination as in truth. The light of truth, you see?"

Mags squeezed her mother's hand. "People come here for the light of truth, but it isn't here?"

"That's right, dear. People come for the light of truth, but all they find is the yoke of tyranny. These churches all across Europe, they make me bloody sick." She spat on the ground. "If you want to conquer a people, Maggie, first you send the missionaries and then the sword. You rob their minds of freedom, then crush their bodies if they resist. The churches of Spain are nothing but symbols of subjugation. They aren't fit to be homes for anyone."

Mags gazed upon the inferno. "They don't sound very nice, Mama." Embers rode the updrafts into the night sky. She thought they looked like little stars. "People should be free. Are there many more of them?"

"Churches? Oh yes, Maggie. Many, many more." She picked up a scrap of lumber and tossed it onto the church's burning wreckage. "How would you like to help me burn every last one of them to the ground?"

Mags rested her head on her mother's arm. If these were evil buildings, she thought, then they deserved to burn, even if people could live in them. Perhaps after the evil was destroyed, then people could build new homes. Homes where they could be free. Homes where they might find the light of truth for real.

The church collapsed upon itself, timbers crashing into a fireball. The heat pressed against her face like a thousand suns. A galaxy of fiery stars exploded, rising in a twisted column up to the sky. Mags envied them in a way. They seemed so free to fly.

She hugged Mollie tightly. "I'd like that, Mama. I'd like that very much."

The steam locomotive thundered across the Spanish countryside towards Barcelona. Mags sat by her mother on the unforgiving wooden bench that served as their seat. She watched the landscape speed past her and fall away. She held her mother's hand.

"Maggie, let's go over your multiplication tables."

"Mama. Do we have to?"

"Yes, we do. You know how important your education is."

Mags sighed. "I know."

"You've been doing so well. Today we can start with sevens. Seven times two is?"

"Fourteen. But I—"

"Seven times three is?"

"Twenty-one. But—"

"Seven times four is?"

"Mama!" Mags stomped her feet.

Mollie watched her daughter's tantrum. She shook her head, then leaned in towards her child. "What's bothering you?"

Mags turned her gaze back to the window. "You don't want to listen to me."

"Of course I do. This is just so important for us to—"

"See? You don't even want to listen."

Mollie stopped and took a deep breath. "Alright, dear. I'm listening. What's bothering you?"

Mags looked into her mother's eyes. She saw frustration, but she also saw love. "Mama, how many prime numbers are there?"

"Prime numbers? Maggie, I—I don't know."

"You don't know?"

"No, I—"

"They start at two. Then three. Five, seven, eleven, thirteen. But when do they end? And what happens if you add all of them up?"

"Where did you learn about prime numbers?"

"It's in one of the books you gave me. The geometry book by Euclid. He wants to know how many prime numbers there are. But I don't understand his equation. Why does he add one to the product of all the primes, and how does he know he can multiply all of them when he doesn't even know how many there are?"

Mollie held a hand to her mouth.

"What is it, Mama?"

"Oh, Maggie. I am so sorry. I didn't realize. You've been reading Euclid?"

"Yes, Mama. And other geometries about curved space instead of flat planes. Parallel lines don't behave the same there. They act like they're on a sphere and they intersect, not like in Euclid where they never meet. But I don't understand his notation on so many things."

Mollie threw her arms around her daughter. "I am such a fool. Please forgive me."

Mags returned her hug. "For what?"

"Here I've been drilling you every day on your multiplication tables, and I had no idea." Mollie pulled away from her daughter. She looked into Mags' eyes and rubbed a hand over her hair, brushing it back. "I promise you, I will help you answer your questions. We don't need to do multiplication any more. You just tell me what you have questions about, okay?"

Mags smiled. "Okay, Mama."

Mollie leaned back in her seat. "My precious child." She felt an enormous pride. Her hopes had become reality.

Mollie remembered when Mags' father had come to Barcelona thirteen years before. She had determined to meet him, for Mollie's revolutionary impulses led her to believe that the future of the world's workers depended on a strong leader. And though Mollie was possessed of an inner strength nearly unequalled in her time, she knew the revolution required more. The revolution required superb intelligence, especially with the growing wave of science that had swept the globe. Mollie had convinced herself she needed to mate not just with any man, but the smartest man on the planet. And, as luck would have it, in 1923, he booked a room at a hotel owned by her mother.

She looked again to her child. Mags had grown into such a wonderful young woman. But Mollie knew this was just the beginning. In time, her daughter's intelligence would outstrip them all, even Margareta and her mother before her.

"Mama? Will we visit Gramma soon?"

Mollie squeezed Mags' hand. "Yes, dear. We will. But we have things to do in Barcelona first. The workers are fighting, and they need our help."

"I miss Gramma."

Mollie felt cold all of a sudden. "I do, too. But Gramma is busy with her business. She can't be bothered with what's happening to the workers here."

"Are you mad at her?"

Mollie turned her gaze away. "Gramma isn't a bad woman. She just doesn't know what it's like for people here. Gramma has her empire to worry about. But who is there to worry about the laborers who build that empire?"

"I don't know, Mama. You and me?"

Mollie's lips spread into a grim smile. "That's right, dear. If not us, then who?"

"Mama? Can I ask you another question?"

"Of course you can."

"If water waves travel in water, and sound waves travel in the air, then what do light waves travel in?"

Mollie laughed. "For that, we need to get you some new books. But I will tell you what I understand of it. Have you ever heard of James Maxwell?"

1937: Barcelona.

Mags pushed the wheelbarrow full of rocks and bags of concrete mix over to the group of women in the street. The laborers of Barcelona, coming together under the anarchist banner, had filled the city streets with barricades. They had become quite effective at resisting interference in their uprising to control the factories where they worked. But from time to time, the barricades needed repairing.

Supplies and functioning weapons had grown scarce. This was why her mother had left the city, but Mags did not at all care to be separated from her. She sang a work song her mother had taught her, and hoped for Mollie's swift return. In the meantime, she worked with the *anarquista* women to protect the city. Mollie would never have entrusted her daughter to a group of men, but the *anarquistas* had proven themselves trustworthy in her eyes.

A group of children her age ran past. "Fucking freak," shouted one of them in Spanish. Mags looked toward the voice just in time for a hail of rotten vegetables to catch her upside the head. She dropped the wheelbarrow to the ground. Raising her hands over her face, she deflected the worst of the barrage. But a stream of stinking tomato juice ran out of her dark curls and down her face.

"*Hijos de putas!*" She grabbed a rock from the wheelbarrow. She flung it with all her might, but the children had already run away. The rock fell short, skittering down the street. Mags' tail flicked back and forth angrily beneath her skirt. She wiped her face on her shirt sleeve.

Mollie had spoken many times of the solidarity between workers, but Mags found the children of Barcelona failed to live up to her mother's ideal. She pulled a knife from her boot, preparing to run down the gang. They never dared torment her when her mother was by her side. But alone—

Just then, one of the anarchist women ran up to her. "Maggie!" The woman dressed in the militaristic shirt and pants of the *anarquistas*, a rifle slung over her shoulder. Mags sheathed the boot knife as the woman approached. "Oh, you poor thing," the woman said.

"*Está bien.*"

The *anarquista* took a rag and wiped what she could from the child's face and hair.

Despite her embarrassment, Mags acquiesced to the kindly touch. "*Gracias.*" Somehow, these women made everything seem alright. She had not known them long, but she believed in their kindness.

"Mollie would have our hides if she thought we let something happen to you."

If only, Mags thought, she could command the sort of respect her mother did. Then those brats would leave her alone.

"It's okay to be different, little comrade. Children don't always understand that." She tucked her rag into her waistband. "I suppose adults don't always understand it either."

"They're mean to me because of my tail."

"They've never—" The woman sighed. "They've never seen anything like it. And frankly," she said, looking Mags over, "neither have I!"

Mags picked up the handles of the wheelbarrow. "But you aren't mean to me."

"Of course not, little one. Why, I remember when I was your age, I was teased all the time for—"

"Do you hear that?" Mags' ears perked up.

"Hear what?"

"Mama!" She set the wheelbarrow back on the ground.

Then the *anarquista* heard the sound of horse hooves approaching. A moment later, the rest of the group working on the barricade heard it, too.

Mags ran down the street. A black speck on the horizon grew larger, and then she saw her mother. "Mama!"

Mollie's horse carried her up the street and pulled to a stop at her daughter's side. Mollie pulled Mags up, and Mags flung her leg over the horse. She settled onto the saddle, holding her mother tightly from behind with both arms. "Mama," she said happily.

Mags did not know this horse had formerly been part of the Spanish cavalry. Mollie had found it nearly rode to death by a militia. She decided she and the horse would ride together. Its captors had little say in the matter, and, in fact, would have no say in anything ever again.

Mollie kicked her heels. The horse sprang into action. When it reached the group of *anarquistas*, the horse reared up, whinnying loudly. The women cheered. They raised their caps in a salute.

Mollie paraded her steed in several circles before bringing it to a stop. She smiled broadly, enjoying her control over the powerful animal. She let Mags slide down to the ground. Mollie dismounted, still holding the reins. "Who wants fresh rifles?"

The women gathered around. Mollie handed out stolen goods right and left. Mags watched her mother with pride. She had seen the pathetic state of the resistance fighters, but only her mother seemed to have the wherewithal to do something about it. Mollie distributed rifles, ammunition, and dozens of pairs of clean socks to the *anarquistas*.

Clean socks especially had become a problem for the resistance fighters in Barcelona, and many of them had rifles which barely functioned. To call their armaments pathetic would be to understate the problem. Where Mollie had gone to get the replacements, and what battles she might have undertaken to bring them back, Mags would never know.

But it was not a sight she would ever forget, even when she had been alive more than a century. Mags saw the respect in her mother's comrades' eyes. The way they deferred to her. The way they counted on her to provide. Mags felt not only an urge to make her mother proud, but to be like her someday.

When Mollie finished distributing her "liberated" goods from the pouches and packs slung across the horse, she placed a hand on her daughter's head but found it wet. She kneeled to look Mags in the eye. "Are you okay?"

"I'm fine." Mags frowned. "Just those asshole kids again."

Mollie looked her daughter over, making sure she was not

injured. "I'm sorry, baby. Did they hurt you?"

"No." Mags fumed. Then she raised her eyes back to Mollie's. "They don't like my tail."

Mollie cupped her daughter's cheek in the palm of her hand. "Maggie, you are absolutely beautiful. Do you know that?"

"Why am I different, Mama?"

Mollie held her daughter close. "I don't know, dear. I really don't know. But I do know this. You are the most special person in the universe to me."

"I love you, Mama."

"I love you, too, Maggie." After some moments had passed, she asked, "Would you like to help me get the rest of these rifles and socks to our comrades in the POUM? They're not very far from here."

Mags clasped her mother's hand. "I would, Mama. Very much."

"Good." Mollie mounted her horse then lifted Mags into the saddle. "*Vivan las anarquistas,*" she cried, raising her fist in salute to the group of women around her.

The women also raised their fists in salute. "*Vivan las anarquistas!*"

Mollie pulled the reins of her stolen horse, and she and her daughter made their way through Barcelona to distribute the rest of her ill-gotten gains.

5 May 1937.

Mags ran down the crude stone street. Only death could await her in this alley. Men with guns had cut off every other route. She ducked into a small alcove, brick on all sides, just wide enough for an adult to stand in, but only a couple meters deep.

The armed workers of the CNT-FAI had forcefully taken the Telephone Exchange building from the fascists nearly a year before. The red and black flag of anarchy had flown from the building ever since. But on the afternoon of May third, a force of two hundred police assaulted the Exchange. The CNT's machine guns and control of the upper levels ensured the police could not advance beyond the first floor. Though opposing forces had exchanged gunfire, they soon reached an uneasy stand-off.

Tension mounted until the evening of the next day, when rifle fire broke out at a barricade near the CNT's headquarters. Soon the armed conflict spread throughout the city. On the fifth of May, the government's assault guards attacked multiple targets throughout Barcelona, including the Medical Union in the city center and the headquarters of the Libertarian Youth.

Through it all, Mags remained close to her mother. The great number of anarchist and communist factions resisting the fascist government would have made little sense to Mags without Mollie there to explain it to her. But even at that young age, Mags intuited this lack of unified purpose did not bode well for the workers. Mags could scarcely tell if the sounds of rifles and machine guns came from friends or foes. And then today's violence happened.

Mags turned her back to the wall and crouched down. With the back of her right hand, she wiped the blood and sweat away from her eyes. Where is Mama, she wondered. The unexpected gun fight had separated them.

Then she heard boots on stone, coming quickly. It sounded like one man. Then another, following him. Mags had little doubt they belonged to the assault guard.

She raised her rifle. Mags had already chambered a round, so she waited silently. She hoped the men would run past her, take another turn, give up and turn back—anything. She had underestimated their determination.

A man appeared in the opening of the alcove with his rifle at the ready. In the split second before he realized his target was not standing, Mags fired from her crouch.

The rifle shot deafened her. If the second man was still coming, she could not hear him. She watched the guard's face turn from hate to shock as he stumbled backwards. Mags had aimed for his center mass, just as her mother had taught her. She chambered another round, as the man spewed a cloud of blood from his mouth.

Mags fired again. In the stark silence, her bullet caught him in the gut. He spun and fell to the ground.

The second man's momentum carried him to the edge of Mags' hiding spot. He had run with his pistol in his right hand. Now he brought it to bear on Mags.

She looked him in the eye. Shaking, she fumbled the rifle trying to chamber a round. The man's finger pulled back on the trigger.

The side of his head exploded. His body fell to the side. In death, he finished pulling the trigger, but the shot went off wildly.

"Maggie!"

Faintly she heard her mother's voice. "Mama!" She peeked around the edge of her hiding spot into the alley.

Her mother lowered a rifle and ran to her. "Maggie! Are you hurt?"

She ran into her mother's arms. They held her tightly. Mags wept.

Mollie kissed her daughter's trembling head. She thought of the dead men on the ground as men first and only second as government police. Two distinct pools of blood formed around the first one. Her daughter had taken him down in two shots, both to center mass—just like she was taught. Mollie felt pride, but she felt no desire to celebrate. She knew her daughter had never killed a man before.

"You're okay, baby. You're okay. Now, listen. The Casa CNT is taking heavy fire right now. They're trying to encircle it and close it off. We can't let that happen. If they cut us off from the Regional Committee, we'll all die in the streets. Just like these poor bastards. Do you understand?"

Mags released her grip on her mother and stood back. She wiped her face, leaving a trail of dirt and tears across her cheeks.

Mollie wet a piece of cloth with water from her canteen. She took Mags' face in her hands and washed off what she could. "It's okay, baby."

Mags sniffed. "I know, Mama. I killed him. He can't hurt me anymore."

"That's right, Maggie. He can't hurt you anymore."

Mags sniffed again and spat into the street. She picked up her rifle from the ground. She did not recall setting it down to hold her mother, but she felt momentarily ashamed. This was no day to be putting down her rifle. "I got lost, Mama. Are we far from the headquarters?"

Mollie smiled. "That's my girl. We're not far at all. Follow me."

7 May 1937.

"Bastards!" Mollie slammed the newspaper on the table. "The papers blame us for all this! Don't they know the CNT wants to end this bloodshed?"

"We were told to return to work yesterday," said the woman beside her. "I thought we'd agreed to an armistice with the government."

A small group of *anarquistas* gathered with Mollie in a boarded-up warehouse. They sat on crates with their daughters. Some of them cleaned their weapons. Others tried nervously to eat.

The sun's fading light crept through tiny gaps in the boards over the windows. Mags watched her mother fume. The tip of her tail twitched anxiously.

"We did." Mollie paced back and forth. "But now Berneri and Barbieri are dead. The police gunned them down yesterday. And the Stalinists helped them do it!" She clenched her fists. "We were fools to trust them."

Another woman spoke up. "So much for solidarity. Now we see the communists' true colors."

"They never wanted to help us at all," said Mollie. "They want to help themselves to Spain. And the workers be damned!"

"They will hunt us down like they did our leaders," said another. "The assault guards control the city already. They force us to give up our guns. They took my husband to prison this morning.

It's the same all over the city."

"Goddamned fascists. And betrayed by our allies. This has all gone to hell."

Mollie was not wrong. The day before, the CNT-FAI had urged workers to return to work. But the hostilities had taken a terrible turn. Two of the anarchist leaders were killed by the police and members of one of the communist groups.

The workers in the Telephone Exchange had formed an ill-fated cease-fire with the invading police. The workers had held the building, but they could not get any food or supplies with the police occupying the first floor. The police agreed to let the workers out, and also to leave the building themselves. That was the end of the CNT's control of the Telephone Exchange. During the cease-fire, the government's assault guards simply took over the entire building.

The assault guards then patrolled the city, arresting workers and confiscating their weapons, though it was the workers' groups who sought an armistice. The press, however, cast the blame for all the violence on the anarchist factions. Now, both the government and the communist groups supported by Russia had turned against the city's workers. In just a few short days, the situation had indeed gone to hell.

"Mollie," said the woman beside her. "We thank you for your help. But we know this isn't your fight."

"Of *course* this is my fight! Every bit as much as the coal miners' fight in Asturias was mine. I can't stand idly by while—"

"Mollie," said the woman again. "We want to ask you for something."

Mollie checked her rage. She placed her hand on the woman's shoulder. "I'm here to help, comrade. What would you have me do?"

"Our children, Mollie. This city may have no hope. But we cannot abandon her. The guards may come to arrest us. Some of us may die. Perhaps all of us. But our children, Mollie. Will you take them to safety? Will you find them somewhere safe until our streets no longer flow with blood?"

Mollie looked to the daughters of the *anarquistas* she had fought beside for nearly a year. They had become as much a family to her as the one she was born into. Their eyes beseeched her. The admiration she had commanded was more than just respect.

She drew a deep breath and slowly let it out. "Is that what you want me to do?"

One by one, the *anarquistas* nodded their heads. They had no more desire than Mollie did to consign their children to imprisonment and death in a losing battle. One of them said softly, "Please."

"Then I will do this for you. Maggie?"

"Mama?"

"Gather your things, dear. We leave tonight."

June 1937.

A branch smacked Mags in the face. She fell to the ground. Then Mollie's hand was in hers, pulling her up. Mags rose to her feet and brandished her rifle. The daughters of the *anarquistas* came rushing up beside her, one by one. "Come on!" Mags shouted at them. "*Ándale!*"

The communist death squad chased after them, only seconds behind. Similar squads swept the countryside, murdering anarchist sympathizers everywhere. The group had sought safety, but in the outbreak of the civil war, no safety was to be found. And so, like many anarchists across the country, they fled before the scourge of death at their heels.

Mollie waved her hand in the air. "This way!" She could not bear to tell the girls the truth, that she no longer had any idea where they should flee. She merely led them away from their pursuers as quickly as she could. She hoped it would be enough.

When the last of the girls made it to their side, mother and daughter aimed their rifles into the forest. They unleashed a barrage in the direction they had come from.

Mags' sensitive ears picked up screaming. She must have gotten lucky. But her luck was about to run out. "Mama."

"Go!" Mollie shouted.

Mags and the girls ran as fast as they could.

Mollie caught up to them where the dense forest opened into a clearing. She was, for a moment, grateful to be out of the tangle of branches and underbrush. But she knew how much easier it was to get a clear line of sight in a landscape such as this.

They all ran across the open space. Mother and daughter reached the other side of the clearing first. They stood at its opposite edge, waving on the girls in their care, rifles at the ready.

Communist soldiers reached the edge of the forest, and Mollie knew all hope was lost. She raised her rifle. "Maggie!"

Gunshots rang out. First one girl and then another fell to the ground. Their bodies flailed in the air then disappeared into the grass.

"Take my ring." Mollie fired at their pursuers then raised her voice. "If I fall, take my ring. Do you understand?"

Mags dropped into a crouch beside her mother. She chambered a round, fired into the forest, and chambered another. One by one, the girls in her group sprayed blood and fell to the ground. They never made it to the other side of the clearing. Mags could not be sure if she was hitting her targets, but she heard shouting.

"Maggie!"

"Yes, Mama." All the girls they had tried to save had fallen. Mags felt nothing but hate and sadness. But her mother's nearness gave her strength. Together, they returned fire at their enemies.

A bullet caught Mollie square in the chest. She fell backwards into the underbrush.

"Mama!"

Mollie sprawled on the broken branches and tangled bushes of the forest floor. Blood gushed from her mouth and down the side of neck into her uniform. "Take it," she whispered.

Mags would never hear her mother speak another word. Mollie's hand quivered above her chest, and the silver ring caught what rays of sun could penetrate the forest canopy.

"Mama!" Mags cried out again. But she knew.

Bullets lacerated the air above her head. One lodged itself in the tree over her shoulder.

Mags grabbed her mother's hand. In one swift motion, she pulled the ring free. Another bullet smacked into Mollie's corpse. Then another. Blood flowed from the wounds.

Mags ducked into the dirt and crawled away. She heard bullets slice the air above her, and the sickening sound of more bullets smashing into her mother's lifeless body.

She leapt to her feet and ran. She left her mother's body there at the edge of the clearing, and she ran harder than she had run in her entire life.

And for that, Mags would never forgive herself.

January 1938.

On her hands and knees, Mags lapped water from the cold stream. It tasted clean. She placed her chin and lips just below the surface and gulped it down. Her tail twitched against her leg inside the thick pants she now wore under her stolen coat.

Winter had come, and she slept outside most nights unless she could find a barn or abandoned house to escape the wind. She no longer had her rifle. She vaguely remembered how it had broken into pieces when, out of ammunition, she had defended herself by bludgeoning an attacker with it.

Winter's arrival meant her fourteenth birthday had come and gone. She had not given it any thought. What few thoughts Mags had this season focused on survival, and little else. Her mind had retreated from a truth she found too painful to face. For seven months, she had lived alone, like an animal. She foraged for food, water, and warm clothing, avoiding the war-torn cities and preying upon more isolated farms across the countryside.

A rustle caught her attention. She raised her head slightly from the water and scanned the opposite bank. There. A movement in the grass. She sniffed the air then lowered her head again to drink. She smelled a bird, but it did her little good on the far side of the stream.

The grass rustled again, and wings beat the air. The bird flew over her head. Mags jumped. Faster than the eye could follow, her hand smacked the bird down from its flight. Stunned, it fell into the grass. She pounced on it, and her fingers closed around it in an instant. She snapped its neck.

Mags was fond of birds, in her own way. Their movements earned her rapt attention. She had grown quite adept at stalking and catching them over the last half a year. She enjoyed their songs, their powers of flight, and their taste. It was this affection which brought them quick deaths at her hands, as opposed to the way most cats play with their prey before eating it.

The taste of blood and raw meat filled her mouth. Had Mags been thinking clearly, she might have headed north to France, toward her grandmother's estate. But how could she face Gramma when she had run like a coward into the forest, leaving Mama's body in the hands of her killers? Surely Gramma would be ashamed of her. So terribly ashamed. Ashamed of her spineless granddaughter who ran and ran like a hunted animal.

On the rare occasions she had encountered other people, she heard talk of the civil war which had broken out following the events in Barcelona. But Mags could not think of the revolution without thinking of her mother. Her mother's body lying still on the ground.

She blotted the thought from her mind. If it were an image on a canvas, she would have painted over it until all its features were buried. Instead, Mags cradled her left hand with her right. She could feel her mother's ring through the gloves she had stolen. Only that familiar sensation brought her any comfort.

Gunshots. And again. Her body tensed. She did not know if the shots came from hunters or soldiers. Either way, they were not her friends. Mags had no friends. She only had a countryside filled with potential enemies. She bolted into the forest and ran until it ended at the top of a hill. Below her, a freight train slowly chugged along.

Mags ran down the hill as fast as she could.

The train picked up speed. Mags saw a car with an open door, perhaps intended for livestock. She ran alongside the train, trying to match its velocity. She reached for a metal bar on the railcar's side. It was only inches from her fingertips. Then it pulled away.

With all the strength she could muster, she willed herself to run faster. Suddenly, her hand closed on the bar. Her feet left the ground. She swung her legs up, frantically seeking a foothold. Her other hand snapped shut around the bar. She pulled herself up, flung her legs inside the doorway, and rolled across the floor.

Crouching on all fours, her belly nearly touching the floor, she studied the hills and forest. Had anyone pursued her? Were the men with guns still following her? She saw no one. But she could not be sure.

That night, huddled in a corner of the railcar, Mags dreamed. She shivered. Her fists clenched and unclenched. The tip of her tail flicked nervously against her leg. She saw a black flag pounded by rain and snapping in a tempest. It bore a white skull above two crossed swords. Its rhythmic dance hypnotized her.

As she watched, the skull and swords turned crimson. The swords liquefied, running like streams of blood to the bottom of the flag. The wind snatched them up and flung them into the storm. But the skull did not run. Instead, it became a heart. It pulsed with a strange light. Mags heard a woman singing, but she could not make out the words above the howling wind. She concentrated, trying to hear the song.

She awoke to find the grey sky glowing with the first pale light of sunrise. Something felt different this morning. For the first time since last summer, Mags felt clear-headed. Faintly, in the back of her mind, she heard the singing woman from her dream. The song slowly burned away her fog of despair just like the rising sun.

She felt an undeniable compulsion to sail, and she caught the scent of the sea. The train had carried her to the coast. Its churning rhythm slowed. Soon it would come to a full stop.

Mags brushed the dirt from her ragged clothes. She did her best to brush her tangled hair away from her face. Then she leapt out of the lazily rolling train. She walked to the sea and stole aboard the first boat she could find.

PART TWO: THE HOUSE ON METEOR STREET

25 January 1938.

Mags knelt before the grave, a stone cross and a small plaque set in the ground. The boat had taken her to England. Once there, she mingled with the crowds, guided by the softly singing voice in her head. Eventually, she arrived at Victoria Station in London.

Near the station sat St. James Park. Just around the way from the park, Mags discovered a small cemetery. She walked among the graves until she found one with her mother's name on it. The woman buried there did not share Mollie's last name, but it was enough for Mags that she shared the first.

"I'm sorry, Mama." The damp earth felt cold against her knees. A constant drizzle of rain masked her tears. "I was just so scared." She sniffed. "I didn't know what else to do."

Just then, a black kitten came running across the gravestones straight toward her. Mags' eyes lit up. She opened her arms and called to him. The kitten leapt into her arms, panting heavily. Mags held him. He nuzzled into her filthy coat. She huddled over him to protect him from the rain.

The kitten had a splash of white on its face and a single white forepaw. Mags made a fist. She ran her thumb over the kitten's closed eye while scratching the fuzz near his ear with her curled fingers. His breathing slowed, and he purred. Mags smiled.

"It went this way!"

At the shout, the kitten opened his eyes and squirmed. Mags stood up.

A boy came crashing through the bushes. "Over here!" He looked to one side then the other, and then at Mags. Three more youths came smashing through the hedge, destroying the quiet of the graveyard with their shouting. They were not much older than Mags and, like her, they wore tattered clothes and dirty faces, disheveled hair, and hunger in their eyes.

"There it is!" The boy pointed at Mags.

Through the damaged break in the hedge stepped another girl, taller than the rest, but just as dirty. Where the others had quick, nervous movements, she moved more confidently and slowly. She eyed Mags with vicious hate. "Who the fuck is that?"

"Yeah," said the boy excitedly. "Who the fuck are you, ya little slag? This is *our* place. Piss off!"

Mags took a step back, unsure if she should stand her ground or run to protect the kitten.

The big girl raised the crude weapon in her right hand. It was merely a cylinder of wood, some kind of post perhaps, with the end taped up for a grip. She grasped it firmly in her woolen glove with the fingers cut out, and pointed it at Mags. "Not so fast, lassie. You'll be giving us that kitten now. Hand it over."

"Tell, her, Emily," said the boy. "Hand it over!"

The other children glared.

"If he was your kitten," said Mags, "he wouldn't be running from you."

"Oi! Ain't ya the smart little cunt?" She smacked the boy beside her on the back of the head. "Get her!"

The gang rushed Mags. Startled, the kitten squirmed free and jumped to the ground. He ran towards the trees on the edge of the cemetery. One of the girls let out a howl and chased after him.

Without a second's hesitation, Mags ran at that girl. The girl ran with the manic speed of a wild dog. She might have caught the cat if left to her own devices. But Mags leapt and tackled her.

The two of them fell to the ground. As they rolled on the ground, Mags' head slammed into a gravestone. She cried out, but she held her grip on her derelict opponent, who elbowed her in the gut.

Two hands grabbed her hair from behind and pulled her up. She swung her arms and legs, trying to find her footing.

The girl she had tackled began to rise to her feet. Mags kicked her as hard as she could in the mouth. The girl screamed, covering her face. Blood spurted from between her fingers.

The rest of the youth joined the fray. "Hold her," ordered Emily. She walked over, brandishing her club.

The boy grabbing Mags by the hair tried to put her in a choke hold. He crooked his arm around her neck.

Mags' fist closed on his hand. She whipped her head back to smash the bridge of his nose. Blood sprayed into her dirty, matted locks.

His grip on her hair loosened enough that she could lean her head forward to his imprisoned hand. She clamped her teeth down on his index finger. He screamed.

Mags bit into the second joint of his finger as hard as she could. Cartilage cracked in her mouth. She forced her teeth together and flung her head to the side.

Emily swung her club. She caught a glancing blow on the side of Mags' head. The severed finger went flying out of Mags' mouth into the grass.

"She bit my fookin' finger off! Aaaaaa!"

"I said hold her, you little sods!"

The blows to the head slowed Mags too much. Before she could charge Emily, the two uninjured youth grabbed her arms.

The girl with the bloodied face punched her in the stomach. She grabbed Mags' legs to keep them from kicking. "Bash this cunt's head in," she yelled. "She knocked my teeth out!"

Mags cursed violently in Spanish, thrashing, trying to free herself. She glared at Emily, who stood before her.

Emily raised her club. "You should have let us have our fun with the cat. When we're done with you, we're gonna go find the little mongrel, and I'm gonna beat it anyway. Just like I'm gonna beat you now."

As the club came down, Mags collapsed, dropping all her weight and pulling her arms in towards her. The boy on her left fell forward, still gripping her. The club came down on the back of his head.

"Bloody fuck," Emily shouted. "Get out of the way!"

Mags and her assailants tumbled to the ground.

Emily kicked them. "Out of the way," she said, not caring whom she hurt.

Just then, a man ran toward them. "Hey! Break it up!" He towered over Emily. His coat made his muscular frame appear even bulkier. He swung a cane as he approached. "Stop it right now! You let her go!"

Emily stopped kicking. "Fun time's over, mates. Let's go!" She took off in the opposite direction. The tangled bodies on the ground separated. The children scrambled away from Mags. They leapt up to follow Emily, barely escaping the wrath of the man's swinging cane. Emily stopped to look at him from the edge of the cemetery.

He pulled off the top of the cane to reveal a blade. "Go on, now," he shouted.

She scowled, then ran off.

He looked down at Mags on the ground. "Are you okay?"

She rolled over onto her hands and knees. "*Está bien,*" she muttered, coming to her feet. "It's fine."

"Are you hurt?"

Mags held her hand to the side of her head. "No," she lied.

She swayed a little. The man held out his hand to her, but she shrank back from him. "Don't touch me! I'm not afraid of you."

The man eyed her thoughtfully and stepped back. "I ain't here to hurt you, little one." He placed his blade back in the top of his cane. "You know," he said, considering the disheveled young woman in front of him, "I was jumped by five guys once. Just minding my own business. Then, out of nowhere, boom. I was fighting for my life. I probably would have died that night. But you know what?"

Mags eyed him cautiously. "What?"

"A friend came to my rescue."

"They wanted to kill you?"

"They sure did. I was in the wrong place at the wrong time for a man with my skin."

"What's wrong with your skin?"

"Not a damn thing. But not everyone back home feels the same way. That's why I left the States to come here. A man's a man here in London, and they don't care so much what color he is."

Mags did not understand what he meant. But he did not seem to mean her any harm. She asked him, "Did you see the kitten? Did he get away?"

"Is that what you were fighting about? That little black cat that went running out of here like a bat out of hell?"

"They wanted to hurt him."

"Goddamn street urchins. I'd hate 'em, if I didn't know a thing or two about being as hungry as they are. By the way," he said, holding out his hand. "My name's Jack."

Mags eyed his hand.

"Are your parents here? Do you need some help getting home?"

Mags shook her head. "Mama's... She's not here anymore. I came here to talk to her."

"And your daddy?"

"He's in the States. I never met him."

"Well. Aren't you in a pickle?"

"A what?"

"A spot of trouble, you know."

Mags did not understand all his slang, but she understood the meaning. "Thank you." She held out her hand. "My name is Mags."

"A pleasure to meet you, young lady." He shook her hand gently a few times then let it go. "Mags. I don't really know what I can do for you, but you're welcome to join me for lunch and some tea if you like. Maybe we can sort something out for you?"

"No one has been nice to me in a long time."

Jack laughed softly. "Let's just say I like to root for the underdog."

"The what?"

"The underdog. That's the fighter no one thinks is gonna win. But you know what? He goes into the ring swinging anyway. And every now and then, that fighter proves everyone wrong. He might even take the title!"

"The title of a book?"

"Mags, you don't follow boxing much, do you?"

She shook her head.

"Why don't you join me for lunch and get out of this bloody rain for a bit, and I'll tell you all about it."

Mags considered. "I want to find that kitten. I'm worried about him."

"You won't be much use to the kitties of this world if you starve to death, will you?"

She looked out to the street beyond the cemetery and saw no sign of the gang or the cat. They could be anywhere by now. And damn it all if she wasn't ravenously hungry. "No," she said. "No, I won't."

The two of them walked south to Clapham, Mags at the boxer's side, and suddenly the rain and the cold and the throbbing in her head did not seem so awful.

She smiled between mouthfuls of her sandwich. The first sandwich had disappeared in the blink of an eye. But she slowed a little on the third one. She grabbed a glass of milk and gulped it down. "Thank you so much."

Jack sat across from her in his modest flat. "My pleasure. Would you like another glass of milk?"

Mags nodded enthusiastically.

"Why don't you tell me your story? How did you end up all by yourself in London?"

Mags guzzled half the glass in a second and set it back on the table. She wiped her mouth with the back of her hand. She started with the fighting in Barcelona, and related her tale to him.

Jack listened, slowly chewing his sandwich as the young woman talked. He raised his eyebrows in amazement. He had seen some brutality as a boxer, but this young lady's tale was something else entirely. He shook his head.

"Then I walked until I found that cemetery," she said, concluding her story.

"And now here you are on Meteor Street, safe and sound."

"Meteor Street? Like meteorites?"

"Mhm. Didn't you see the street sign?"

"I love the stars."

"Do you, now? Here, let me show you something." Jack walked

to his bookshelf and picked up a wooden case the size of a cigar box, with a hinged lid. Standing at Mags' side, he set it on the table. "I picked these up when I went to Sydney for a fight. Must have been about twenty years ago now. Open it up."

Mags lifted the lid. She looked in awe at the contents, then up to Jack.

"Go ahead," he said, returning to his seat. "You can hold them."

She lifted a polished stone from the box. It sparkled in her hand. She set it on the table and took out another. "Where is Sydney?"

"Australia. Where they send all the criminals."

"Really?"

"I'm just kidding. They send boxers there, too. It's really a beautiful place. Most people don't know England sent criminals all over the world, even the States. Forced transportation, they called it. Anyway, if you're up for exploring, you can find all sorts of craters and meteorites there."

Mags took out the meteorites one by one, some rough, some polished smooth. "Oooh," she exclaimed. "This one's pretty." She held a meteorite which had been sliced into a slab, flat on two sides. All around the edges, it was only black and brown. But the interior was filled with chips of colorful rock, all packed together. A hole had been drilled in the stone, and a metal ring set in it. Mags could not take her eyes off it.

"That's a beauty."

"It came from the stars?"

"Some people say we all came from the stars. But these rocks came from asteroids. Bigger rocks that float in space. And sometimes they get smashed up, and the little pieces fall to earth. They say these ones from Oz mostly came from the same asteroid, a real big one out past Mars. A place called Vesta."

She closed her fingers around the stone. "I want to go there."

"Australia? You could buy a ticket and sail there, I suppose. Or work on a ship."

"No," said Mags. "Not Australia. Vesta."

Jack's belly shook with laughter. "You're something else, young lady. I tell you what. Why don't you hold on to that little rock for me, okay? And someday, when you get to Vesta, you can tell her old Jack sent you to bring that rock home."

"Okay," she said. "But I don't want to lose it!"

"Take the chain that's in the bottom of that box. Do you see it in there?"

Mags pushed the pile of stones to the side. She saw the links of a silver necklace, and she pulled it out of the box.

"There you go. Put your new pendant on that, and then it won't get lost." Jack watched her string the pendant and clasp the necklace. It had sat unused in that box ever since his last wife passed away. It felt right to give it to this girl who had lost so much, yet could hope for something so obviously impossible.

"How does it look?"

"Like it belongs," he said.

Mags purred.

"Now that's a very special rock. But a girl that gets in as many scraps as you needs an edge. Otherwise, who's gonna keep that meteorite safe until you take it home?" He went to the living room. "Come here, young lady. I'm going to show you a couple things that will help you in a fight."

"Yes!" Mags joined him.

"First, if a fight's coming, you want to stand like this. See? Get your fists up like this, to protect your face. And stand with your body like this."

She imitated his stance. "Like this?"

"That's good. But," he said, pushing her elbows up slightly, "you want your arms raised a little more. There you go. Good. Now let me show you some footwork. Have you ever danced before?"

"Mama taught me how to dance."

"Good. Because when you're in a fight, you need to do more than just swing your fists. You gotta dance."

"Okay," said Mags. A broad smile formed on her lips. "Let's dance!"

For the next few hours, Jack taught her basic sparring moves and methods. "You're a natural," he declared. "I've never seen anyone pick up footwork so fast."

"It's just like dancing."

"It sure is. How about another sandwich?"

"You've been kind to me, Jack. But I'm worried about that little kitten. I feel like I should go find him. He could be lost."

Jack sighed. "You've been great company, Mags. And you seem like you can take care of yourself. Let me make you a few sandwiches to take with you, at least." He busied himself in the kitchen. "And in this corner," he said, "the reigning champion, Battlin' Roast Beef Bronson!" He wrapped up a sandwich and handed it to her. "And in this corner, a bold new contender. The one, the only, Meteor Mags!"

She clapped her hands. "Is that my boxing name? Hahaha! I like it."

"Every fighter needs a fightin' good name." He looked at her seriously. "Now, if things get too rough out there, young lady, you just drop by any time. You're always welcome at the house on Meteor Street."

Mags threw her arms around him. The old fighter held her like a father holds his daughter. When she finally left, Jack immediately missed her.

It would be many years before Mags could keep her promise to take that meteorite home. And by the time she did, Jack had been dead a long, long time.

Mags walked across town towards the park and the graveyard, sniffing the air for the scent of the little black cat. "Kitten," she called out now and then, alternating words with mews only a cat could understand. Eventually, she heard a response. She crouched at the entrance to an alley and called again.

The kitten emerged from the shadows. He peered around the corner of the alley, blinking his eyes. He rubbed his face on the corner. "Meow?"

"It's okay, baby." She held out her hand for him to sniff. He rubbed his face on her fingers. "Are you lost?" The kitten bumped against her and curled his tail to rest on her leg.

Mags scooped up the cat in her arms. He purred on the ledge of her forearm as she talked quietly to him and scratched the side of his face. "Let's get out of this part of town. Then we can have a roast beef sandwich. Doesn't that sound nice? Yes, it does." Mags chattered on and on.

People filled the streets that evening. They cast disapproving looks at the young woman, seeing nothing more than an untidy urchin. It was half past six.

Mags ignored the frowns, the stares, and the throng. But as she passed the park, she caught another familiar scent. This one, she did not like. This one smelled like an enemy.

From beyond the line of trees surrounding the park came a shout. "Emily! That little slag is back!"

Mags recognized the boy's voice. And a second later, Emily's.

"Where?"

"Over here!"

Mags could have run. She could have fled. But the idea of enemies charging her through the trees brought back savage, horrible feelings. This time, she did not even consider escape.

She whispered to the kitten. He leapt from her arms and darted up a tree. By the time he had safely reached a limb high above the ground, Mags was already running full speed into the park.

She tackled the boy. His body slammed into the ground. Something inside him cracked. Mags grabbed a fistful of his hair. She pounded his head into the ground until his eyes glazed over.

Emily screamed. She raised her club and charged.

Mags rose from her prey like a beast and stepped forward into a boxer's stance. When Emily was upon her, Mags danced out of the way. Emily flew past. Mags turned to face her, hands raised and clenched.

Emily charged again. She swung her club.

But Mags stepped quickly inside the swing. With her right arm, she deflected the blow, blocking Emily's arm. With her left, she jabbed the girl in the face.

Emily's free hand swung into the side of Mag's head. It took a firm hold of her hair. Instead of pulling away, Mags danced even closer. She smacked her head into the girl's teeth. Then she flung herself upon Emily.

They fell to the ground, twisting and turning. Emily screamed incoherently, swiping her fingers like claws. They raked the side of Mags' face and drew blood.

Mags hissed. Her hands locked on Emily's club. She tore it loose from her enemy's grasp.

Gripping it like a barbell, Mags smashed it lengthwise into Emily's face. Blood spurted from the ridge above the girl's eye. "Don't!" Smash. "Fucking!" Smash. "Hit me!" Smash.

Mags swung the club again and again. She had no awareness of her own screaming, a long wail broken only by her shuddering sobs. Tears streamed down her dirty face, rendering her field of view a cloudy, swirling purple.

Mags wanted the girl to stop. Stop tormenting her. Stop teasing her. Stop making sounds. Stop moving. Stop. Stop. Stop. Stop. Stop.

Mags took a deep breath. Her tail twitched sharply. She tossed the blood-smeared weapon to one side. With a filthy sleeve, she rubbed streaks of snot and tears away from her face, sniffing now and then.

"*Puta*," she said, drawing herself to her feet. She sniffed, then spat on the ground. "You fucking bitch." She wiped another stream of tears from her cheek.

"Mew," came a voice from the edge of the park.

"Kitten? Kitten!" Mags held out her hands. The little black cat came trotting up to her. "*Mi bebé.*" She stroked the cat's side.

He wrapped his tail around her forearm. "Mew," he asked again.

"Agreed. *Vámonos!*" Mags quickly walked away. The kitten followed her, glancing back nervously at every sound.

She thought the screaming and the fighting would have attracted some attention. But no one paid her any attention at all, not even the slightest bit. In fact, quite a noise had begun in the streets during her struggle. When she left the park, she found everyone looking up. People in the crowd talked loudly, agitatedly, pointing their fingers at the sky.

She looked up, too, and she saw. The entire sky was on fire. She scooped up the kitten, pushed her way through the crowd, and ran from the city.

Mags sat on a hill overlooking London, watching the sky blaze with mysterious lights. They sparkled through her haze of tears. She wiped her eyes then patted the kitten at her side, wondering what it would be like to be up there, flying in the burning borealis. The adrenaline rush subsided from her body. Fatigue mingled with her sadness.

A fiery finger from the blazing curtain stretched out to Earth. It reached the foot of the hill. The kitten ran for cover in the forest. Mags placed her palm to the dirt to push herself up. But she saw something that stopped her.

Where the light touched the hill, an incandescent globe appeared. The outline of a figure appeared inside it. The figure raised its hands above its head, clasping them. The white globe expanded, illuminating the entire hill.

Mags shielded her eyes with her hand. But she felt no fear. Something about the light burned too purely, too powerfully, too divinely to be a threat.

The globe contracted, forming an aura around the figure, twinkling like a robe of stars. The figure stepped forward. It looked up the hill, and it spoke. "Maggie," said the voice, not questioning, not asking—simply knowing. It sounded just like the voice from Mags' dream.

Then she recognized the figure from portraits she had seen at her gramma's house long ago. "Great-gramma," she cried, and ran down the hill.

Magdalena opened her arms to greet her great-granddaughter. "Maggie."

Mags wrapped her arms around her great-grandmother and wept into the black lace of the woman's cloak. She heard ravens singing. She felt warm like blood. She smelled the ocean. In the woman's embrace, Mags felt a peace unlike anything she had ever felt before.

"My daughter, don't be sad. What a lovely young woman you've become."

"Great-gramma! How can you be here? Didn't you—"

Magdalena's white hair stood gathered on her head like a mighty temple. She arched an eyebrow. "I did, dear. I died. After two hundred years. Bloody hell, I'm exhausted. Come sit with me." They walked hand-in-hand to the top of the hill.

The kitten peered out of the forest. He ran down to inspect them as they took a seat on the hilltop.

"What do you think of my light show, Maggie?" She scratched the kitten behind the ears, and he promptly plopped down in the grass beside her.

"You made this happen? It's beautiful."

"Why, thank you. I don't mind telling you it was harder than hell." Magdalena brushed a strand of hair back from her face. "That should give them something to write about for a few years, anyway." She put her arm around Mags. "I tried to reach you sooner, but it's taken all my power to pierce the veil between our worlds. These lights, this curtain of fire, is the result. That, and being with you now."

"I'm so glad you're here! It's been so awful. We were fighting, and the war went against us and we had to run, and then Mama—" She hugged her great-grandmother and cried.

Magdalena pet Mags' hair and rubbed her head. "I'm sorry I couldn't save Mollie. I could see what was happening, but there was nothing I could do."

"You could see us?"

"I could. And I tried to help but—oh, Maggie. I felt so powerless."

"So did I. I wanted to save her. I wanted to help her. But I couldn't. I couldn't do anything but run. I'm so ashamed of myself." She put her head down and sobbed.

"I know, baby. I know." The woman placed her hand on Mags' cheek. "You did everything you could. That's all anyone could ever ask of you. We can never give more than everything we are. Do you understand?"

Mags sniffed. "Yes. But she was just lying there and I—"

"Shhh. It's okay, baby." Magdalena held her, letting her cry until the trembling subsided. "Maggie, I'm proud of you." She lifted the young woman's head. "You fought, and you survived. No one your age should have to go through what you did. No one. But you didn't let it destroy you, did you?"

"No, Great-gramma. It was so hard afterward. I was so sad. But I had to keep fighting."

"That's right." Magdalena sighed. "You remind me so much of myself when I was your age. So much fire. So much spirit. Did you know when I was your age I was already sailing under the black flag?"

"Were you?"

"Oh, most certainly. It was a rough life, and I could have let it destroy me. Grind me down to nothing. I could have given in to despair. But like you, I had more fight in me than that. You just have to keep going, Maggie. You keep fighting until you can't fight any more. There's no other choice. Not for us."

"I'll never give up, Great-gramma. I want to be just like you."

Magdalena laughed and laughed. "Oh, my dear. You had better be prepared to leave a pile of bodies behind you, then. And to make quite a few enemies along the way."

Mags wiped her face. She recognized some of her mother in this glowing woman, the same rage and determination. But the power radiating from Great-gramma was like nothing she had ever witnessed before. Mags believed this night she sat in the presence of a goddess. She would never forget the awe she felt for this woman whose blood flowed in her own veins, this ancient woman who made the sky fill with fire.

She grasped Magdalena's hand. Her mother's ring and Magdalena's ring touched. When they made contact, a mystical flame bloomed, lighting up their faces, yet burning neither of them. The rings were exactly the same.

"I see Mollie gave you my ring. I'm glad."

"She made sure I took it, Great-gramma. Like it was the most important thing in the world, even as she was—" Mags tightened her grasp on her great-grandmother's hand. "Even as she was dying."

"Do you know why that is?"

"No."

"That's *my* ring, Maggie. Look at them. Do you see how they look just like one another?"

"Yes."

"There were only two ever made. One for me. And one for my husband, your great-grandfather. I obtained them at considerable cost. And I don't mean money. I mean many good members of my crew went to their graves for me to have them. Maggie, I have seen so many people die. But when I met your great-grandfather, I wanted more. I wanted something that would last. Something beyond these pale constraints of flesh. We deserved more than that. Our love deserved more than that. Our love…"

Magdalena's voice trailed off. She focused on the curtain of fire shimmering between this realm and the other. How many skies would she have gladly burned to the ground to regain her love? How many empires would she have gladly toppled? How many lives would she have snuffed like candles to spend one more hour with him? But she knew all of that was fantasy.

"Our love deserved to last forever," she said, holding her great-granddaughter's hand. "But since that isn't possible, I obtained these rings. They would let us live to the age of two hundred years, and in relatively good health that whole time."

"You weren't immortal?"

Magdalena laughed. "No, darling. More like charmed than immortal. We were never sick. We never aged. But our time was limited. We had until we lived two hundred years, and then we would die as everyone else. But even that was denied my husband." Her gaze fell to the ground.

"What happened, Great-gramma? You can tell me."

"Of course I can, Maggie. Of course I can." She raised her eyes to the burning sky. "My enemies came for us as we slept. They slew my husband. And they would have slain me, too. But I lead them to their deaths. I discovered who sent them, and I killed them, too. Not that it eased the pain at all. Vengeance is its own satisfaction, my daughter, but it can never heal."

"They killed him even though he had your ring?"

"Oh, yes. The gift of long life did not come with invincibility. We could certainly be killed before our appointed time." Magdalena paused. "And he was. But Maggie, those two rings have been handed down from mother to daughter. Before I buried him, I took the ring from his finger. I gave it to your grandmother when she was born, so she would live in good health for a long, long time. When I died, my ring passed to her daughter, Mollie. And that, my darling, is the ring you wear right now, taken from her hand as she died."

Mags' eyes shone with understanding. "We wear the same ring. You and me."

"Yes."

"I love you so much, Great-gramma. Will you stay with me?"

"I would love nothing more than that. But I can't."

"Please!"

"I'm sorry, my beautiful daughter. Nothing would make me happier. But the strain of crossing over to this side—I can't stay here long."

"Please stay, Great-gramma!"

Magdalena cupped the young woman's face in her hands. "Maggie. I will always be with you. Do you understand? I will always be close to you. Even when you cannot see me. Even when you cannot hear me. I will be there, with you. I will watch over you the best I can. I can't say I understand exactly what's happened to me. But I can feel the bond between us. Can you feel it, too, Maggie? Can you feel me with you now?"

"I can."

"Then that is all that matters. It's no mistake you wear my ring and wear my name, is it?"

"No. Mama named me after you."

"Good. Now, listen to me. This is an important time in your life. You've become a woman. A young woman, with much to learn, but still a woman, do you understand?"

"Yes. My body has changed. And I had to fight to live."

"That's right. But it's even more than that. You have important times ahead of you, Maggie. All of history lies before you, and there will come times people of my day and age never dreamed possible. You will be a part of that. But you need to get out of Europe. Things are about to happen here that no one can stop. Terrible things. I worry for you. Tomorrow, a ship leaves from this country to go to the States, and I want you to get on that ship. Do you understand?"

"No, not at all! What's coming, Great-gramma?"

Magdalena rubbed a hand back and forth across her crimson lips. "This city here will be bombed into oblivion, for starters."

"Should I go back to France?" Mags' face fell. "I don't know how Gramma could ever forgive me."

"Margareta would never turn you away. But she will have her hands full with the destruction of our adopted nation. It will be brutal, merciless, and quite hopeless for several years. I want you to go to the States. Do you trust me?"

Mags squeezed her great-grandmother's hand. "Yes."

"Good." Then Magdalena told her where to go the next day, and which train she needed to take south.

When she was done, Mags asked her, "Were you really a pirate? Before Gramma was born?"

In Magdalena's laughter, Mags heard sails snapping in gale-force winds. She heard waves crashing against wooden hulls with enough power to throw sailors into the watery depths forever. Blood flowed down the length of a saber and splattered on a deck worn smooth by leather boots. Magdalena's laughter was death spilling over the waves in a relentless storm. It filled Mags with a strange and savage joy. She imagined that one day she, too, might have that kind of laugh.

"Indeed I was." Magdalena eyed the waving sheets of cosmic

fire scorching the skies above them. "I can't stay here much longer, Maggie. The gateway will close soon, and I will have to go. But I could tell you a few stories in the meantime."

"I'd love that. Did you ever capture a treasure?"

Once again, the oceanic laughter. Magdalena ran her hands over her great-granddaughter's hair, brushing it back. "My darling daughter, you have no idea. Let me tell you a story."

Mags cuddled up to her great-grandmother's breast. She listened to tales of piracy and seafaring mayhem until she fell asleep, purring in Magdalena's arms, the tip of her tail slowly curling and uncurling.

When she awoke in the morning, no one but her kitten was around. She looked to the bottom of the hill. The scorched earth proved to her the visitation was more than just a dream. She scooped the kitten into her arms.

As her great-grandmother had instructed her, she stole aboard a train, heading southward to the docks.

26 January 1938.
The New York Times: Late City Edition, page 25.

Reporting on the events of the evening of 25 January: Aurora Borealis Startles Europe, People Flee in Fear, Call Firemen. Britons Thought Windsor Castle Ablaze. Scots See Ill Omen. Snow-Clad Swiss Alps Glow.

From 6:30 to 8:30 P.M., the people of London watched two magnificent arcs rising in the east and west, from which radiated pulsating beams like searchlights in dark red, greenish blue, and purple. From an airplane, the display looked like a shimmering curtain of fire. Police stations, fire brigades, and newspaper offices all over the country were inundated by calls tonight asking, "Where is the fire?" The phenomenon was seen as far south as Vienna. It spread fear in parts of Portugal and

Lower Austria while thousands of Britons were brought running into the streets in wonderment. The ruddy glow led many to think half the city was ablaze. The Windsor Fire Department was called out in the belief that Windsor Castle was afire.

Celina strode down the dock towards the scuffle. Her expensive skirts snapped in the breeze. Three dock workers had their hands full trying to subdue a filthy terror raging and kicking in their midst. As Celina approached, she could see the upstart was a girl, and her fists clenched reflexively. "Rack off," she shouted. "Leave her alone!"

One of the workers scowled at her. Then a black bolt leapt out of the struggling girl's arms and onto his face. The kitten howled, digging in its claws.

Celina called out, "Starry!"

The kitten jumped down to the dock and ran for her. Celina scooped him up. "I said stop it!" She drew a knife. Cradling Starry in one arm, she stepped up to the fray.

A dock worker held the ragged girl in a chokehold. "I got the little bitch!"

A second worker closed in on her. The girl kicked him in the testicles. She brought her heel down on her captor's foot as hard as she could. He screamed.

She broke free from his grasp and stepped away. But instead of running, she adopted a boxer's stance. The worker with the bleeding face drew a knife of his own.

Celina acted on instinct. "What the hell do you think you're doing? She's with me!"

"This brat's nothing but a stowaway."

"Pig's arse! She found my cat, and you whackers are trying to kill her! I should have you strung up by your bollocks and left for vultures!"

Mags stepped away from her assailants. She did not know this finely dressed, outspoken young woman at all, but the stranger seemed to be helping.

"She tried to board without a ticket," said the man with the clawed face, "and fought us when we tried to run her off."

"And that's a reason for you to beat on a young lady? You should be ashamed of yourselves!"

"No ticket, no ride. That's the rules."

"She's sharing my cabin, you bloody yobbo! I have her ticket right here." Celina sheathed her knife. She pulled a wad of bills from her brassiere. "Do you see?" She held out the money to the man.

He looked from the cash, to her face, and back to the cash. Then he took the money from her. He unfolded the bills, raising his eyebrows. One of his companions whistled softly. He stuffed the money into his pants pocket. "I see, ma'am. We just had a little misunderstanding, is all." He gestured past him to the ship. "Welcome aboard."

"Thank you, kind sir." To Mags, she said, "Come with me, dear. Let's get you cleaned up." She walked past the ragged young woman to the ship. "Coming?"

Mags relaxed her stance and unclenched her fists. "Sí." She boarded the ship and caught up to the older girl. "I could have beat those men."

Celina laughed. "Oh, too right. But then what? Were you planning to fight every drongo on the boat all the way across the ocean? By the way, my name is Celina." She held out her hand, smiling.

Mags considered the hand, then Celina's eyes. She saw no malice in their sparkle. She took the offered hand, closing it firmly in her grip. "My name is Mags. Meteor Mags."

Celina held her hand warmly. "A pleasure, Meteor Mags. Good on ya for finding my little Starry. I was worried sick about him! Where did you find him?"

"The cemetery in London. Some people were being mean to him. But I made them stop. Forever."

Celina raised an eyebrow, looking Mags up and down. "You're

quite the scrappy little wagtail, aren't you?"

Mags blushed. "What do you mean?"

Celina's laughter played on her ears like golden bells. "Oh, it's just a bird we have back home. Feisty little wagtails. They're like crows, you know?"

"I thought you were making fun of me." Mags' tail whisked the salty ocean air.

"I'd rather not poke fun at any sheila willing to have a blue with those three louts all by herself. Now please, come to my cabin. Don't take this the wrong way, love, but you look dirtier than a dead dingo's donger in a dunnycan."

"A—what?" The young woman seemed to be speaking English, but Mags was not entirely sure.

"Why don't we find you something to wear, okay? Maybe a bath and a bite to eat?"

"I'd like that." She followed Celina to her cabin. "You said home. Do you live in the States?"

"I will for a little while. My oldies have some business there. But home will always be Australia for me."

"Australia? Where they send all the criminals?"

"Our reputation precedes us. But there's more to Oz than a bunch of convicts. You should go see it for yourself sometime." Celina opened the door to her cabin. She walked in and set Starry on the narrow bed. Then she pulled out the chair at the tiny writing desk. "Be my guest."

Mags shut the cabin door behind her. She accepted the offered seat and looked out the circular window towards the ocean. Starry calmly laid down and groomed himself.

"There isn't much room for the two of us," said Celina, "but we can sort something."

"You lied to those men about sharing a cabin." Mags stated this fact without a hint of accusation in her voice.

"I sure did. But let me tell you something, little wagtail. There are very few problems in the shipping industry that can't be solved by the application of cash to the proper hands."

"That sounds like something Mama would say."

"I see," said Celina. "Your mama is in the shipping business, too?"

Mags shook her head. "No. She's—she smuggled guns and supplies for the revolution."

Celina clapped her hands and laughed. "Mags," she said. "I can tell you and I are going to be *very* good mates."

Within the hour, the ship set out for the States, and Meteor Mags' life would never be the same again.

EPILOGUE: MOTHERS AND DAUGHTERS

November 1923: France.

"I do wish Mother could be here for this," said Margareta. "Rest her soul."

"Me too." Mollie groaned as another contraction came.

"Breathe, dear."

Mollie squeezed her mother's hand. She sat partially submerged in a circular tub. Its tiled interior was supplied with warm water which was heated over a fire and pumped slowly through a pipe to maintain the perfect temperature. Mollie rested on a bench set below the water level.

Katerina, her mother's personal nurse, appeared in the doorway of the birthing chamber. "Are you comfortable?"

"Ungh." Mollie grimaced. "Comfy as can be. My little one will be here soon."

Katerina set a pile of fresh, warm towels on the edge of the tub. To Margareta, she said, "I checked on the businessmen, ma'am. They were none too happy at first, but now they seem content to enjoy dinner and drinks in the billiards room."

"Good. The acquisition is very important to the future of the Plaza. But they can entertain themselves until after my grandchild is born."

Mollie cried out again.

"Breathe! Breathe, dear. Just relax." Margareta clasped her daughter's hand and breathed with her.

Katerina sat on the edge of the tub, placing her hand on Mollie's shoulder. She joined them in the rhythmic breathing they had practiced together. "I recall when you were born in this tub," she said to Mollie. "It seems like only yesterday." She checked the water for any sign of blood or meconium, but the water was clear and clean. "Everything seems well so far."

"Oh, god, I can feel it!" Mollie rocked her hips back and forth. "It's coming."

Katerina leaned over the side of the tub. "I can see the top of the head!" She reached her hands below the surface to help guide the baby into the water.

Mollie let go of her mother's hand. She held a firm grip on the sides of the tub. She pushed without straining. The warm water eased her pain.

Margareta hugged her daughter from behind, looking over her shoulder into the water. "The head is clear! Here it comes. Nice and easy, dear."

Katerina deftly unwound the umbilical cord from around the baby's neck. "It's okay," she told Mollie. "Everything is fine. Just a little more." The baby, submerged, had yet to take a breath, instead drawing all her oxygen from the umbilical cord.

Then, in one smooth motion, the baby slid out of Mollie's body, into the water and Katerina's waiting hands. She scooped the child up and brought her to the surface, right into Mollie's open arms. But doing so, she noticed something unusual about the child.

"Oh, my baby!" Mollie cradled the child in her arms, holding her daughter close to her breast.

Katerina did not know how to explain what she had seen. So, she quietly took a towel from the side of the tub. With gentle care, she wiped the baby's face. She checked the infant's nose and mouth to make sure they were clear of any obstruction. The baby appeared supremely calm as she took her first breath of air.

"My beautiful little girl," said Mollie. Then a look of shock formed on her face. She moved her hand to see her daughter's backside.

Margareta looked, too. "What is that?"

"It looks like a tail!" She held her daughter higher, close to her face, and pressed her cheek to the newborn infant.

"Is she alright?" Margareta asked. "Is anything wrong? I've never seen anything like that."

Mollie shook her head. "She's perfect." She found it strangely comforting to feel her child purring in her arms. "She's a perfect little girl." Mollie looked into her mother's eyes. "I'll name her after her great-grandmother."

"Mother would be very pleased with that."

149

"Let her breathe for a couple minutes," said Katerina. "Then I will cut the cord."

"Magdalena," Mollie said softly. She kissed her daughter's face, moving gently over the tender cheeks and forehead. "My sweet little Maggie."

And that was how Meteor Mags came into this world.

ASTEROID UNDERGROUND INTERVIEW: HYO-SONN

Hyo-Sonn, welcome to *Asteroid Underground*.

Thank you.

Does your name have a meaning?

Yeah, I guess so. It's Korean. It means like gentle daughter.

Does it fit your personality?

Ha. I guess it used to. I don't feel like it does so much these days.

You're not gentle?

After what's happened to me and my friends, I'm kind of pissed off a lot. And as far as being a daughter...

Yes? What happened?

It's hard to feel like a daughter when your parents abandon you. When they just leave you at some "treatment facility" instead of listening to you. And then you try to tell them what really happens in this place, and they don't believe you. Or maybe they just didn't care. Fuck them.

It was, what? A rehab clinic for teenagers?

Yeah, that's what they tell people. But really, it's just a place where kids who didn't do anything wrong get drugged up, beaten, and—other creepy stuff. If you try to speak up or have a problem with what's going on there, they just drug you senseless. Strap you down. I can't even talk about what they did to little Sarah. It's so horrible. How could anyone who loves their kid do that to them?

Maybe they didn't know?

Maybe they just didn't give a fuck. Mags and Celina are different though. They're more of a family to us than most of us ever had. They care about us.

How did you meet them?

I heard of Mags' band because of Sarah. She was super into that one song they did, you know.

Something to Destroy?

Yeah, that one. Where Mags sings. I think it meant a lot to Sarah. But we met Mags after we'd been captured by the lizards. They had us in some kind of pen. If Mags hadn't rescued us... Mags and Tarzi, of course. And Patches. And Tarzi's little seahorse.

So you know Tarzi, too. What do you think of him?

He's nice and all, but I wish he would quit smoking. It's so gross. And I don't know how he can listen to that stuff he calls music. Sounds like a lot of noise to me.

What kind of music do you like?

I like all kinds of stuff. Mags and Celina have been playing us music we didn't even know existed. Weird, old jazz, stuff from Africa, Japan, South America. I mean, I don't like all of it. I like stuff you can dance to, or sing along with. Not like Tarzi's bands.

Do you like the Psycho 78s?

They're alright. I mean, they're a fun bunch of guys. They talk all tough, but it's just like a lot of hot air, you know? I thought maybe they were creepy at first, but you have to get to know them.

Do you have any hobbies? What do you do for fun?

I like to draw a little bit. But Kala's so much better at it than me. She's amazing. I think she was born to do it. Celina's teaching me some dance stuff. And not just pole dancing but like all kinds of things. Pole dancing is... It's a little too sexy for me. I just want to dance, not have men drooling all over me like a—I don't know. Like some kind of chicken on a rotisserie.

(Laughs)

Seriously though. I mean, nothing against Mags and Celina. They've been dancing for like a gazillion years. It's just not my thing. Other than that, I help with teaching.

You mean dance lessons?

No, no. Reading. And math. You probably wouldn't guess from talking to her, but Mags is *crazy* good at math. I don't even know what she's talking about sometimes, differential this and integrate that. But she's pretty serious about making sure all of us are putting our minds to work. So, I help some of the younger girls with basic math and algebra. And Mags has some crazy antique books I never even heard of before.

So it's not just a constant party at Club Assteroid?

Oh, god no. Celina keeps us pretty busy. But, I mean, it's not like awful work. Some of the girls bitched at first about, you know, cleaning their rooms and stuff like that. And helping in the garden or whatever. But Celina knows how to make it fun. I mean, Mags might be all like, "Just clean your fucking room!" Hahaha. But Celina makes it seem not like work at all.

How so?

Oh, you know, we have contests, or we have to do *some* stuff, but then we can pick our own projects to work on most of the time. We always work together, so you're basically just hanging out with your friends and talking. And we make little groups of our own to do stuff. Kala is giving drawing lessons, and she's planning out a big mural for the club with her group.

And do you have a group?

No, not really. I mean, I sit in on Kala's lessons, especially the figure drawing ones. But I haven't thought of a project I'd want to lead. Honestly, I'd rather just do my own thing most of the time.

Do you think the other girls look up to you?

Me? Hahaha. Maybe some of them. They must think I'm a total bitch sometimes. I might have been a little too hard on them before. But I was just worried about them. I'm trying to be more chill these days. More like Celina.

And less like Mags?

I don't have anything bad to say about Mags. Except she should quit smoking. It's so *gross*.

But she can be pretty rough on people, can't she?

I guess. It's just how she is.

Why do you think that is?

Maybe how she grew up? I don't know. I'm just glad she's on our side. And most people don't know her, I mean like *really* know her. They just see one side of her. Her pirate side or whatever. They don't really know her like we do.

So, do you have any plans to return to Earth in the future?

Yeah, I don't know. Maybe. Earth is so fucked up right now. I think I'll stick with Mags and Celina for a while. Like I said, they really care about us, and things are so much better for us than they were before.

10

Daughter of Lightning

Every nature, every modeled form, every creature, exists in and with each other. They will dissolve again into their own proper root. For the nature of matter is dissolved into what belongs to its nature.

...There is no such thing as sin.

—The Gospel of Mary; Text from the *Papyrus Berolinensis.*

PART ONE: THE VESTAL VIRGIN

October 2029.

Against the star-splattered canvas of space, Plutonian listened to the fabric of reality singing. His Siamese cat, Tesla, lay across his lap and purred. This soothed him. He stopped rubbing Tesla's face just long enough to turn up the volume on the ship's speaker system.

Tesla opened his eyes. His pupils rolled up lazily to survey his human friend. Tesla did not know what they listened to, but he knew it was unlike anything they had ever heard.

This was no small feat, considering the two of them had listened to every form of music imaginable in their years together. But this sound was something different, something Plutonian could not find words to describe.

Below them smoldered the desolate husk of the Ghost Moon. Only a few months before, this moon had housed the machinery which transformed Patches from an ordinary calico cat into her adorably invulnerable self. But in the wake of the instantaneous reversal of its magnetic poles, it now orbited like a broken thing around its ringed planet. Fully two thirds of the moon had disintegrated and become part of the asteroids circling the planet. Little remained but a ragged chunk of destruction.

Tears streamed from the corners of Plutonian's eyes. "I thought we'd heard it all. But this—" With a gesture on the monitor's touch screen, the Club Assteroid DJ activated a recorder. "We need to record this." Waveforms sprang into life on his screen.

He cradled his cat in his arms and stood before the window on the bridge. Plutonian scratched the side of Tesla's face with one hand. He cried like he hadn't cried since he was a boy. "So beautiful," he whispered.

If he had been the religious sort, the music playing over his speakers might have convinced him of the deistic nature of reality. Surely, he thought, this was what the ancient Hindus meant by the sound of Om, that original sonic vibration which caused the universe to spring into being and gave rise to all the forms we know. But he had abandoned deism long ago. He simply heard the music without any expectations. It washed over him and through him and in some way became him.

Only a few days before, Meteor Mags had given him the coordinates of the now-obliterated Ghost Moon. "Knock knock, Mister DJ! What are you up to? Nobody's seen a trace of you in weeks!" She stood in the doorway of his quarters, her tail swishing back and forth, her eyes shining over the rims of her tinted glasses.

He set down his soldering iron and rested his safety glasses on top of his head. "Mags! So good to see you. Come in, come in." He stood and opened his arms.

She gave him a friendly hug. "Seriously, dude. What the fuck? People are getting worried."

"I think I've got it. Finally."

"Got what?"

"Come here. Look at this." He swept his hand in an arc to present the circuits on his workbench. "This is the recording project I was telling you about."

"Oh! No wonder you've been hiding out down here. How's it coming?"

"It hasn't been easy. I fried the first dozen circuits. But those capacitors you gave me—wow. Perfect!"

Mags smiled. "Superconductivity at room temperature is something else, isn't it?" She walked over to his bench. "You don't even want to know how many motherfuckers I had to waste to get my hands on those. Friggin' bloodbath! If not for Patches, I probably would have been FUBAR on that little excursion. But I thought we could use them."

"And how. Mags, these circuits are picking up stuff I never thought possible. Listen." He flipped a switch. "Hear that? That's Hawking Radiation coming out of the black holes at the core of the Andromeda galaxy."

"No way. That's gorgeous." She put her arms up, closed her eyes, and swayed. "I could dance to that for a million years."

"And these are residual wavelengths from a dying supernova."

He turned a dial. "This one here is a pulsar in the same sector."

"Damn. Did you just get bored of rock and roll or what?"

"I'll never get bored of that. But, you know, Tesla and I have archived damn near everything humans ever recorded. We thought it would be cool to record some things no one has ever heard before. Stuff technology just hasn't been up to recording."

"Until now."

"Until now."

Mags looked her friend up and down. Then she decided something. "Listen, dear. If you're really into this thing—and obviously you are—there's a little something I'd be curious to hear. I mean, if you have the time and all."

Plutonian placed his palms on the bench and leaned towards her. "You name it."

She laughed. "I don't know if it has a name. Hell, I don't even know if it exists." Mags pulled a pack of cigarettes from her bra and took out a pair of them. She offered one.

He took it and looked for a lighter.

"I got this one." She produced a lighter for him. "Now listen. Something weird went down this summer, when Patches and Tarzi and I were on the Ghost Moon." Mags walked around to his side of the bench. She rested her backside on the edge of the bench and puffed leisurely. "Now, you've heard the story before, but I still have some unanswered questions. And I'd be willing to bet that whatever we did to that sodding moon left some interesting traces behind. Maybe radiation, electromagnetic disturbances, maybe some gravity signatures. I don't know. But," she said, leaning in closely to him, "I'd be hella curious to find out."

Plutonian took the coordinates from her, loaded up a ship with his new recording circuits, and went in search of whatever he could find.

A soft beeping from the console broke his reverie. He set the cat down in his seat, glancing at the waveforms on the screen. Radar brought him unexpected news.

"Check this out, Tesla."

Tesla did not check it out. He stretched out his body and rolled over. His claws kneaded the chair's fabric. He purred.

"These readings. It's like we're picking up two distinct signal sources. This one here," he said, pointing to the screen, "is the remains of the moon itself. That's giving us some radiation from what's left of that rock. But this one here—" Tap, tap, tap. "This is something else entirely. A totally different source."

He pulled up his camera controls and zoomed in. "I wish Mags was here. I can't even do the math on this. It's like the carcass of the moon isn't just orbiting the planet. It's got some secondary orbit, like a binary star. It's orbiting something else *within* that orbit." Plutonian ran a hand over his face, thinking. He took the camera controls to their limit.

"I can't see a bloody thing. We don't have high enough resolution." He brought the ship in closer to the wrecked moon. "It's got to be right there, but—"

Then the alarms went off.

"Okay, just give it a little turn, Mags." In the shop at Club Assteroid, Fuzzlow held a piece of machinery on the workbench. "Don't over-crank it."

"I know, I know. Jeez, calm down."

Donny held a nut in place with a wrench on one side of the machinery. He lacked Fuzzlow's magic touch with machines, but he had spent enough time repairing mining equipment to have proven quite handy in the shop. The two of them had spent many hours together, tinkering with all kinds of things since Donny had joined the band. "That's a laugh! The great Meteor Mags telling anyone to keep calm."

She tightened the bolt from the other side. "What?! I'm as sweet as a little angel!" She cranked it some more.

"Easy there, Magatha," said Fuzzlow. "Don't—"

The bolt suddenly snapped in half, clattering down into the guts of the machinery.

"Goddamn fuck!" She whipped her wrench across the shop. It

smacked against the wall and fell into the piles of parts stacked there.

"Mags!" Fuzzlow shook his head. "I told you—"

"I know. I know! It was just a little bit loose."

"Well," said Donny, "now we gotta drill out that damn bolt and start all over. How about a smoke break?"

Mags' eyes lit up. "Now there's an idea!"

"Fine, you two." Fuzz set the machinery aside. "I'd get more work done in here if I had less help."

Donny snorted. "Go ahead and hold your own nuts, then!"

"Yeah, Fuzz. Nut holder."

"Mags, can I just have my wrench back?"

She sighed then searched for the wrench. "So when are you guys recording your next album?"

"What do you mean, *you guys*? Aren't you going to be on it with us?"

"Fuzz, you know I can't commit to rehearsals and sessions and all that. I got cargo to liberate! Lizards to exterminate!" Mags walked back to the bench and handed him his wrench.

Donny offered his pack of smokes. "Come on, Mags. You can't even do one song?"

"Listen to this guy." She took the pack. "Then we have to write the bloody thing, rehearse it, record it, decide that take sucked, record it again, do overdubs. It's never just one song."

"What if we do it live? I mean, we've got a huge show next month. It's your birthday, for crying out loud. You aren't going to sing on your birthday?"

Mags thought this over. "You've got a point. But I don't want to be on record doing a cover. So what song goes on the album?"

"Let's do that one you're always talking about but we never arranged."

Mags laughed. "That old thing? Oh, come on. No one wants to hear that."

"I want to hear it," said Donny. "What is it?"

"Oh, god. It's just this thing I used to drive Gramma nuts with. It's not even a real song!"

Fuzzlow grinned. "Yeah, but it's got a great title: Stone cold blasted at the edge of infinity!"

"Now I gotta hear it," said Donny.

Mags rolled her eyes. "Okay. Fuzzlow, dear, would you give me a beat? Something like—" Mags drummed her fingers on the table.

He put his hands to his mouth and beatboxed.

"Yeah, like that. Okay, it goes something like this."

Stone cold blasted at the edge of infinity!

Mags emulated the sound of a guitar riff: *Duh duh duh DUH nuh nuh nuh nana NUH.*

You were plastered on the day that you lost your virginity!
Duh duh duh NUHNUH duh duh duh duh dada WEEEER

You were kicked outta house
You were kicked outta school
But you'll never build a rocket ship
Flogging your tool!

Take me to the stars now baby
Take me to the—

"Mags!" Donny held his belly and shook.

"Donny," she said, "what the fuck is so funny? Hahahahaha!"

"Mags, that's some real poetry there."

She threw her hands in the air. "I told you it wasn't even a real song!"

Donny laughed and laughed. "No, no. Go on! What's the rest of it?"

"There was only ever one verse! I was kind of wasted one night at La Plaza and started banging on the piano, belting this thing out. Suddenly Gramma storms in and yells, 'Maggie, what in the name of god are you doing? It's three in the bloody morning!' So, that was the end of that."

"Gramma put the hammer down."

"She sure did." Mags stubbed out her cigarette.

Donny said, "I never would have rhymed infinity and virginity. Were you really plastered when you lost it?"

Mags glared at him. "I assure you it was purely for comedic effect. There's nothing about me in that line."

"Oh, quit yanking my chain. A wild woman like you? Dancing naked across the solar system for decades? I bet you have the best first time story of anyone."

"There's no story, Donny. Get your mind out of whatever filthy gutter it's crawled into."

"Are you trying to tell me that you never, like—you know? Ever?"

Mags put her hands on her hips, looking over the rims of her tinted glasses at him. "As if it's any of your bloody business, Donald!"

Fuzzlow laughed. "They don't call this asteroid 'Vesta' for nothing, Donny."

"What's that supposed to mean?" Mags asked.

"You know, this crater all around us is Rheasilvia, right?" Fuzzlow leaned against the bench. "That's from Roman mythology. Rhea Silvia gave birth to twins: Romulus and Remus. And you know who their father was?"

Donny shrugged. "Who?"

"Mars, the god of war."

"Damn, Fuzz!" Mags furrowed her brow. "Did you read a book or something?"

"Whatever. I read lots of books."

"Yeah, but I mean one that wasn't all pictures?"

Donny laughed, but Fuzz slugged him in the arm. "Screw you, Donny."

"She said it, not me!"

"Alright," said Mags. "Settle down, numb nuts. What's your point?"

Fuzzlow ran his hands over his mane of dreadlocks. "Rhea was the daughter of some king or other. And his dickhead brother forced her take a vow of chastity, to be what they called a Vestal Virgin. They were like priestesses or some shit. They never married and never had kids. Instead, they had a duty to guard this sacred fire so it could never go out. And that's where this asteroid Vesta gets its name: the Vestal Virgins."

"But you said she did the nasty with the god of war," said Donny.

Fuzzlow chuckled. "Right. That's why dickhead threw her babies into the river to drown. But a she-wolf found them, and suckled them, and they survived."

"You mean they sucked on wolf titties?"

Fuzzlow slapped his forehead. "Yes, Donny. They sucked on wolf titties."

"That's awesome. Wait, is that legal?"

"Donny, you are such a tard sometimes," said Mags.

Fuzzlow picked up his wrench and got back to work. "Legal or not, it must have been some good milk. Those two kids went on to found Rome."

"Whoa."

Celina's voice came over the shop's intercom. "Hey! Is anybody down there?"

"Hi, sweetheart."

"Hi, Fuzzy love. Have you seen Mags?"

"I'm right here, Celina."

"Mags, come up to the club please. Right away. Plutonian's here, and he's—I don't know exactly. But he keeps asking for you."

"I'm on it. Let me get Patches."

Plutonian's head rested on the table. He slumped over a black box and clutched its handle, his knuckles white with exertion. "The world," he mumbled. "A sacred instrument."

Celina sat next to him, resting her hand on his arm. Tesla lay under the chair, whining nervously.

"What's wrong with him?" Mags asked. Patches dashed past her feet and made a bee-line for Tesla. She licked his face and mewed. "Is he hurt?"

"I don't know. He seems okay, physically. But when he came off his ship, he just collapsed. I practically had to drag him here."

Mags pulled out a chair, taking a seat next to the DJ. "Plutonian. Hey. Talk to me, man."

"A sacred instrument." His voice slurred. "Can't control it."

"Come on, dear. Look at me." She picked his head up, grasping his hair and supporting his cheek in her gloved hand. "Look at me."

He opened his eyes without seeing her. Mags inspected them, looking for signs of concussion. Then she said, "The world is a sacred instrument."

"Yes," he said. "One..."

"One cannot control it. He who controls it will fail."

"Yes. Yes! The one who—"

"The one who grasps it will fail."

"Yes," he said. "The one who grasps it." He released his grasp on the black box. The color came back into his knuckles.

Mags slid the box away from him, to the opposite edge of the table. "There you go, dear. It's going to be okay. You just relax."

"What are you saying to him?" Celina asked. "Is it some kind of secret code?"

"Hardly. It's a verse from the *Tao Te Ching*. It must mean something to him."

A light dawned in Plutonian's eyes. He rubbed his hands over his face. "The space between Heaven and Earth. Is it not like a bellows?" He took Mag's hand and squeezed it.

"Empty, yet never exhausted," she replied. "It moves and produces more."

"Empty." Plutonian shook his head as if to clear it. "Oh, my god. Mags. Celina. I was freaking out, wasn't I?"

"I've seen worse," said Celina. "What happened to you?"

"Did you go the Ghost Moon? Talk to us, man!"

Underneath his chair, the cats curled up together. Patches purred, calming her friend.

"I did. And I'll tell you what happened. But, first. We got any rum in this joint?"

Mags laughed. "I think you'll be just fine. Let me get some

glasses and a bottle."

"So there I was," Plutonian began, "just listening to the most wondrous song. It couldn't have been sound, not in the vacuum of space. But my new receiver was picking it up loud and clear."

"From where? The Ghost Moon?"

"That's what I thought at first. And to be sure, that ragged scrap of rubble Mags and Tarzi left behind is kicking out some interesting radiation. But then I realized I had a second signal in the mix. And it seemed to be coming from something locked in orbit with the moon. So I checked it out." He took a sip of spiced black rum then swished the liquid over the ice cubes in his glass. He watched the way the light made tiny rainbows on the liquid's surface.

"Well?" Mags demanded. "Did you record it? Is that what's in this box?" She reached for the box, but his hand gripped her arm.

"Don't."

"Come on! I want to hear it!"

"Wagtail, would you let the man finish his story?"

"Fine." She slammed a shot of rum. Then she pulled out a pack of cigarettes, passed it around, and lit everyone up.

Plutonian exhaled a puff of smoke. "I got the recording, Mags. And it's amazing. But I don't even know if it's safe to listen to."

"Is that why you came in all fucked up?"

Plutonian nodded. "Maybe. See, there was something else out there. But it was small. Much smaller than the moon. So I moved in closer. And the sound... Did you ever read Goethe?"

"I read *Faust*, years ago," said Celina.

Mags puffed her cigarette. "I hate German poetry. It sounds like a train falling down the stairs."

Celina laughed. "That's bullshit. You liked the Rilke I read to you!"

"Yeah," said Mags. "But Rilke's cool."

"Listen. There's a verse where he describes this sound. 'As it moves about, there is music without cease. In heavenly tones, it pours out who-knows-what. And while it moves, all is turned to melody now: The pillared shafts, even the triglyph, ring. I think the whole temple sings.' That's what it was like."

"Sounds pretty," said Celina.

"That's because it was in bloody English."

"I mean the music!" Celina tossed back a shot of rum and slammed her glass on the table. "Go on, Dr. P. Don't listen to her."

"As soon as I moved in and got a lock on the signal source, guess who showed up?"

"Don't tell me," said Mags. "Those goddamn lizards."

"The MFA?"

"You're both right," said Plutonian.

Mags pounded the table with her fist. "Fuck! Together?"

"Yeah. Can you believe that?"

She shook her head. "It's worse than I thought. If those creeps have cut some kind of deal, it ain't gonna be a happy ending for anyone. Not Earth. Not us. And not anyone in the Belt."

"You got that right. The lizard's ship looked like the big one you described, and with it were two standard MFA patrol boats. My alarms started going off to beat the band. I figure they all came from my blind spot around the other side of the planet."

"The MFA never gets out that far. They stick around the Belt, where the smuggling action is. So what the hell were they doing out there?"

"Nothing good," said Celina.

"Fuckin' A," said Plutonian. "I knew I was outgunned. So I decided to get the hell out of there. Except I couldn't. It was like the ship was frozen in space. I panicked a little right then, but I noticed the other ships weren't moving anymore either. And then..." Plutonian stopped to sip the last of the rum from his glass.

"Then what?"

Plutonian, lost in thought, watched the liquid run over the melting ice cubes. Then he looked into Celina's eyes, and then to Mags. "I know it sounds crazy, but this music got even louder. And with it, this incredible light. Like every color of the rainbow. No, that's not right. It was like colors that don't even exist. Millions of them. And the music kept building and building, and the light got brighter and brighter. I couldn't see Tesla at all, or anything really.

It was like we were engulfed. But it wasn't scary. I mean, it was at first, but then totally calm. I don't know how to explain it, but I felt like I wasn't just listening. I was being listened *to*. Then I guess I blacked out."

"I felt like that before," said Celina.

"For real?"

"Strewth. But it's been a long, long time."

"What happened?"

Mags chuckled. "We still don't have any idea."

"It's a long story," said Celina, "but the short version is that once upon a time, me and wagtail went on a little walkabout in the outback. And by the time it was over, I got what I wished for."

"What's that?"

Mags smiled and took another shot of rum. She looked at Celina with loving eyes.

"I wanted to live as long as my best friend here. But that story can wait, Dr. P. You finish yours!"

"Right, right," he said. "After my blackout or whatever, I woke up. And it was the damnedest thing. There wasn't anything left of the other ships but some wreckage floating near the Ghost Moon, getting sucked into its orbit. And there in the middle of the cabin, just floating in the middle of the air, was this—this *thing*."

"This *thing*?" Mags asked. "Can you think of a better word, man?"

Plutonian laughed. "No, I can't. You just have to see it for yourself."

"Is that what's in the bloody box already?"

"I didn't know what else to do, so I just walked up to it with this soundproof box, and closed it in."

"What difference does it make if it's soundproof?" Celina asked. "Didn't you say it was broadcasting in the vacuum?"

"Like I said, I didn't know what else to do. And it didn't really stop the music. Not until I turned off my new recording gear. So for all I know, it's still broadcasting right now."

"Okay, let's have a gander at it."

"Not here in the club!" Celina shouted. "You just want to open

Pandora's Box and let out who knows what the fuck right here in the club?"

"Come on now, convict. I'm not daft! But I bet the ship's got a recording we can look at."

"I can do better than that," said Plutonian. He pulled a small tablet from the side pocket of his cargo pants. "I made a video first." He touched the screen a couple times then handed it to Mags. "But I've never seen anything like it."

She watched in silence for a moment. "I have. I've just never seen one that wasn't a computer model." Mags held the tablet so Celina could see, too.

"Oh, wow. That's gorgeous. What is it?"

"I don't know," said Mags. "It reminds me of a rectified 5-cell. But if I had to guess, I'd say it's more complex. Like a 24-cell. Or more."

"A what?"

"A rectified 24-cell. See how this thing looks like it's spinning? But as it spins, the shapes inside it seem to change? It's like watching a projection of a rectified 24-cell rotating through 3-D space. You'd never see one in real life, because we can only perceive objects in three-dimensional space. But the bloody thing exists in four spatial dimensions. As it rotates, it looks like—it looks a hell of a lot like what's on this screen right now. Only this thing—this is way more complex. Look at how the shapes seem to become other shapes as it moves."

"It's like every shape imaginable is stacked inside that thing, somehow."

"Exactly. And you think this is the same thing that was orbiting near the Ghost Moon?"

"It has to be," said Plutonian. "It's what was making all that music."

Mags covered her mouth with one hand and then rubbed her face. "There's only one thing this can be. This is part of the machine that saved Patches."

"Bloody hell," said Celina. "It destroyed an entire moon, and then a bunch of ships, and nearly drove our DJ bonkers—and we've got it sitting in a box on the table? Get it the fuck out of here!"

"Relax, dear. I think if it wanted to kill us, we'd be dead already."

"Still," said Plutonian, "it wouldn't be a bad idea to find somewhere else to store it. Wait. What do you mean if it *wanted* to? Are you suggesting it's intelligent?"

"We know it works on more levels than just sound. But it seems to be totally chilling in that soundproof box. Maybe it's cooperating?"

Fuzzlow appeared in the doorway. "Hey! Everything okay in here?"

"We're fine, Fuzz." Celina waved him over.

"Are we still on for that test run? Donny and I got everything ready to go on our end."

"Shit, I nearly forgot." Mags placed her hand on Plutonian's shoulder. "Listen, dear. We got a thing we gotta do. What do you suggest we do with your little discovery here?"

"I think Celina's right. This is no place for it. But it's too amazing to just toss into space again. Why don't I take it to an uninhabited asteroid, for starters?"

"Are you sure you're up for it?"

"Yeah. But do me a favor. Keep Tesla here. And give me the rest of that bottle of rum!"

Mags smiled. "Alright, Mister DJ. But if things get hairy out there, you radio back, okay?"

"Deal. And what are the three of you testing?"

A wicked grin formed on Mags' face. "My new pets. I'll tell you all about it when you get back."

Plutonian knelt down to scratch Tesla's face, taking a moment to rub Patches' ears too. "You stay here, buddy. I'll be back before you know it." Then to Mags, "Watch out for Tesla for me. And when you're done with your tests, check out the audio files on that tablet. Just be careful."

Then he left, carrying his incredible discovery with him.

"Can you hear me up there?"

"Got you loud and clear, willie wagtail. How does the suit feel?" Celina and Fuzzlow watched Mags on a monitor from inside Club Assteroid.

Mags spoke into the microphone inside her protective suit. "It feels like Rick James is grabbing my arse. Hard. But other than that, okay I guess. Better than the first time I tried it on."

She surveyed the selection of potential victims at her shooting range on the surface of Vesta 4. Three cybernetic eels hovered around her, slowly circling. The Faraday suits she and Tarzi had "liberated" from the asteroid lab on their last adventure had clearly been designed for men, as Mags discovered to her dismay minutes before taking on a ship full of dragons. But after a few weeks of work in the machine shop, she and Fuzzlow tailored one of them to her curvaceous specifications, with enough room to tuck in her tail. "Tell Fuzz he needs to learn how to measure a woman's butt."

Celina's voice responded in her earpiece. "He says to tell you to learn how to not slap the shit out a tailor who is trying to measure your butt."

Mags grinned. "Let's do this before I have any second thoughts." Unlike Tarzi's seahorse, which had operated under control of a ring, the trio of electric eels was ostensibly controlled by panels on the back of Mags' gloves. But Fuzzlow had shown her circuitry inside the Faraday suit's helmet, circuitry unlike anything either of them had ever seen before.

"What the fuck is all this then?"

Fuzzlow had scratched his head. "Can't say, Mags. But seeing as how it's in the helmet, I would guess it picks up on mental signals."

"Great. All I need is my brain fried—again!"

He shrugged. "Worst case is, you give yourself an electric lobotomy. Then you'll suck at math as much as the rest of us."

"Ugh. You just make sure Slim has my notes on wireless power if that happens, okay? We've come too far on that project to lose it all to an eel migraine from hell."

"You could always, like, just not try out a totally alien technology you don't have a clue about, you know?"

"Fuck that. Let's fire these bitches up, Captain G-Style. I've got a war to wage!"

Now she wondered if that was really such a good idea. She had seen what Tarzi's little seahorse had done to a dragon warship. She hoped a trio of meter-long eels would not vaporize the entire asteroid.

Celina's voice came through the earpiece again. "What's first, Mags? Target practice?"

"Yeah. But not with the eels. Let's see if they can stay the hell out of my way first." She took hold of an FN MAG machine gun from her armory. She had spliced together a few fifty-round belts to feed into it. Pointing it downrange at a rusted van three hundred meters away, she pulled the trigger.

Her eels instantly snapped into a new configuration around her. They stopped circling her to take up positions above and behind her. Their tails crackled, whipping the air as they prowled behind her back.

Mags almost forgot they were there. She riddled the van with bullets. She hit the gas tank. The van exploded in a ball of fire.

"Mags?"

"Um, whoops? Must have forgot to drain the petrol."

"Sure you did."

"When have I ever lied to you?"

Celina chuckled on the other end. "Did you see what the eels did?"

"They got the fuck out of the way."

"They're watching your flank."

"They are, aren't they? Let's see how they like this." Mags picked up a bullwhip. She swung it around and around in a circle above her head, then snapped the handle forward. The whip cracked in front of her. But the eels simply spread out. "They know when to step off. Now let's see if they can keep up." Mags grabbed her shotgun and ran towards her targets.

The trio of eels followed her, keeping pace, never advancing beyond her, never falling behind. When her eight rounds were exhausted, the eels resumed their circular swarm around her. She felt a strange thrill come over her. They certainly were paying attention.

She lifted her hand into the air, crooked her finger, and said, "Come let your auntie pet you, ya little freaks." And sure enough, one of the eels stopped circling, swam in close to her hand, and let her pet it. Mags smiled inside her mask.

"Having fun, Mags?" Celina asked.

"You know what? I am! Now let's see what kind of juice they can kick out."

She had set up several targets shaped like dragons. She snapped her fingers and pointed at them. "Eels, electrocute these motherfuckers!"

She did not expect what happened next. Still circling around her, the eels unleashed a barrage of lightning. Electric tendrils surged out of them, enveloping the targets. Inside her suit, Mags felt not so much as a tickle from the current. But the electromagnetic force blasted her backwards. She twisted in mid-air, landing on all fours on the rugged surface of the asteroid.

Electric current assaulted her targets. The lights inside Club Assteroid flickered. Celina said something, but her voice turned to garbled static in Mags' ears.

"Fuck yeah!" Mags yelled. "Pour it on!" The eels did just that. Her entire field of view turned white. The power ripped apart not just her dragon targets but every target on the range.

Electrons whipped across the jagged plains of Vesta 4. All the bullets on Mags' table uprange exploded. She dove to the ground and covered her head. The eels savagely cranked the air, their bodies undulating, writhing in the center of a massive ball of lightning. Targets burst into flame. Elements broke down into isotopes as their electrons were ripped away and drawn up into the storm.

Mags looked though her visor in awe. "Bloody fuck," she whispered. The ground on the asteroid fused into black glass. The glass circle formed below the eels, then spread. Within seconds, it reached a diameter of twenty meters and kept growing. Cracks ran through it ringing out like bullets and thunder in Mags' ears.

"Stop!" She waved her hands. "Stop!"

Just as suddenly as they had begun, the eels ended their attack. They swarmed around Mags, taking up their circling positions as if nothing had happened. With infinite robotic patience, they hovered around her.

She stood up and held out her hand. One by one, each eel circled around to rub its metallic snout against her open palm.

A vicious smile spread across her face. She heard the static crackle of Celina's voice in her earpiece again, but she ignored it. She ran her suited fingertips along the length of each eel. Their teeth sparkled in the starlight.

Mags turned off her communicator. She stayed out there for as long as she liked, saying things to her eels no one else would ever hear. Eventually, she went back to the club. Her eels followed her faithfully.

That night, Meteor Mags dreamed. In her dream, her headphones' puffy pads pressed her ears. All of her favorite Kyuss songs played at an utterly unreasonable volume. The singer's raspy voice called to her, describing her body in song.

"Goddamn sonofabitch," Mags mumbled in her sleep. She felt the riff not just in her eardrums but on her skin. It moved over her body, caressing her curves. Her back arched. Her hands gripped the sheets.

A rippling light surrounded her. The hair on her tail stood on end. She felt herself wet and swollen. One by one, her trio of eels floated around her body in the darkness. Her fingers touched their sleek metal surfaces. She could not hear their electricity, but she felt it humming an electromagnetic serenade all around her. Her hand closed on one of the eels' rounded snouts.

Mags dreamed another eel nuzzled her cheek. Its chrome tail

wrapped around her breasts and cupped them. The third eel ran its metallic face over her thighs. Mags imagined the empires she could topple with such incredible power in her thrall. She envisioned the four of them, together, forging a new era, one electron at a time.

A snout pressed against her, warming its cold metal on her skin. She opened herself to it. The music blared in her ears. She hooked a leg around the eel and firmly clutched it.

Mags pressed its nose between her legs. She rubbed it in little circles. Then faster, faster—faster than a Kerry King guitar solo. Mags glistened. She eased the eel's snout into her body. She stretched to grip its sinewy, cybernetic form.

The eel pulsed and crackled. Her womb glowed red from its electric light. Her body trembled. The eel writhed inside her. "Yes," she whispered.

She cried out, shaking uncontrollably as her womb accepted the eel's cybernetic seed. She gasped for breath.

The seed took root inside her. The eel's tail spasmed in her hand. Mags gripped it tighter, squeezed it, and wrapped both of her legs around it.

Then she slept, and dreamed no more.

"Thanks for coming with us, Donny. I don't expect any trouble, but we sure don't mind having back-up just in case." Patches bumped Donny's leg. Mags brought up Coltrane's *Crescent* album on the speakers of the *Queen Anne*. The ship took a course for the asteroid lab she and Tarzi had raided in September.

Donny kicked back with a beer. He thought Mags seemed especially mellow today. "No sweat. I've been curious to check this place out anyway. What did we bring for the little critters?"

"Crabs and polychaete worms, mostly. Yum! I hope they like them."

He frowned and stuck out his tongue. "Ugh. Who wouldn't?"

"Give me a break! It's the best I could do on short notice."

Patches mewed.

"That's right, dear. It wouldn't be very nice of us to help them all get born and then let them starve out here." Mags recalled the sight of the decayed bodies in the tanks. Tarzi's cybernetic seahorse had flooded the asteroid so the baby octopuses could hatch, but Mags knew they had nothing to eat on that rock.

"Congratulations," said Donny. "Now you've got yourself the biggest aquarium in the System! Are you just going to keep dropping in and feeding them?"

"I don't know what else to do! I feel responsible for them now. But—yeah. They don't make very practical pets out here, do they?"

Donny shrugged. "You could take them back to Earth, maybe? Or build a giant aquarium on Vesta 4 and charge admission to the octopus zoo?"

Mags laughed. "That's so bloody ridiculous it sounds fun. Let me know if you have any other bright ideas." She walked to the bow of the ship and stared into space. She swayed in time with Elvin's ride cymbal. "Love this tune."

Donny quietly sipped his beer for a few minutes, letting her enjoy the music. Then he cleared his throat. "Listen, Mags. I just wanted to say sorry about getting in your personal business in the shop the other day. I just—I don't know. I had you all wrong. I didn't mean any offense."

"Donny, you know what I like about you? You may be a grade-A fuck-up, but at least you know when to say you're sorry!"

"Um—thanks?"

Mags sauntered over to hand him a cigarette. "But you don't owe me an apology. I have seen and heard some shit as a dancer that makes the Psycho 78s' locker room talk sound G-rated by comparison. You just hit a nerve, that's all."

"Good. The last time you were mad at me, I ended up getting shot at and losing my job." Donny lit her cigarette, then his own.

"Such a gentleman. But that's all water under the bridge now. You're a stellar saxophonist, and a big help to Fuzzlow in the shop, regardless of what he says. I'm glad you came aboard."

"Thanks, Mags."

"So, look. Let me explain something." She walked back to the window. She took in the sight of the stars, the planets, and the moons, undimmed by atmosphere. Her eyes traced the path of a distant comet. "You know what pheromones are?"

"Yeah, like scents and stuff."

"Close enough. In mammals, they play a huge role in how two animals decide to get it on. But look at me, Donny." She curled her tail up into her hand and pet it gently. "Do I look entirely human to you?"

He took a swig. "Now that you mention it, uh, not really? Are you like part cat or something?"

"Who knows? But I do know this. People just don't smell right to me. I mean, they don't smell disgusting. But they don't smell..."

"Sexy?"

Mags chuckled. "Precisely."

"I know this is none of my business but—do cats?"

"Ugh, no. As if that's even physically feasible if they did."

Donny scratched his chin. "You know, I can't say I ever met anyone like you Mags. I mean, with the tail and all. If you're not human, and you're not cat, then—you're one of a kind, aren't you?"

The sparkle left her eyes. She turned back to the window. "Lucky me."

Donny looked her over as she stood with her back to him. The tip of her tail flicked the air. She wasn't exactly his type, but he had always found something strangely compelling about her: the way she moved when she danced, the carefree joy she took in displaying her ample yet agile body. But now he felt an unfamiliar sympathy for her. She had friends who loved her. She even had fans who admired her. But he had never stopped to think that the infamous Meteor Mags might feel all alone in the universe.

She stubbed out her smoke in an ashtray. "Anyway," she said. "Sorry to get all mopey on you. It's just been on my mind lately." She walked back to the console and brought up a display. "Let me show you how to track me and Patches when we're down there, okay?"

"What? I gotta stay on the ship while you two visit the zoo?"

"At least until we scope it out. I'll have my mic with me. But Donny, last time we were here, Patches and I got our minds merged with the mama octopus, and it was like having your soul laid completely bare. Now, I like you, Donny, but I don't want you in my friggin' brain!"

"Fair enough. I don't think I want to be in your brain either."

"Hey, doorknob! What's wrong with my brain?" Mags slugged him playfully on the arm.

"Whatever it is, I don't want to find out!"

Then she showed him the tracking system, and the two of them chatted about music until the asteroid came into view.

"Okay, Donny. This is as far as you go." Mags stood at the elevator entrance to the former laboratory. Donny had helped her wheel the shipping crates full of crabs and worms from the *Queen Anne* to the elevator, but now she waved him off. "Patches and I will take it from here. Just keep an eye on us on the monitor."

"Uh, you're welcome?"

"Sorry, Captain Sensitive. Thanks for your help."

"Don't mention it. I'll be helping myself to all your beers now! Good luck."

Patches stood in the doorway, holding it open as Mags rolled the crates in. They descended into the asteroid.

"Meow?"

"I don't know, baby kitty. I hope they're alright, but who knows what we'll find down there." She scratched her cat behind the ears until the doors opened.

Darkness greeted them. Mags switched on her headlamp. Only weeks before, Tarzi's poor little seahorse had released a flood. His electric storm had killed all the lighting circuits, and apparently every sub-surface system but the GravGens. Mags' light swept across the lab. Fog diffused it into a misty glow. Water dripped from fixtures and walls. The enclosure had thwarted evaporation. Now everything was damp and dripping.

"Hmpf. How bloody cheerful." She wheeled the crates out of the elevator one by one, through the foggy laboratory, to the doorway leading to the caverns beyond. "At least we knew about the elevator this time around. Sodding mapmaker had one job to do."

Patches offered no assistance but stopped to rub her face on every stone and corner along her path. She scampered to the door, meowing ceaselessly until Mags joined her with the final crate.

Mags punched buttons on the keypad, but nothing happened. "Hell. Sparky fried the shit out of everything down here. Time for Plan B, dear. Step back now."

Patches complained.

Mags wheeled the crates along the wall to a safe place. "Yeah, yeah. You can't be hurt. I should probably stop yelling at you to get out of the way in firefights, huh? Sorry." She took a few blocks of C4 explosives from her kit and stuck them on the door. "I guess I still can't get over it. Cut your auntie some slack, will you?" Mags set the detonator. "But seriously, unless you want to get shot through the air like a cannonball, I suggest you get the hell back now."

They followed the wall until they were well out of blast range. "Fire in the hole!" Mags pressed her handheld switch. The doorway exploded.

Once the smoke cleared, she wheeled the crates back to the decimated doorway. "Shit, maybe we should have brought Donny down to move these things. At least men are good for something!"

She felt a familiar tug on her mind, and so did Patches. "I guess they know we're here." She called into the caverns. "Ahoy, krakens and krakenettes! Did you miss us? We brought you some din-din!"

Patches ran out onto the rocky bridge which rose only centimeters above the water filling the cavern. Mags wheeled the crates onto it and looked around for the giant tentacles of the mother octopus, but she saw nothing.

"Mama kraken," she called out. "Babies! Nom-noms are here." She aimed her headlamp into the water, searching. Slowly at first, and then in a cephalopodic chorus, tentacles rose from the water.

First one, then two, and then hundreds upon hundreds of tentacles waved, swishing the fog that had settled over them.

Mags could hear them. They hummed to her, not in sound waves, but in telepathic communion. She smiled, unfastening the lids of the crates and pulling them off. "Could you all try to *not* fry my brain this time? I'm still having whacked-out dreams, you know."

She hummed along with them and felt their approval. She kicked down the locks on the wheels of the first crate. With a generous heave, she pushed it over onto its side. The crate slammed onto the bridge, disgorging its contents into the water, splashing onto the waving tentacles. The octopuses greeted the slop of crabs and worms, crunching open the tasty prizes. Mags felt their excitement tickle her mind.

"There's more where that came from! Hold on, little darlings." She dumped another crate onto its side, emptying it on the opposite side of the bridge. Before she got to the third crate, their humming grew louder.

Patches ran back and forth. Waves of happiness flowed over her as her brain flooded with pleasure chemicals.

Mags smiled so hard her face hurt. She dumped the contents of the third crate into the water.

All along the sides of the bridge, tentacles splashed playfully. Mags knelt. Patches rubbed on her leg, purring wildly. Mags reached down to the nearest tentacle. "Do you like that, babies?" The tentacle wrapped around her hand in response.

Then she discovered what happened to the mother octopus.

Something inhuman grew inside Club Assteroid. Unbeknownst to Meteor Mags, her eel dream was more than just a dream. But in reality, her eel did not impregnate her. Its technology removed a single ovum from her uterus to bond with its own synthetic DNA. As she slept, two of the eels returned to the black box which stored them in her room. The third forced its way into the club's ductwork to nest.

While Mags and Donny traveled to the asteroid where it had originated, the eel curled into a ball, motionless, hidden from sight. The eel's internal machinery spliced Mags' genetic sample to its own.

Fueled by the eel's electric energy, a tiny zygote quickly grew into a fetus. The fetus assembled a body using the eel's metal and machinery within a matter of hours. The eel felt neither pain nor remorse as its components broke down and became something else. The eel merely followed its programming.

By the time Mags was feeding the octopuses, a cybernetic organism the size of a child flexed its newly-formed fingers. It blinked its metallic eyelids and crawled through the club's ductwork. It smelled machinery, and organic matter nearby. It needed more material to assemble a larger body.

Soon, it would need to feed.

"Don't be scared."

Mags heard the voice all around her. With her free hand, she ran her fingers along the tentacle encircling her wrist. The fog glowed white. But unlike her experience with the mother octopus, the white light did not completely envelop her. Sparkles like distant fireflies played over the water's surface. They could not possibly be real, but Mags watched their movements anyway. They flowed in a non-repeating pattern which calmed her and drew her in.

Patches made a raspy meow showing the tips of her tiny teeth. She stretched out beside her friend and purred.

"It's alright," said Mags. "I'm not scared at all."

"Good." Hundreds of voices in multi-part harmony said at once, "Mama wanted us to show you something."

Mags took a deep breath. She sat cross-legged on the barren bridge. "Okay, babies. Show me." She closed her eyes.

The white light consumed Mags and Patches. They experienced

floating below the water's surface. The light faded to present a scene which had taken place after their last visit to the asteroid. They swept their tentacles through the water—Mags covered in stars, Patches covered in calico, but their bodies now resembling the octopuses. The cold pressed all around them, but they felt no fear. With gentle care, the baby octopuses regulated their neurochemicals so they would feel no distress.

Before them floated the mother octopus. Her giant eyes were cloudy now, and dim. Her babies swam around her, circling her in the pit, conversing with her on the mental plane. In a language composed of images and emotions rather than words, she gave them everything she had learned from the minds of Mags, and Patches, and the researchers who had mutated her. She taught the babies words from the humans' minds, and their meanings. This knowledge, she made her children understand, would help them communicate with Mags and Patches when they returned.

The mother octopus had neither guarantee nor promise the two of them would return, but she had an unassailable, animal faith in Mags. She told her offspring the story of meeting Mags and Patches, how they had communed with her and kept their promise to help hatch the babies.

The octopuses swarmed around their mother, raising their tentacles in union. They formed an image in their minds of Meteor Mags and Patches as goddesses of the great waters and the vast unknown space which lay beyond. Though they lacked voices, they filled the mental plane with what could only be called singing.

"Bloody hell," she whispered. "They think I'm some sort of deity."

Patches whined.

"And you too, dear."

Then the mother octopus gave her final instructions to the young cephalopods, and she sank to the bottom of the pit.

"Oh no," cried Mags. "We were too late!" She dove into the obsidian depths, joined by Patches and the hundreds of babies. She ran her star-covered tentacles over the gigantic octopus head, hoping against all hope. But there was nothing she could do—

nothing but witness the past.

The mother octopus had watched over her unhatched children for years without any food at all. If not for Mags, she knew, she would have starved to death before they were ever born. She had impressed this on her offspring, and also the necessity of the terrible action they must take to survive.

Opening their beaks, the young octopuses fed on their mother's lifeless body. Mags turned away from the sight, but it was no use. Locked in telepathic communion with the babies, she lived the horrifying feast. Patches swam into her arms.

Mags tasted the mother's body. She devoured the tentacles and the network of neurons in them. Memories of losing her own mother came to her. She wept into the water. Her heart ached and pounded in her chest.

Then she felt the wave of calm again. The octopuses sensed her stress. They regulated her neurochemicals, soothing her. Her terror subsided. Patches purred in her embrace.

As one being, Mags, Patches, and the baby octopuses consumed the brain of the great mutant octopus. All of the mother's knowledge became their knowledge. All they had ever felt, they felt together.

As one living creature with thousands of tentacles, the swirling mass realized the mother was not gone at all. She had become a part of them, and they had become a part of her. There was nothing to mourn, as no one had gone away. A hum filled the water. It begged for a melody. The sound turned into white light. It filled everything.

Mags opened her eyes. She scooped Patches into her arms and stood up. She switched off her headlamp and removed her mask. She no longer felt any fear or sadness—only joy, only unity, only love.

The humming rose in volume all around her. Mags wiped tears from her eyes. She felt the minds of the octopuses touching hers, communing with her still. She understood the unspoken question in their hum.

"Of course I will, darlings. Of course I will."

There, in the darkened recesses of the asteroid caverns, Meteor Mags lifted her head, began a melody, and led the gathered octopuses in song.

Aboard the *Queen Anne*, Donny popped the cap off another beer. The dots on the monitor had not moved in several minutes. If Mags and Patches weren't moving, he reasoned, they might be in trouble. Or they could just be feeding their weird little pets. He decided to give them one more minute.

He looked out the window of the ship. Mags never seemed to grow tired of looking at the stars, thought Donny, but as an asteroid miner he had grown a bit sick of them. It wasn't like you could touch them. They just hung there, stupidly, probably burned out millions of years ago and nothing but dead husks floating in space. Dead, dying, and death as far as the eyes could see.

Donny frowned. "Getting morbid in your old age, aren't you, Donald?" Then he hunched over. The bottle fell from his hand. Beer sloshed across the deck. "Ungh!" He dropped to his hands and knees, but he did not see the deck. Instead, he saw death.

Darkness surrounded him, endless wet darkness. His arm struck out, meeting nothing. A giant skull hovered before him. Blood ran from its eyes. Piece by piece, it crumbled into fragments. A horde of smaller skulls descended upon it, devouring it.

Donny stared. "What the—" An unusual thought came to him. "That was metal as fuck!"

Donny's fear suddenly vanished. The blackness around him faded. His hands found his chair. He pulled himself to his feet.

A song came to Donny. It did not come over the ship's speakers. It simply came to him, a chorus of voices, a wash of emotions and images, hundreds of singers alive with joy, and love, and unity.

His eyes fell upon the stars. He no longer saw endless death in their distant lights. In fact, he saw them as a child, as if he had never seen them before. The Milky Way Galaxy sprawled before him, as if some god had splashed it on a canvas. It no longer seemed a dull, inhuman thing taunting him from afar. He felt he was a part of it, that he could never leave it, nor ever want to. It sang to him in a star-covered voice.

And the melody, he realized, was led by Meteor Mags.

Later, when he would tell this story, he could never pin down how long this went on. It might have been minutes or maybe hours. He only knew that while he listened, time had no meaning.

Eventually, the song subsided. Mags' voice came over the speakers. "Donny? Donny? Are you there?"

"I'm here. What's happening? I swear I thought I heard you singing."

Laughter chimed over the speakers. "Oh, did you hear that? All the way up there?"

"It was like I heard it in my head. What the hell are you doing down there?"

Donny heard nothing for a minute. Then the speakers came to life again. "I'll tell you all about it when I get up there. Oh, and Donny?"

"Yeah?"

"I know what song we're gonna put on the next album. See you in a few."

"Check this out." Mags tossed him a leather-bound book. "Patches found it."

Donny caught it. "What was going on down there? I had the craziest feeling up here and—whoa. What is this?" He flipped through the pages. They appeared to contain writing, but in a script he had never seen before. Some pages contained mechanical drawings for parts he did not recognize, machines he had never encountered. But strangest of all, the illustrations depicted some sort of dinosaur.

"I don't know, but it sure is a trip. Look at it! It's like a manual to build some kind of spaceship, and a bunch of those bloody lizards!"

"These aren't lizards, Mags. These are dinosaurs. Look at this page here." He held up the book for her to see.

"That's the bastard who chained me up and electrocuted me! If not for Tarzi—"

"This thing chained you up?"

"Yes, dickweed! Or something that looked just like it. He had me chained up and was frying me with those electric rods they carry. It—"

"Mags. This is a Dracorex. It's been extinct for more than, I don't know, a hundred seventy-five million years or something. It's fucking dead."

Her cigarette fell onto the deck.

"Patches found this?"

Mags picked up her cigarette. She almost took a puff, then looked at it. She walked over to the console and stubbed it out on an ashtray. She produced another and lit up. "A Dracorex."

"That's what I said."

"Aren't you the little paleontologist?" Mags blew a series of smoke rings, staring out the window into space. "Yes," she said. "Patches found it. We were on our way out, and she was sniffing around. As she does."

Donny looked over at Patches, sprawled on the corner of Mags' bed. The tip of her tail flicked back and forth. Her face had relaxed into a feline scowl. She rested her chin on one of her legs. Donny was never sure how much of what Mags told him about Patches was real and how much she just made up. "What happened to you two down there?"

Mags laughed. "I got two words for you, Donny. Sentient tentacles." She strolled over to her portable keyboard, set on a stand by the edge of her bunk. "Those things aren't just alive and hungry, Donny. They're intelligent." She flipped a switch and sat down. Brushing her bangs back from her forehead, she told Donny exactly what she had learned inside the asteroid.

"So that's what I was feeling."

Mags arched an eyebrow at him. "What were you feeling?"

Donny looked away, embarrassed. "It was—I don't know how

to say it without sounding like some kind of fucking hippie."

Mags smiled and leaned forward. "Let me help you, dear. You felt like everything you ever loved had died. Your whole life was meaningless, empty, and dead. Then all of that melted away. You felt the whole universe was an endless reservoir of love, and you were a part of everything."

She knew, somehow. "That's exactly it, Mags."

Her lips curled into an evil smile. She laughed and laughed. "You fucking hippie!"

Donny could not help but join her laughter. "Fuck you, Mags."

"Fuck you, too! Do you want me to get your tie-dye and sandals ready?"

"Hahaha. Damn it, Mags! Why do you always have to bust my balls?"

"Cause I like you, ya sodding useless space miner. Now listen. You ever hear that Deftones song *Diamond Eyes*? Do you think you can get that sort of guitar and bass sound at the end out of your sax?"

"Oh, for sure. Love that album."

"Good. And maybe keep it going for like thirty minutes like a Swans riff?"

"Now *that* sounds fun."

"Good. Because this is the song I want to put on the next album. It's called *Octopus Mother*. It goes something like this." Accompanying herself on the keyboard, Mags sang.

Give myself to you
So that you may live
All my everything
All I have to give

See the stars that shine
If they all were mine
They would never fall
I give you my all

There's no future here
But the one we make
If we can't have that
Then the one we take

Nothing ever but forever
Nothing ever but forever
We will all become as one

Donny sat entranced. He had never mentioned it to anyone, but his favorite part of jamming with the Psycho 78s was listening to her sing. She had something so pure, so raw in her voice.

Suddenly, an inbound message lit up the control console. "Incoming! And it's marked priority." He switched on the communicator to play the message.

"Mags," said Celina's voice over the cabin's speakers. "All hell is breaking loose here! There's some kind of robot running wild and tearing everything apart! Fuzz and I are going to take it on, but we sure could use all the help we can get, wagtail. When you get this, get back to the club. And put the pedal to the metal!"

Mags stormed over to the console without a word. She knew the distance between the club and the ship would mean a delay in the signal, but she opened a channel anyway. "Celina! If you get this, hold down the fort, convict. We're on our way and ready to bring the noise. Mags out."

She took her seat. "Strap in, Donny. And get ready to kick some arse." She looked over her shoulder. "You too, Patches. Celina's in trouble."

Patches ignored the command, but she jumped onto Donny's lap. He clicked his safety restraints into place. Donny did not know Patches now understood every word Celina said. Nor did he know Mags' very life would soon depend on her little calico cat.

The *Queen Anne* kicked into high gear and sped back to the club.

PART TWO: THE LADDER OF LIFE

Hyo-Sonn, Kala, and Suzi sat in Club Assteroid's garden. The garden provided fresh food for the club. It also indulged Mags' floral passions. La Plaza Margareta may have ended years ago, but she had moved the statue of her great-grandmother here and surrounded it with magnolia trees. She had bolted a plaque over the garden's entrance. It read, "Maggie's Farm."

When Celina pointed out that Maggie in Bob Dylan's tune was the villain, Mags responded, "So what? It's anti-establishment, it's got my name in it, and Rage Against The Machine covered it. Close enough!"

The three young women discussed a mural Kala wanted to paint and unveil at Mags' birthday party in November.

"What about a historical mural?" Kala asked.

"You mean like great women of history?" Hyo-Sonn bit into a peach plucked from a nearby tree. "We could do ones from that book she has, like Annie Besant and all them."

"She'd rather have pirates," Suzi said.

Kala laughed. "She so would. Oh, that gives me an idea. We could do a mural of her great-gramma."

"And her gramma, and her mom," said Hyo-Sonn. "That way we get pirates *and* great women of history!"

Suzi chomped on a fresh orange. "It narrows down how many people we have to paint. Damn, these things are good."

"You've really turned this garden around, Suzi. It was kind of a shambles when we got here, wasn't it?"

"Ah, it's no big deal." She spat out a seed. "If you want farming done right, hire a farm girl!"

Kala smiled. She had never cared for Suzi's provincial and frankly racist attitude. But she could tell something had changed in the young woman since they were captured and subsequently rescued by Meteor Mags. Kala supposed anyone could change, given enough time and the right setting. "I don't know if we have enough details to paint all that. Do you think Mags would tell us some more stories?"

Hyo-Sonn laughed. "Oh, you know how Mags is. Every time we try to get her to commit to something, she says the same thing: I've got cargo to 'liberate!' Lizards to exterminate!"

"Dance poles to lubricate."

"Ewww! Gross, Suzi."

"What? I'm just sayin'."

Above them, unseen, a pair of cybernetic eyes watched them converse. The young cyborg did not understand the conversation, but it sensed the presence of organic material, machinery, and meat. This would be a good place to grow. It flexed its metallic fingers.

Suzi continued, "But seriously, I think it's a good idea. Maybe we could do like one scene from each of their lives, real big. And don't forget Patches."

"No, we can't forget Patches," said Kala. "But which scenes?"

"Do you remember that story Mags told us about her ring?" Hyo-Sonn asked. "And then something about the GravGens."

Kala sketched in her notebook. "Yeah, and that scene where she met—"

Suddenly, the ductwork above them exploded. The cybernetic infant fell through the shrapnel to the ground. Its metallic lips parted in a roar.

The young women fell to the dirt, shielding their faces. Suzi looked over her arm. She had no idea what she was looking at, but it was not good. Kala screamed something, but it only registered as noise. Suzi rolled out of the way. A chunk of ductwork crashed beside her. Her hand closed on a shovel's handle.

Suzi rose to her feet, growling like an animal. Behind her, Kala and Hyo-Sonn scrambled away from the monster. Suzi gripped the shovel with both hands. She ran at the snarling thing, and with all the force she could muster, swung the shovel like a baseball bat.

The metal blade smashed into the attacker. A shower of sparks and lightning erupted from the point of contact. The wooden handle insulated Suzi from the electricity, but the force pummeled her backwards through the air. She landed on her back in the dirt, knocking the wind from her lungs. The shovel fell from her hands.

But her attack was not in vain. She had smacked the cyborg several meters backwards. As it struggled to regain its footing, Hyo-Sonn's arms encircled her, pulling her away from the monster and towards the exit. Another chunk of the ceiling fell where Suzi had been gasping just seconds before.

The cybernetic infant stood and hissed at the trio. Its metal tongue lashed the air between two rows of sharpened teeth. An orb of sparks crackled around its body, and its eyes glowed red. It was not yet as tall as the girls in the garden, but its diminutive stature did nothing to soften its horrifying visage. It charged.

Suzi scrambled to her feet.

Hyo-Sonn released her. "Come on," she shouted. "Come on!"

Kala made it to the door. She stood ready to punch the access button and slam it shut as soon as her friends made it through. As Suzi and Hyo-Sonn ran towards her, Kala got a good view of the thing attacking them. Her artistic eyes captured its details. What she saw sent a chill through her soul. For the attacker was not entirely alien. In fact, its face looked incredibly familiar.

Hyo-Sonn and Suzi ran past her. She punched the button outside the doorway. The door to the garden slid shut. Though sturdy, it was not opaque. A Plexiglas sheet six inches thick and set in a metal frame, it gave Kala a perfect view of the monster who pursued them.

The cyborg slammed into the Plexiglas. Kala watched it howl in anger. Its metal fingernails raked the other side of the door. The plastic curled up and fell away in strips. She looked into its red eyes and memorized them.

"What in the fuck is *that*?" Suzi shouted.

"Let's go," said Hyo-Sonn. "We need Celina!"

The cyborg placed its hand on the metal doorframe. A bolt of lightning erupted from its hand, engulfing the frame.

Kala screamed. She fell back from the door.

"Kala!" Hyo-Sonn caught her friend. The doorframe crackled with sparks. The controls smoked and sizzled.

"Fucking hell, let's go!" Suzi yelled.

They ran down the hall as fast as they could.

Hyo-Sonn pounded her fist on the door again and again. "Celina!"

The door slid open to reveal Celina wrapped in a sheet of cloth. "What in the name of sweet bleeding Christ do you—" Then she saw the horrified looks on their faces. "What's wrong?" Behind her, Fuzzlow slipped on a pair of boxer briefs.

"There's something in the garden!"

"And it's mad as hell!" Suzi added. "Fucking came out of the ceiling and tried to kill us!"

"What is it?" Celina looked up and down the hall. "Come in, come in." She motioned the girls inside.

Celina had adorned her room with tapestries on the walls and pillows for sitting on the floor. Oils dispersed their scents from a pair of oil warmers on her bookshelf. A candle in a glass jar cast a soothing glow below the dimmed electric lights. Tesla quietly napped on a padded chair. But the romantic refuge was about to be shattered.

"I can draw it," said Kala. She had dropped her pencil and pad of paper in the attack. "Do you have a tablet?" Her hands shook as she took a tablet and a stylus from Celina. "It was like some kind of robot," she said, sketching on the screen. "But its face. Its face—" Kala drew quickly on the tablet.

"You saw its face?"

Suzi answered. "I smashed its fucking face with a shovel. And it didn't do a damn thing to stop it!"

"It had red eyes," said Hyo-Sonn, "and it growled at us, and it came out of the ceiling, and there were sparks everywhere and—"

Kala handed the tablet back to Celina.

She stared in disbelief. "That's its face?"

"It had a face like Mags. *Just* like Mags. Only metal."

Fuzzlow looked over Celina's shoulder. "What in the actual fuck?"

"Look at that, Fuzz. Do those panels and circuit lines look familiar?"

"Hell yes, they do. It looks just like those eels we tested. But that face..."

"Is it still in the garden?" Celina set the tablet down and stepped up to an emergency panel by her doorway. Pushing a tapestry aside, she revealed a panel of screens displaying feeds from the club's security cameras.

"It was up against the door, clawing its way through the Plexiglas. It made these lightning bolts come out of its fingers!"

Celina's mouth fell open when she saw the video from the garden's camera. The cyborg scratched madly at the door. Tendrils of electricity poured into the door frame and surrounding circuitry. Circuits tore loose from the wall. They flew through the air, attaching to the cyborg's body. The monster assimilated the new parts, and it grew. The video feed went black.

"Fuck me dead." Celina picked up a handset from the panel on the wall. "I don't know what that thing is, but we aren't sticking around to find out." She scooped up Tesla from the chair and handed him to Hyo-Sonn.

"Mew?" Tesla asked, squirming. Hyo-Sonn held him close.

"You girls get to emergency exit three *right* fucking now and do *not* stop for anything. Get everyone inside Mags' private hangar and lock it down! I'll sound the alarm. Fuzz, you stick with me." Celina opened the door. "What are you waiting for? Go! Go! Go!"

Sarah happily hammered her new keyboard in the room she shared with Kala. Meteor Mags had shown her a handful of chords. All week, she had practiced changing from one to the next without breaking her rhythm.

She loved the promotional poster Mags had given her with the keyboard. Printed for the release of the Psycho 78s' first album, it portrayed Mags viciously screaming *Something to Destroy* with the band backing her up. Mags gripped the microphone with one hand, snapping a bullwhip into a fierce "S" shape with the other. Silk-screened blood splattered the image and its bold text reading *The Psycho 78s: HyperSonicHatred.*

Sarah's parents had told her Meteor Mags was evil. They had told her all kinds of things were evil, even Sarah herself. She believed them for many years. But when her body began to change, Sarah prayed. Sarah prayed between the beatings and the other things she would rather not remember.

In her prayers, she believed an angel talked to her. The angel said Sarah was made of light, the same light that powered the stars. When her family hurt her, and when they sent her to The Clinic where the hurt grew even worse, Sarah silently sang her favorite songs into the light. They made the pain go away, washed it from her mind, and made it fade to nothing. Of all her favorite singers, Meteor Mags was her most favorite.

"Come on, Sarah. Sing it for us!" A few of her new friends sat on the chairs and beds in the room with her. Some of them were dancers at the club. Some of them helped staff the parties. Some of them just had nowhere else to go. But all of them loved Mags and Celina, and together they worked to make the club a home.

"Okay, promise me you won't laugh," she said.

"Sarah!"

"Promise."

"Alright, we promise," said one of the girls.

"But what if it's funny?" asked another.

What would Mags say? "Fine!" Some of these young women were much older than Sarah and had been at the club far longer than the new arrivals in her group. Yet none of them had ever tried to make her feel bad about anything. "So, Mags showed me some chords, and I wanted to see if I could make a song with them."

Sarah picked out a D Major chord. Then she switched to an F Major, then back to D, then up to a G Major and back, all without hesitation. She sang.

Fuckin' bacteria
Voices in my heard, I'm hearin' ya
You make me feel inferi-a
When you colonize my exteri-a

Get up off my planet, all you bastards
Get up off my planet, all you—

The laughter stopped her.

"You promised not to laugh!"

The laughter continued, then clapping. One of the girls spoke up. "Oh, Sarah! Don't stop. That's awesome!"

"You really think so?"

"Oh, my fucking god, Mags will love it. You have to play it for her."

Her frown relaxed into a smile. She laughed with them. "I thought you didn't like it. I really don't want to disappoint Mags."

"Sarah, believe me. I've known Mags for a while now, and the one thing your song will *not* do is disappoint her. Do you have a name for it?"

"I was thinking about calling it *Bastard Virus Plan*—"

Celina's voice blared over the loudspeaker. "Emergency evacuation! Attention! Emergency evacuation! This is not a drill! Everyone to exit number three *now*. This is *not* a drill!" Klaxons rang out their shrill pulse. Red LED's flashed on the walls of every room, and every few meters in the hallways.

The young women looked to each other in shock, then leapt to their feet. They raced from the room, taking Sarah with them.

Next to the video screens for the security cameras, Celina's tapestries covered the door to her gun safe. She punched in the combination. "We can't let that thing get loose in the club."

Fuzzlow pulled on his shirt, pants, and boots in a flash. "Looks like it's *already* loose," he said. "If that thing came out of the ceiling, what's to stop it from crawling wherever it wants through the ductwork? What if it fried that door?"

"Damn it." She handed Fuzzlow a laser rifle. "I knew those eels would be trouble."

"You think they're to blame?"

"Didn't Mags say she got them from some genetics lab? Put two and two together, love. That bloody monstrosity is half machine, half Mags. Where else could it have come from?"

"I've got an idea. Mags controlled the eels with that Faraday suit. If we can get that suit from her room, maybe we can control this—this Magbot thing!"

"Magbot!" Celina laughed. "You have such a way with words, Fuzzy love."

He took a pair of holstered revolvers from the safe. "Hey, I don't get songwriting credits for nothing."

"I can get us into her room. Even if your idea doesn't work, at least that suit will keep Magbot from frying us."

"Just in case, let's take this bad boy with us." He grabbed one more weapon from the safe.

"Fuzz! We don't want to shoot *that* bloody thing inside the club!"

"You saw what those eels did in the trial run. I'm not taking any chances with Magbot."

"Word." Celina quickly recorded a message to Mags and hit send. "We can't wait to hear back from her. Let's go."

"What the hell? Mags told me she had all these cases locked up in her armory." Fuzzlow stood over the black case in her room.

"Looks like she made an exception," said Celina. "Should we open it?"

"Let's suit up first. I don't feel like riding the lightning today. That looks like Mags' suit on the back of the chair there. It should fit you. Let me see if she's hiding one of the spares in here." Fuzzlow opened her closet. A pile of clothes a meter high slumped over and fell through the door. He found himself knee-deep in a pile of socks and panties. "Damn it, Magatha. Do your bloody laundry sometime!"

Celina pulled Mags' tailored Faraday suit over her clothes. "I think she'd rather steal new socks than wash the old ones."

"You say pirate, I say kleptomaniac. At least we've got a spare suit in this mess." He pulled a Faraday suit from a hanger and got busy pulling it over his clothes.

"Kiss me before we get sealed in, Fuzzy."

The two of them shared a deep kiss. They pulled the suits closed over their faces. Celina stood to the side of the black case, her laser rifle ready. Fuzzlow lifted the lid, slowly, ready to slam it shut.

Inside, two of the three eels lay quietly in their molded housings. But one slot sat empty.

"I guess that solves that," said Fuzz.

A red glow appeared in the eels' eyes.

"Fuck!" Celina aimed her rifle.

He slammed the lid shut.

"Doesn't this thing have a lock?"

"Got it, babe." He set the locking mechanism. "But if it's electric, couldn't they fry the lock?"

"Stand back. I don't want those bastards getting out." She took the butt of her rifle and smashed the lock's keypad. Then she pulled on the lid. It refused to open. "There. Best we can do." She picked up her tablet. A moving dot on the screen tracked the cyborg through the club's security system. "Everyone's out of the club except us, Fuzz. Magbot's heading for the smaller concert room. If we get there fast, we can box her in."

Fuzzlow followed her into the hall. "Let's go show this robot why you don't fuck with the Psycho 78s."

Celina set the lock on Mags' door. "Race you."

The two of them sprinted down the hall.

Magbot grew to full size after feasting on the metal and circuits in the garden. Now she sat on the piano bench where Meteor Mags enjoyed playing by candlelight late at night. Her fingers pounded the keys, making dissonant chunks of sound that more resembled a demolition than a song. An inhuman, guttural noise issued from her throat.

Celina and Fuzzlow stood outside the entrance to the small concert room.

"What the hell is it doing?" Fuzzlow whispered.

"I'd say she's trying to play piano."

"She's not very good, is she?"

"What a godawful racket."

Magbot grimaced. She felt something like a dim, forgotten memory, a compulsion to make this inert block of wood and wire do—what? Like metal sledgehammers full of fury, her hands beat the keyboard. Possessed by an uncontrollable urge her newly formed mind could not comprehend, she opened her mouth to do—what? Only a wild roar escaped.

"That's just fucking sad," whispered Celina. "Are you ready?" She took aim.

He raised his laser rifle to his shoulder. "Let's take this thing down." His finger squeezed the trigger.

But the part of Magbot that was cybernetic eel sensed the control circuits in Celina's suit. She felt them tug at her willpower, and she did not like it. She jumped to her feet. The bench flew back and tumbled across the stage. A barrage of laser beams assaulted her.

Their bright bursts ricocheted off her body. The piano splintered as they smashed into it. Its wires snapped, filling the bandshell with a terrible din. The deflected beams burned smoldering holes in the stage curtains.

The humans advanced, pouring on the lasers. "Don't let her get away!" They pressed forward, firing round after round of searing light.

Magbot howled. She grabbed the bench from the floor and hurled it at them. Celina ducked. Fuzzlow dropped to the ground and rolled away. He pulled a .44 Magnum revolver from a holster at his side. It blasted like a cannon.

The round caught Magbot in the shoulder. The force spun her around.

He fired again and again until the pistol was empty. The bullets smacked Magbot to the ground. "Damn," he said, eyeing the weapon appreciatively. "Mags was right about this sucker." He slipped it back into its holster and picked up his rifle. "Celina! She's down!"

Celina moved in closer to the stage. "How does this bloody suit work?"

"I don't know! Just think about what you want it to do."

She furrowed her brow in concentration. "I want it to stop."

"Rarrrgh," roared Magbot. She felt the mental signals amplified by Celina's suit. They tried to tell her what to do. They tried to calm her down. They tried to make her stop. Stop. Stop. The part of her that was eel felt itself submitting to Celina's will.

But the part of her that was Mags refused. "Eeeyaarrr," she yelled. She forced herself to her feet. Her skin crackled with electricity. A seething mass of lightning took shape around her.

Celina screamed. The mental feedback from the cyborg pierced her mind. The sharp blade of its resistance stabbed into her skull. She staggered backwards.

"Celina!" Fuzzlow fired his rifle, but it was too late.

Magbot leapt from the stage. Roaring, she fell on Celina, driving the woman to the ground. Her metal hands closed around Celina's throat in a blaze of current.

Fuzzlow's boot bashed the side of her cybernetic head, but Magbot held on. She shook Celina like a ragdoll, trying to crush her windpipe.

Celina tried to shout, but she only made a rasping, choking noise.

Fuzzlow drew the other Magnum from its holster with his left hand. He fired it into the side of Magbot's head, point blank. The force blew off a chunk of the cyborg's metallic hair. An oily kind of blood spewed over Celina's suit. He fired again. Magbot's head snapped to the side. Fuzzlow kicked her in the face as hard as he could. Her grip on Celina broke, and she fell to the side.

Fuzzlow fired a third round. "Get out of here!"

Celina, gasping, scrambled to her feet. Nearly blinded by a migraine, she stumbled, turned, and ran for the doorway.

Magbot bared her teeth and hissed. Fuzzlow shot another bullet into her chest. The force racked her body. A bolt of energy lashed out from her to engulf his revolver.

It grew hot in his gloved hand. "Shit!" He flung it at the cyborg. The electricity exploded the powder in the remaining bullets. Fuzzlow ducked. In his crouch, his hand fell upon the chunk he had blasted off Magbot's head. His fist closed around it and he ran.

Dented, damaged, and bleeding, Magbot raised her arms to the sky. A scream of pure hate burst from her cybernetic lungs. The tortured sphere of electricity expanded all around her. It scorched the wooden dance floor in the concert hall. The stage curtains burst into flame. The scraps of the piano caught fire.

Reaching the entryway where Celina stood, Fuzzlow asked, "Are you okay?"

She merely waved her hand in the air.

"I guess it was a good idea to bring this after all." He swung up the AA-12 he had slung over his shoulder. "Auto-assault, baby!" Its magazine held eight high-explosive rounds, each with the force of a grenade. "Let's see how eel face likes a fucking Frag-12!"

The rounds punched through the lightning and exploded all around Magbot. Their concussive force smashed her backwards into a wall. Fuzzlow slammed a second magazine into the AA-12 and shot another eight rounds. The explosions battered her to the floor and cracked the wall. A section of it collapsed, burying her in a pile of rubble. A cloud of dust rose in the rays of light coming through the hole in the wall.

Celina peeled back the helmet of her Faraday suit. "Bloody hell. Remember when I said we didn't want to fire that thing in the club? I take it back."

As if in reply, a stone fell from the top of the pile of rubble. Then another.

"Fuck," said Fuzzlow. "Let's get out of here!"

They ran for the emergency exit.

Moments later, a faint crackle ended the silence in the bandshell. One by one, chunks of broken concrete fell from the pile and onto the ruined floor. A cybernetic hand shoved its way through the wreckage. A hateful growl emanated from the pile of stone.

Magbot pushed her way free. Her shiny body now blackened with soot, she staggered in the dusty beams of light. She kicked a rock out of her path.

The daughter of lightning made her way out to the surface of Vesta 4.

"Are we close enough to talk in real time yet, Donny?"

"Close enough. Bringing up a channel right now."

"Celina!" Mags called into the microphone. "Celina! Are you there?" No response. "Damn it, Donny!"

"Give her a minute," said the sax player. "Who knows what's breaking loose down there?"

She fumed. Then Celina's voice came over the speakers.

"Mags? Can you hear me?"

"Loud and clear. What's the situation?"

"Everyone's okay. We're all in your hangar."

"Good," said Mags. "We built it bloody nuke-proof. Have you got hostiles?"

"Just one," said Celina. "But she's a doozy! Fuzzlow and I attacked her, but we got our arses kicked."

"Her? Who is she? I thought you said it was a robot?"

"It *is* a robot! Or some kind of cyborg. Mags, it's one of those eels of yours! We checked in your room, and one of them was missing."

"You went in my room?"

"Yes! We had to get those suits! And that's when we found one of the eels was missing."

"You went in my closet?"

"Goddamnit, wagtail! No one gives a rat's arse about your three-year-old pile of dirty socks! We're under attack here! But something's gone wrong. That thing isn't an eel anymore. It's got electricity and armor and shit like your eels, but—but it looks just like you!"

"It *what* now, mate?"

"It looks like you! It's—Mags, it has your face. It attacked the girls. Then we found it trying to play piano in the bandshell. It damn near killed me! Fuzz blasted it with Frag-12s, caved the whole sodding wall down on it, and the fucking thing still got up and walked away!"

"Fuzz blew up my fucking concert hall?"

"We didn't have any choice! It was shooting out bolts of lightning and bloody choking me to death!"

Mags sighed. "Are you okay, dear?"

"I'm fine now, thanks."

"Good. You clear everyone off the landing area in the hangar. I'll open it from the ship once we make sure there's no hostiles outside. Okay?"

"Sounds like a plan. Love you."

"Love you too, ya blasted convict. Now try not to blow up any more concert halls until we get there!"

Soon, Mags brought the ship into the hangar. She strode down the ramp from the *Queen Anne*. Patches scampered past her to the group of young women, bumping her side against their legs one by one. Donny followed behind.

Sarah ran up to her. "Mags," she cried out, throwing her arms around the space pirate.

Mags' face lit up. She scruffed the girl's thick black curls with a gloved hand. "Heya, kiddo. You doing okay?"

"There's a monster on the loose!"

Mags picked her up and carried her with one arm. Sarah's arms wrapped around her neck.

"Don't be scared, baby." She kissed Sarah's cheek. "Your sweet auntie Mags is gonna bring down total hellfire on that thing. Celina!"

"Over here! We're tracking the cyborg on the surface."

Mags had a bad a feeling about all this. She recalled her intimate dream with the eels. She had written it off as a pleasant dream, nothing more. But now this had happened. Could it have been more than a dream? Could her eels have really spawned some kind of hideous monster using her DNA? "Does anybody have a clue how we can take this thing down short of a bleedin' atom bomb?"

"No, but check it out," said Fuzzlow. He pulled the piece of cyborg from his pocket. "I got a chunk of the Magbot."

Mags stared at the scrap of blood-soaked, sticky machinery. "A chunk of the what?"

"The Magbot! The thing that's—"

She snatched it from his hand. "I bloody heard you the first time! What the fuck is wrong with you? You named it after me?"

"We could call it RoboMags. Or Maggotron, but—"

"Stick it up your arse, Fuzz! I can't believe this shit." Mags eyed the chunk in her hand. "Named it after me, you twisted son of a bitch." She stormed over to the panel of video feeds, cursing a blue streak.

"At least the fire's out," said Celina.

On one monitor, Mags could see the fire in the bandshell had been snuffed out by the rubble from Fuzzlow's grenade launcher attack. On another screen, the cyborg moved across the plains of Vesta 4.

"We could open the hangar," Celina suggested, "and use the *Queen Anne's* missiles on her. But if she could survive sixteen grenade rounds, I don't really know if that would do any good."

"Let her go. Better to have her out there than wreaking havoc in the club. Besides, I have an idea. Patches!"

The calico cat's ears perked up. She trotted over.

Mags set Sarah down and knelt before her cat. "This is serious, Patches. Do you remember that nice octopus we met?"

Patches rubbed the side of her face against Mags' hand.

"Mhm. Do you remember what we learned there?"

"Mew."

"Now it's time to put it to work. Come with me, dear. Sarah? We could use your help, too."

"Me?"

"That's right. Now the rest of you, keep an eye on that sodding cyborg. Sarah, Patches—come with me."

Inside the armory of the *Queen Anne*, Mags opened a panel on the wall. She pulled out a massive black case, sliding it on its wheels into the room. She lifted the lid to reveal the portable genetics lab she and Tarzi had plundered in September.

"You see," she explained, "when Patches and I got our minds merged with the octopus, we were exposed to everything she knew. What she knew included everything she'd picked up from the minds of the eggheads who created her. That means Patches and I ought to be bloody geneticists by now. But let's just say it was all a bit much to assimilate at one time. That's why you're here, Sarah."

The young woman stared at the components in the case. "What do you want me to do?"

Mags set the sticky chunk of cyborg in the case. "Do you remember when I heard you singing? And came to rescue you?"

"Yes."

"How do you think that happened, Sarah?"

"I don't know. I just sang. In my mind. As hard as I could."

"Mhm." Mags bent down and placed a hand on Sarah's cheek. "I think you have a gift, Sarah. A very special gift."

"I do?"

"That's right. Now, maybe it was just because I was fresh from bonding with that kraken. Maybe I was just on the right wavelength or something. But I think your mind can reach out and touch other minds."

"Like a psychic?"

"Whatever you want to call it. So, I'm hoping you can help me and Patches sort something."

"I'd do anything for you, Mags."

Mags hugged her. "Help me remember. Patches will be there with us."

She pulled equipment out of the case and set it up. "This bloody thing will sequence the gene. And I'm pretty sure this is the other gizmo we need. Patches?"

Patches rubbed on the machinery. It looked like the bastard son of a microscope and a centrifuge, with plastic tubes protruding from it, wrapping around and through it, and down into plastic reservoirs.

"Mhm. I thought so, too." Mags lifted a computer from the case and plugged both pieces of equipment into it. She pulled out her boot knife and sliced off the thinnest piece she could from the chunk of cyborg. She placed it in the gene sequencer and turned it on.

"Come sit with me, Sarah." Mags sat cross-legged on the floor. Patches crawled into her lap, turned around several times, and made herself comfortable. Sarah took Mags' hand and sat next to her. "Now, just focus on me and Patches together. And sing."

"Sing?"

"Sing the way you sang that day when I first heard you, okay?"

"Okay."

Mags placed her hands on Patches, closed her eyes, and tried to recall anything she could about ubiquitin.

Mags had mastered advanced mathematics at a fairly young age, devoting her free time to studying it after moving to the States nearly a century ago. Much of genetics, however, remained uncharted waters for her. This much she knew: When the body decided it was time for a cell to die, enzymes attached a protein called ubiquitin to proteins in that cell. Mags had already decided it was time for that cybernetic monstrosity to die. Now, she needed to know how to synthesize an enzyme that would attach ubiquitin to the synthetic proteins which made up half the DNA of the cybernetic sea creatures she and Tarzi had discovered.

Mags relaxed and focused on Patches, who had been exposed to all this information in the octopus' mind, too. She hoped that linking their minds again would increase their processing power on this problem, much like computers on a network can contribute processing power to each other. She hoped she had correctly judged Sarah's talents, and that the young woman could facilitate this mental networking.

Mags heard a beep from the lab equipment. She opened her eyes and marveled at what she saw on the screen. The computer had sequenced the cyborg's entire genome. Like a forgotten memory returning from a distant time, an understanding of the sequence dawned on Mags. Alongside the four nucleotide bases of adenine, cytosine, guanine, and thymine, four synthetic bases designed by the original researchers attached in a cybernetic double helix. Mags just needed to know how to attack them.

She heard Sarah singing in her mind. With Sarah, she felt Patches, too. Maybe this idea really was crazy, she thought, but she had been called crazy before. And here she was, still alive, outliving her detractors, and ready to rock. Mags surrendered to the white light of Sarah's song.

On the mental plane, they stood in a circle, joining hands and paws. Sarah's song held them aloft, like a prayer rising up to heaven. A pair of wings grew from the young woman's back. Patches sprouted a pair of wings, and Mags felt wings grow from her own shoulders. "Sing it, Sarah."

Mags saw her great-grandmother's ring hovering above them in the white space, but it was much larger than life-size, meters wide. The ring unfolded into a double helix.

On angels' wings, the three of them flew up into it. Like a giant spiral ladder, it stretched upwards as far as they could see. Patches met Mags' eyes and meowed. "That's right, dear. Remember." They sped into the blank oblivion above them, surrounded by the helix.

Suddenly, Mags understood how to engineer the enzyme she needed. She perceived its atomic structure and its folded proteins. She saw them in the white space all around her, attaching to the double helix. They attacked the synthetic nucleotides, unlatching them from their bonds in the genome.

Then the twisted ladder of genetics began to unravel all around her. From top to bottom, it collapsed and fell apart. Gigantic, broken proteins fell from above like girders falling from a shattered crane.

"Keep singing, dear. That's it. That's what we need!" Mags

opened her eyes. Her fingers flew over the keyboard of the geneticists' computer. She told it exactly what she needed the enzyme to do, and how to do it. The equipment hummed in response, singing its own mechanical song. Numbers and letters raced up the monitor faster than anyone could read. "Got it!" She squeezed Sarah's hand.

Sarah opened her eyes. "Did it work?"

"On a wing and a bloody prayer, beautiful. You did great."

"What *was* that? It was like a ladder to heaven!"

"That," said Mags, "was the basic blueprint of all life. And we were inside it."

Patches meowed incessantly and pawed at Sarah's leg.

"Patches wants to destroy something, too," said Mags. She produced a length of string for Sarah. "Here. Play with her. And give me a moment, dear. Auntie Mags needs to find some decent artillery to deliver our love note to that sodding cyborg."

Soon, Mags strolled out of the *Queen Anne*. In one hand, she held her trusty Benelli shotgun. She had a pouch slung across her shoulder like a purse. In her other hand, she held Sarah's. "Go on, dear. Join your friends."

Sarah ran down the ramp. "Kala! I saw the ladder of life!"

Kala hugged her friend. "You saw what?"

"Listen up," said Mags to the assembled crowd. "I just want to say you all did a bang-up job. Now you know why we run emergency evacuation drills! This could have been a whole lot worse. Hats off to Celina and Fuzz for leading the charge. Now I want you to do one more thing for me. Just stay here and keep your cool. I got a little surprise for that cast-iron robot bitch, and she ain't gonna like it one bit."

"You're going to take her on all by yourself? She damn near killed me and Fuzz!"

"Yeah, Mags. At least let us help."

"If you want to help, hand me that Faraday suit," said Mags.

"And then get the bloody fuck out of my way. That monster came out of *my* uterus, so *I'm* gonna be the one to send it to straight to hell!"

With that, Meteor Mags and Patches left the hangar to hunt.

"There she is, Patches." Mags set her binoculars down. She lay on her stomach on a low ridge overlooking her shooting range.

Below and a hundred meters away, with her back to them, Magbot tore jagged shards of metal from the various household appliances Mags used as targets. The cyborg shoved the scraps into her mouth. Her teeth sparked as she chewed and swallowed. Her body used the metal to heal from the earlier attack.

Patches meowed softly.

"Yeah. Bitch thinks she's bad as fuck, eating a laundry machine. I got something else for her to chew on." Mags wore the Faraday suit with the helmet open, hanging down the back of her neck. Celina had described to her the cyborg's reaction to the suit's mental controls. Mags realized she would only be warning the beast of her presence if she tried approaching while wearing the helmet.

She quietly brought the Benelli up to a firing position. "This is just going to piss her off, sweetie. But we need to get up close and personal to finish this. Cover your ears."

Patches laid her head down on the rock. She placed her paws over her ears.

Mags brought the cyborg into her sights. The Benelli roared like thunder. Within seconds, eight three-inch Magnum slugs pounded into Magbot's center mass.

She fell forward into a dilapidated water heater. The bullets hammered her relentlessly. Every time she tried to move, another slug beat her down. Her respite came after the eighth round. She made a blood-curdling howl. A web of lightning bolts erupted from her metallic skin.

Mags beat her own personal speed record for reloading the

Benelli. "Gotta have a soft spot in that armor somewhere, you bloody cunt. Come and get some!" As Magbot advanced toward the ridge, Mags aimed for her chest.

Again the shotgun blasted round after round. Finally, a slug caught the cyborg in her mouth. Magbot stumbled, gushing oily blood into the air. She screamed. Electric tendrils raced along the ground up to the ridge.

"If it can bleed, it can die." Mags pulled the helmet over her face and sealed it. She reloaded the Benelli and squeezed off another eight rounds, then the lightning was upon her. Mags dropped the shotgun and tossed the rest of her shells far away from her. Magbot charged the ridge at full speed.

Where Celina had failed by trying to impose her will on the cyborg, Mags simply encouraged her rage. "Atta girl," she said. "Come and get me!" As Magbot reached the base of the ridge, Mags leapt into the air. Lightning crackled up to meet her, blazing along the exterior of her suit. The sky burned.

"Raaawwrrr!" Mags landed full force on top of her foe. They tumbled to the ground together. Wrestling, they rolled over and over each other. Magbot came out on top. She poured waves of current at the object of her hatred.

From the pouch she had slung across the Faraday suit, Mags pulled out a capsule full of enzymes. She popped the top off with her thumb.

The cyborg's hands closed around her throat. Magbot shook her violently. Mags' head struck the asteroid's unforgiving surface. Then again. The pain blinded her for a second. She gasped for breath but could not draw any air.

Patches leapt onto Magbot's face. With her invincible claws, she tore at the cyborg's eyes.

Magbot howled. She let go of Mags to clutch the calico demon with both hands. She tried to crush the cat, but failed. Patches swung her claws furiously. They dug long scratches in Magbot's metal face. The cyborg clamped its razor-sharp teeth on the cat's head, but Patches bit back.

Mags saw her opening. She pulled another capsule from her

pouch, popped the top, and grabbed a fistful of cybernetic hair with her free hand. Holding tight, she jammed the capsule into Magbot's open mouth and slammed the flat of her hand into the cyborg's face as hard as she could.

Magbot screamed. She fell off Mags, then scrambled to her feet. She held Patches prisoner with one hand.

Mags sprung up. She landed a roundhouse kick on Magbot's ribcage. "Take your meds, bitch!"

Magbot unleashed the storm. As the eels had done in their trial run, she generated a massive field. The ground below her fused into glass.

Patches wailed a high-pitched feline scream. Her body thrashed wildly in Magbot's grip.

"Patches!" Mags dove at the cyborg, tackling her, and took her to the ground. Metal squealed against rock as they slid across the expanding field of glass.

The blow loosened Magbot's grip. Patches' body skidded across the asteroid, spasming out of control.

Magbot's hands closed on Mags again, but their grip was weaker now. Mags pulled them away. She picked up a chunk of space rock and bashed Magbot in the face. The cyborg convulsed. The enzymes did their work, destroying it from the inside, on the cellular level.

"Not so tough now, are you?" Mags grabbed her by the hair. She took the jagged point of the rock and drove it into the side of Magbot's throat.

A thick substance like blood and motor oil burst from the cyborg's eyes and mouth. The tremors of a thousand earthquakes ran through her body. Her limbs flailed helplessly.

"Teach you to threaten my fucking friends!" Mags stomped the cyborg's head in a rage, again and again.

The lightning vanished. The trembling ended.

Mags stepped away. She peeled back the helmet of her suit. "Right on, Patches. That's how you take down a—Patches? Oh, no!"

Patches lay as still and silent as a corpse on the barren rock of

Vesta 4.

"Oh, baby." Mags knelt beside her calico cat and cried. She ran her hands over Patches, but she felt not a sign of life. Mags scooped up the still body and cradled it in her arms, rocking it gently back and forth. She looked up to the stars and said a silent prayer.

She carried Patches back to the hangar.

Celina, Fuzzlow, and Donny gathered around Mags. They stood at Fuzzlow's workbench in the shop.

"I sure as hell hope this works," he said.

Mags stood quietly, wiping a tear from her cheek.

"If Mags is right," offered Donny, "it can't hurt to try. If Patches can't be injured, then she's just been, like, shut down, you know?"

Fuzzlow agreed. "A massive disruption of the electrical signals in her brain, and to her muscles and organs. But if her organs are physically indestructible, then there's a chance we just need to turn the juice back on. Are you sure you want to do this, Mags?"

She placed a hand on Patches' inert body. Where normally she felt purring, Mags now felt nothing. "My baby kitten." To one of Patches' forepaws, Fuzzlow had lightly clamped a cable. A second cable affixed to her opposite hind paw. "All wired up like a bloody car battery." Mags sniffed.

"We don't have to do this," Celina said. "We could just—"

"Just what? Give up?" Mags set her face in a mask of resolution. "Patches would *never* give up. Let's fucking do this."

"Alright. Stand back," said Donny. "Mags?"

"I heard you." She joined her friends in stepping away from the bench.

Donny said, "We've calibrated the power to that of a human defibrillator, about three hundred joules, and then stepped it back down according to Patches' weight." He placed his hand on a lever. "Here goes nothing."

The lever clicked into place. A stream of electricity poured through Patches' body. Her hair stood on end.

Suddenly, her eyes slammed open. Her pupils widened, contracted, and widened again. "Mrrrooowwwlll!" Patches sprung to her feet and thrashed wildly, tugging at the cables.

"Donny!" Mags shouted. "Turn it off!"

Donny shoved the lever back to the off position. Patches furiously tore at the cables.

"It's okay, kitten!" Mags rushed to her calico cat. She reached for the cable on Patches' forepaw to unclamp it.

Patches hissed and clawed the air.

"Chill, sweetie! Relax!"

Patches looked around and saw her friends. The last thing she knew, she had been fighting for her life. But now, she was surrounded with love. She held up her paw to Mags, who gently removed the cable. Patches shook it off. She rolled back on her hindquarters to bite at the cable on her back paw.

Celina laughed. "Feisty as ever!"

"That's my girl," said Mags, removing the second cable. She scooped up Patches in her arms. Walking over to Fuzzlow and Donny, she said, "You guys are the best. Thank you." She kissed each of them on the cheek.

Patches meowed loudly.

Mags laughed and scruffed Patches' hair, rubbing her ear. "Fine, dear! We'll get you some beef jerky, pronto." She kissed Patches on the top of her head. "You deserve it."

"Donny," said Fuzzlow, "good work, my man."

Donny slapped his hand in a hearty high-five. "Shit, man. It was nothing. If you need your heavy equipment jump-started, just call a space miner!"

"*Ex*-space miner," Fuzzlow said. "You're stuck playing sax with us for the rest of your goddamn life."

Donny grinned. "I wouldn't have it any other way."

Mags watched her mates celebrate. "All's well that ends well, as my adorable nephew likes to say." A cold grimace fell across her face. "But there's one more thing we need to do. Celina? Would you come with me, please?"

She stormed out the door.

Patches happily chomped on bits of dehydrated beef and kibble at her bowl in Mags' room. Quite satisfied, she licked her chops. She ran a paw over her face, licking the side of it and running it over her face again from ear to cheek.

"I can't even imagine how horrible it must have been," said Celina. "I mean, that cyborg was practically your baby."

"That fucking monster wasn't any baby of mine. Let's finish this job. Cover me."

Celina stood to one side of the black case on the floor. She held Mags' Benelli shotgun, loaded with three-inch slugs. "Careful, wagtail."

"Not a word in my vocabulary, dear." She brought the back of an axe head down on the lock panel Celina shorted out earlier. The broken electronics fell to the floor. Mags adjusted her grip on the axe handle and kicked open the case.

As if sensing her presence, the eels' eyes glowed red.

"Fucking bastards!" Mags swung the axe down, chopping an eel in half. "I loved you!" She hacked open the second eel. "I trusted you!" The mangled pieces of the eels writhed and sparked. "And this is how you fucking repay me?" She swung the axe again and again with all her might.

At some point, Celina lowered the shotgun. She could tell it would not be necessary. She watched as Mags chopped the eels into tiny chunks, smashing them, obliterating them in a barrage of hatred.

Eventually, they stopped sparking. But Celina knew better than to tell Mags to stop. She let her friend take as long as she needed.

When her rage was sated, Mags turned away, with her back to Celina.

"Mags?"

"I'm fine."

But by the shaking of her shoulders, Celina knew Mags wept. She could not have known what transpired between Mags and her eels in the darkness. But she had known Mags a long time. She knew Mags' secret loneliness. Perhaps these evil cybernetic weapons, in their own way, had meant something special to her unique and wonderful friend.

At last Mags turned to face her. Without speaking a word, she knew her best friend understood. "Thank you, Celina." Mags sniffed, then brushed her white bangs back from her forehead. "Now help me wheel this case to the bloody incinerator."

And that was the last of the eels.

That night, Celina and Fuzzlow sat next to each other on the bed in her room. Tesla had happily returned to napping on her padded chair. His paws kneaded the fabric.

Fuzzlow strummed power chords on an acoustic guitar. "It's in F sharp minor," he said, "but Mags will probably want to sing it in a different key."

"Sing it for me," said Celina. "What's it called?"

"*The End of Love.*"

"What a cheerful little title."

"Yeah, but—just listen."

She had dimmed the lights and set out candles. Shadows and flames flickered on the walls. Fuzzlow closed his eyes and sang, picking the guitar with incessant, driving eighth notes.

Let them burn their bridges
Let them run inside
They can never touch this love of mine

Let them hide in shadow boxes
Hanging from a rope
They can never desecrate our hope

Don't believe them when they say
This is the end, this is the end of love today

Celina stared into the candle's shimmering light. She had known Mags longer than anyone alive. She knew her resilient friend would be okay, eventually. But Fuzzlow's song captured something few people understood about her friend: that sense of infinite love, yet always tinged with so many loves lost. Celina placed her hand on Fuzzlow's leg. He sang the next verse.

Make me a promise lover
Make it one you mean
Will you come and watch me while I dream

We are safe together
In our eternal place
We can disappear without a trace

Don't believe them when they say
Don't believe them, baby
Don't believe them when they say
This is the end
This is the end of love today

Fuzzlow stretched out the last line. He ended it by slowly arpeggiating the F sharp minor chord. He let it linger in the candlelight. The vibrations from his guitar soaked into the night and faded away. "So," he said. "What do you think?"

"I think the next Psycho 78s album is going to be the greatest fucking thing ever recorded."

"Better than all the Electric Moon albums put together?"

Celina stood up from the bed. "A *million* times better." She unbuttoned her blouse and threw it to the floor. "Now. Sing it to me one more time, lover."

EPILOGUE: BANNED AND BEAUTIFUL

Kaufman hated calling Earth. He drummed his fingers on his desk. He slapped it with his palm. He stood up to pace back and forth.

The distance between Mars and Earth led to pauses in any real-time conversation as the signals traveled back and forth. Depending on where the planets were in their orbits, a brief conversation could take all afternoon. Kaufman would have preferred to simply exchange data files and go about his business. But even as head of the Port Authority for the Martian Warehousing Zone, he had superiors who demanded his compliance on certain formalities.

The files on his tablet were perfectly clear. Meteor Mags had been moved to the top of the list of known criminals in the System. An amendment to the Musical Freedoms Act had effectively banned her from all locations in the Belt and the Martian Warehousing Zone. The amendment criminalized possession of any images or recordings of her, and it authorized the termination of all violators of this ban. Finally, all citizens had been granted provisional authority to terminate her under any circumstances, with a sizeable reward at stake.

Earth had declared open season on Meteor Mags.

At last, the response came. "Good, Kaufman. So you have read the orders on file and understood them. We need full cooperation from the MWZ on this, and you may need to redirect your resources appropriately. This is priority number one now. Vesta 4 is simply too large a mining opportunity to let it go to waste due to the interference of a known felon. We will no longer tolerate piracy within the Belt. This operation will send a clear message that Earth is willing to fully commit to eradicating such interference. We will be sending a team from the MFA to assist you in all organizational aspects of these orders. Please give the team all due courtesy. Understood?"

A series of beeps signaled the end of the transmission.

Off-camera, Kaufman rolled his eyes. They certainly did like to talk, he thought. He sat down at his desk and opened the transmission channel. "Understood, sir. We look forward to having such distinguished guests. The Port Authority is at your disposal. Kaufman out." He pressed 'send' before returning to his pacing.

Kaufman no longer had any doubts his corrupt superiors were in league with the dragons. The Belt was littered with countless asteroids known to have far more profitable mining potential than Vesta 4. And though acts of piracy, such as the ones his covert tips had helped Meteor Mags carry out these past few years, did place a financial burden on the Martian Warehousing Zone, the cost paled in comparison to that of carrying out a major military strike within the Belt. That left only one good reason for these new orders.

"Very good, Kaufman," came the response. "Transmission complete."

He shut off his transmitter. Commander Cragg had not threatened him and his son in months, but the dragons' activities in the Outer Planets continued unabated. Kaufman's intelligence network had informed him of several raids the dragons had carried out on Earth, and their buildup of force showed no signs of slowing down. Where then, he wondered, was Cragg? Had the awful beast died in one of the conflicts rumored to have taken place beyond the Belt? Were he and his son finally free of the reptile's interference in their lives?

Kaufman rubbed the bridge of his nose between his thumb and fingers. Closing his eyes, he thought of the last time he had seen Meteor Mags. She had danced so incredibly. He had woken up more than once dreaming of her star-covered body. She had spoken to him in trust, as a friend, and then single-handedly taken out an entire bar of degenerate space miners. Well, he thought, not single-handedly. She also had that adorable calico cat she traveled with now. And the boy she called her nephew.

Kaufman made his decision. He had to see her again. He had to warn Meteor Mags of the impending attack. But first, he needed to get his son to safety.

METEOR MAGS

OMNIBUS EDITION
BY MATTHEW HOWARD

www.ingramcontent.com/pod-product-compliance
Lightning Source LLC
Chambersburg PA
CBHW070815120626
46556CB00002B/516